PAX BR...

D1635562

BLOOD ROYAL

They moved from streets open to the sky into the near-dark of the tunnels, from windswept corridors that lay between the towering shells of fire-twisted financial buildings into the damp, dripping depths of cellar underpasses. And they were always on the lookout for signs of life, fingers hooked around the triggers of their flame-throwers, the vigilante with a hand to his pocket mine dispenser, just in case.

The first of the monstrous insects came scuttling out of a collapsed alleyway. Each was roughly the size of a man, and each was a horrific hybrid of mantis and locust.

Ulysses gunned the trigger of his Smith and Winchester. A jet of liquid fire roared from the end of the weapon. One of the creatures fell shrieking from its precarious perch on the tunnel wall, landing on its back amidst the black puddles of fetid water, its legs frantically pawing the air.

A moment later, Nimrod's flame-thrower sprayed fire into the dark hole and another wall-crawler went tumbling to the ground. It ran past them, giving a high-pitched scream, and disappeared along the alleyway behind them, its chitinous shell aflame and trailing black smoke.

V ... OM

An Abaddon Books™ Publication
www.abaddonbooks.com
abaddon@rebellion.co.uk

First published in 2010 by Abaddon Books™, Rebellion Intellectual
Property Limited, Riverside House, Osney Mead, Oxford, OX2 0ES, UK.

10 9 8 7 6 5 4 3 2 1

Editors: Jennifer-Anne Hill & Jonathan Oliver
Cover: Mark Harrison
Design: Simon Parr & Luke Preece
Marketing and PR: Keith Richardson
Creative Director and CEO: Jason Kingsley
Chief Technical Officer: Chris Kingsley
Pax Britannia™ created by Jonathan Green

ISBN: 978-1-906735-30-2

Printed in Denmark by Norhaven A/S

PAX BRITANNIA

BLOOD
ROYAL

JONATHAN GREEN

Abaddon
Books

WWW.ABADDONBOOKS.COM

For Sam and Nick

And

For Lisa and Tony

ACT ONE

Insect Nation

March 1998

CHAPTER ONE

The Handover

Four hours after curfew – in the shadow of the St Paul's Cathedral – an unmarked hansom cab rattled to a halt. The door opened and Dr Victor Gallowglass stepped down onto the street. His heart beat a nervous tattoo against his ribs, although he was concentrating hard so that his nerves and his fear did not show in his face.

A gang of five men, skulking in the shadows, watched him from the other side of the street, their dark clothing making them almost invisible. Except for the debonair gent who stood slightly apart from the others.

"Good evening, Doctor," the man said.

He was immaculately turned out, wearing a fine green frock coat, charcoal grey trousers, spats and a silver-embroidered waistcoat. A gold silk cravat finished off the ensemble, held in place with a ruby-tipped pin. In one hand he swung an ebony cane as if keeping time, like a metronome. His face was as sharp, his brown hair – greying at the temples and slicked back from a pronounced widow's peak – glistened with a copious helping of hair oil.

He looked from the grim face of the doctor to the pall of Smog that hung over the city like a shroud, the glowing yellow streetlamps turning its clammy mantle a sallow tinge. The hazy white disc of the moon struggled through the banks of pollutant cloud that still plagued the city, despite former Prime Minister Valentine's best efforts. Its milky luminescence added an eerie, unsettling quality to the night's illicit proceedings.

"A fine evening, is it not?" the man continued, as if they were all there for no other reason than to pass the time of day.

"Where is she?"

The man raised an eyebrow. "Do not worry, Dr Gallowglass, your daughter is safe."

"I want to see her."

The debonair gent regarded Gallowglass for a moment, an incalculable expression in his eyes.

He turned and nodded to one of the suspicious-looking characters waiting in the darkness behind him.

The darkly dressed ruffian took a step forward. He was of burly build but weighed down by the large sack he was carrying over his shoulder. Carefully, he set the sack down and fumbled with the rope tying it shut. He pulled the sack down around the body of the small girl bound inside.

The girl looked terrified and, on seeing her father, fresh tears began to stream from her eyes, but she said nothing. She couldn't – the gag prevented her from doing so.

"Oh, Miranda, my poor darling," Gallowglass gasped. Tears welled in his eyes too. "It's alright now. It's going to be alright, my darling. This will all be over very soon, I promise." Blinking the tears away he fixed the kidnappers' spokesman with a look of black, unadulterated hatred. "If you have harmed a single hair on her head..." He did not need to say any more.

"I can assure you that she has been as well looked after as Her Majesty might expect to be," the other said, his voice oozing charm and charisma despite the direness of the situation.

Gallowglass reached out his arms to the frightened child but didn't dare take a step towards her.

"I doubt that distinctly," he growled. "Now let her go." His tone was more pleading than he would have liked.

"All in good time, doctor. All in good time." The debonair gentleman slapped the shaft of his cane into his hand. "But before we hand her over to your care you must give us certain assurances."

"What is it you want from me?"

"Your continued, faithful, patriotic service. That is all, Doctor Gallowglass. All that we ask is that you see your vital work through to completion."

Gallowglass's expression didn't change.

"I will continue with my research until my labours bear fruit," Gallowglass conceded.

"And we have your word on that?"

"You have my word."

"Well, we can't ask for more than that, can we? After all, an Englishman's word is his bond, is it not?"

At another nod from their leader, the ruffian freed the girl from her bonds.

An expectant hush hung over the street, the shadowy silhouette of the cathedral on the other side of the barricade a threatening presence nonetheless. It was a silence disturbed only by the Smog-muffled clatter of Overground trains – although there were a lot fewer of them running on the elevated tracks now at this time of night – and the sudden clatter of roof tiles above.

Anxious glances shot to the rooftops of the burnt out buildings on the other side of the wall.

"What was that?" the debonair gent demanded.

"Don't know, boss," one of his unshaven lackeys replied.

The man put a steadying hand to the shoulder of the one still struggling to free the girl and turned cold, black eyes on the equally anxious-looking doctor. "You were told to come alone!"

The debonair dandy took a step back towards the wall, eyes fixed on the rooftops on the other side of the road. His companion took a step back too, pulling the girl after him.

"I did!" Gallowglass screamed.

The unshaven lackey suddenly shot an anxious glance up at the wall behind them. "Here, boss, you don't think it could be –"

"Silence!" the other snapped, never once taking his eyes from the buildings on the other side of the street. "I thought I heard..." The dandy's words trailed off into silence and then: "Look! Up there!"

All eyes followed his trembling finger.

At first Gallowglass could see nothing amongst the shadows shrouding the rooftops, not until one of those shadows detached itself from the darkness and unfurled bat-like wings.

Like some animated gargoyle it leapt from the guttering at the edge of the roof.

Gallowglass gasped and a number of the kidnappers began to whimper. All of them recognising the night stalker for who he was.

The skin of its leathery wings rippling as it dropped from the parapet, the figure swooped towards them.

"Get out of here!" the dandy shouted and took off down the street, keeping close to the wall as he ran. His burly comrade was close on his heels, dragging the terrified girl after him.

As the bat-winged terror came within a few feet of the ground, his legs swung forwards and he planted the soles of two heavy boots squarely in the chest of one of the panicking rogues. The man was hurled onto his back and a solid kick to the head made sure that he stayed there.

Two remained. The crack of gunfire shattered the night.

Gallowglass watched, his jaw slack with shock, as the armoured bat-man bore down on the kidnappers. Their shots must have missed, Gallowglass decided, for the figure did not even break his stride as he closed on them.

But their second volley of shots certainly didn't miss. How could they? The vigilante was right on top of them now. Gallowglass heard the pang of metal on metal and the advancing colossus wavered.

But his hesitation was only momentary. One last bounding stride and he was on top of them. Dully gleaming claws sliced through the night. Blood sprayed black in the darkness.

Another threat neutralized.

The masked vigilante – the one the press had dubbed Spring-Heeled Jack – was the only man who dared stalk the streets of London once the curfew sirens had been sounded. During the hours of darkness he delivered his own brand of justice to those who had taken advantage of the fact that, in the aftermath of the Wormwood Catastrophe, the capital had become a more lawless place than ever. The authorities' resources had been stretched to breaking point and were no longer able to cope with the rise in opportunistic crime and gang-related warfare.

With three down and two to go, the vigilante didn't hesitate for a moment but, leaving the motionless bodies of his victims behind, launched himself after the gang's leader, his burly companion and the still captive child.

The first any of them – doctor, vigilante and kidnapper – knew of the locusts' arrival was the zinging buzz of chitinous wings, as the gigantic insects rose over the west wall and descended on the fleeing felons.

For the first time since taking on the kidnappers, Spring-Heeled Jack faltered, stumbling and losing his balance as he tried to arrest his forward charge. There were two of the things – their bodies as long as a man was tall, their huge wings a blur of movement.

They paused for a moment, hovering several feet above the cobbled street, their mantis-like heads jerking from side to side as they regarded Gallowglass and the vigilante with compound eyes the size of footballs.

As if at some unspoken command, one of the locusts moved towards the vigilante; the second targeted the dumbstruck, paralysed doctor. Regaining his feet, the vigilante put a gauntleted hand to a dispenser on his belt. A second later, he tossed something small and metallic towards the insects. The object hit the road as the giant insects passed overhead.

There was a soft click and then with a great whooshing noise, like air escaping from a punctured dirigible, a thick jet of smoke erupted from the device.

It was as if the locusts had hit a wall. The two insects, buzzing angrily, withdrew, turning away from the expanding gas cloud. Repelled by the smoke bomb they left the vigilante and the doctor, and set off after easier prey.

Even through the smoky haze, Gallowglass saw what followed clearly enough.

"No!" he screamed, his paralysis suddenly gone, his legs carrying him after the insects. But he was too late.

First to be plucked from the ground was the unshaven ruffian, the girl stumbling to her hands and knees as the startled man lost his grip on her. The locust lifted the kidnapper, kicking and screaming, into the air. It took off back over the wall, holding the wailing man fast in its pincer-grip, labouring its way towards the black dome of St Paul's.

Just for a moment Victor Gallowglass thought that perhaps his daughter might escape from her ordeal unscathed. But his moment of desperate hope was short-lived.

The second locust dropped onto her back before he could reach her. With the child clutched in its chitinous embrace, it rose again into the Smoggy air.

Gallowglass was sprinting now, arms outstretched towards his daughter, as if he might somehow still be able to pluck her out of the sky and to safety, but against the airborne assailant, he was utterly helpless.

As the locust rose over the wall after the other, the girl's gag came free and he heard her cry.

"Daddy!"

Hearing her scream his name only made the already desperate situation infinitely worse.

But then his faltering steps found purpose again and, within a few strides, he was at the wall. He had already managed to scramble a good six feet up the barricade when the vigilante grabbed him.

"Stop!" the vigilante's voice boomed from the speaker grille in the front of his goggle-eyed mask.

With one strong tug, Spring-Heeled Jack pulled him off the wall.

"You cannot go in there. The whole area is contaminated!"

With a snarl born of rage and frustration, Gallowglass pulled himself free of Jack's grasp and then, turning, began to pummel the vigilante's bullet-proof breastplate with his fists, until at last, realising that that too was futile, he gave up and fell to his knees. The soul-wrenching sobs came freely now in an outpouring of agonised grief.

"There must be a way!" he wailed through the tears. "And if you can't do it, then we must get help!"

CHAPTER TWO

A Friend in Need

"Have you seen this?" Ulysses Quicksilver said, as he and his brother – Bartholomew Quicksilver – enjoyed cigars and a glass of brandy in the library after supper. They had dined late that evening on beef *en croute*, prepared, as ever, by their inestimable housekeeper Mrs Prufrock. The poor woman had only just left for her own home across town, but not before Ulysses made sure that Nimrod – his manservant, valet, butler and general all round dogsbody – had called her a cab first. Travelling by foot after curfew was a dangerous business.

Barty grunted and looked up from his copy of *The Racing Post*. "What?"

"Have you seen this piece in *The Times*?" Ulysses waved the newspaper he had been perusing at his brother.

"Always got your head in the paper, haven't you?" the younger man said without any hint of actual interest. "If you're not making the news, you're reading it."

"It pays to keep up with what's going on in the world, Barty, old chap. Anyway, this item."

Ulysses thrust the paper, folded open at the appropriate page, under his brother's nose.

"There's been another murder." He stabbed a finger at the article buried among the column inches at the bottom of the page. Barty followed his brother's probing digit.

"In Whitechapel?"

"In Whitechapel."

"Another prostitute?"

"Another prostitute. Jointed like a Sunday roast."

"How many's that now?"

"Four by my reckoning," Ulysses said, having already totted up the total in his head.

"Jack the Ripper up to his old tricks again, is he?"

"I doubt it very much," Ulysses laughed dismissively, "but it remains a mystery nonetheless. I should contact Eliza, just to make sure she's alright."

"Would that be your friend Eliza Do-Alot?" Barty smirked.

Ulysses shot him a look that soon wiped the ribald smile from his face.

"So, who do you think is behind it then?" Barty pressed, quickly changing the subject. He was intrigued now, much to his annoyance.

"I'd hardly like to hazard a guess without having all the facts at my disposal," Ulysses said. "I would be making a complete stab in the dark."

"Like this strumpet slasher." Bartholomew Quicksilver knew his elder brother better than that. "But you have an inkling, don't you?"

"Of course I do. Well, one or two ideas have sprung to mind, as it happens."

"Go on," Barty encouraged, although he knew that he didn't really have to draw the information out of Ulysses. He was just playing along.

"Well, I've often found myself wondering what happened to Gabriel Wraith's lost boys, the ones who ended up at his House of

Monkeys. And it's always possible that the police never actually managed to round up all of the escaped inmates from the Tower following Wormwood's intervention at the Queen's jubilee last year. And then again..."

"Hmm?" Barty grunted. "Then again what?"

"The fact that someone's cutting up street-walkers in the East End, one hundred and ten years after that fiend the Ripper did the self-same thing..." Ulysses left the thought hanging.

"So you think it's a copycat."

"It doesn't look like it. The murders themselves don't appear to be actual copies of those killings ascribed to the Ripper."

"It's just that the *modus operandi's* the same."

"Indeed."

"So who would be the likely killer?"

"Well – and I realise that this is going to sound ridiculous – but if I were a gambling man, which I am not," he added, giving his younger brother a look heavy with meaning, "I would say that it looked as though it was the self-same killer getting back into the swing of things, having had the last century and a bit off."

Barty said nothing in response to Ulysses' outrageous claim. He was staring unseeingly at *The Times*, a distant look in his unfocused eyes.

"Obviously wasn't as preposterous as I thought it sounded," Ulysses muttered.

"Hmm? What?" Barty managed, looking up from the paper. "Sorry, you lost me there for a moment."

"I can see that," Ulysses said. "Anyway, what's wrong with you? You've been away with the fairies this evening." He retrieved his paper, taking his seat by the fire again.

"I wish I was."

"What?"

"It's nothing. I'm fine."

For a moment neither of them said anything more, both returning to their perusal of their papers, the library clock marking the passing seconds *tick* after *tock,* after *tick* after *tock.*

Ulysses looked at his brother. "You're not in any kind of trouble, are you?"

"Well, it's funny you should mention how you're not a gambling man." Barty shifted uncomfortably in his chair. They said confession was good for the soul; what they didn't say was that it was terrible for your pride and sense of self-worth.

"You haven't been gambling again have you?"

Barty winced at his brother's parental tone.

Ulysses glowered at him from over the top of *The Times*.

"When did this start?"

"Well, it didn't ever really stop."

"What? You mcan to tell me that ever since you tried to have me declared dead, so that you might come into your inheritance prematurely – just so you could pay off your gambling debts – and even then, after I bailed you out and invited you to join me in our father's house once again, you still didn't learn from your mistakes and continued to fritter away our father's legacy until – now what? – loan sharks are after your blood, you've got heavies breathing down your neck for non-payment of blackjack table fees? What?"

Slowly, Barty opened his mouth to speak.

Elsewhere within the Mayfair townhouse, the jangling of the doorbell disturbed the peace of the tiled hallway. At any other time Ulysses may well have stopped to wonder who had dared break curfew to come calling at such an hour, but at present he was too caught up in his brother's tangled affairs.

"No, I don't want to hear it," Ulysses declared angrily, interrupting his brother before he could even speak. "Just tell me how much it is you need this time to get you out of whatever mess it is you've got yourself into, and then *I'm* going to tell *you* how things are going to be around here from now on!"

Barty returned his brother's glowering gaze and Ulysses was able to read the fear writ large within his sorrowful eyes.

"It's not as simple as that this time," he said quietly. "I wish it was, but money's not going to cut it."

Seeing his brother like this Ulysses relented and his expression softened.

"Look, don't be ridiculous. No matter what your debt, I'll settle it; even if I have to sell the Warwickshire pad. Don't worry, little brother, we'll sort this out together. It'll be alright."

"I wish I could believe that. I really do."

With a polite cough, Nimrod announced himself, standing at the threshold to the library. It was as if he had appeared out of nowhere, his prize-fighter's physique and straight-backed butler's stance giving him a certain presence. Grey-haired, broken nosed and with a hawkish countenance, Ulysses' butler nevertheless wore his uniform as if he had been born to the profession.

Still scowling, Ulysses looked from his brother to his manservant and adventuring companion. "What is it, Nimrod?"

"I'm sorry to interrupt, sir, but there is a gentleman here to see you."

"A gentleman?"

"One Doctor Gallowglass, sir. I believe you are old acquaintances."

"Gallowglass?" Ulysses said, suddenly elated, his mood having taken a turn for the better now that something had distracted him from his concerns over his brother's frivolous lifestyle. "Victor? Victor Gallowglass? We were at Eton together. What's the old bugger doing here and at this time of night, after curfew and all? It's a long time since the two of us have wasted an evening in the company of the green fairy, or with a bottle or two of Beaujolais," he said, recalling happy memories of more carefree times. "I wonder what he wants."

The manservant fixed him with those piercing, sapphire-blue eyes of his. "I think the matter might be an urgent one, sir."

"Really? Well I'd better not dally a moment longer then." He rose to his feet. "Look, Barty, I'm sorry, but I need to deal with this." Ulysses moved towards the door. "But we'll talk again later, old chap? Stiff upper lip and all that, alright? We'll sort it out. Whatever it is you've got yourself mixed up in, we'll sort it – *together*."

He left the room, his younger brother slowly shaking his head in denial as he stared despondently at the fire dying in the grate.

The moment Ulysses set eyes on his old school friend he knew that something was wrong. The man's face was the colour of a bloodless corpse, his eyes sunken and his shoulders slumped.

He was pacing around the drawing room, fretting like a man facing imminent fatherhood; either worrying at his neatly-trimmed goatee or wringing his hands together until his bony knuckles showed white.

"It's been a long time, Victor," Ulysses said as he entered the room. "What is it that brings you to my door?"

Victor Gallowglass stopped his pacing and looked at Ulysses. Relief and sorrow warred for dominance of the features surrounding his permanently doleful eyes.

"Quicksilver," he said, clasping Ulysses' hands in his, "it is so good to see you."

He was shaking; Ulysses could feel it through his grasp.

"Here, have a seat." He guided Gallowglass to a chair beside the cold stones of the hearth. Ulysses released himself from his old acquaintance's clinging grip, and took the chair opposite. "Can I get you anything to drink? Barty and I were just enjoying a nightcap."

"No. Thank you," his guest said hastily. Ulysses could see sweat beading on his forehead. "This can't wait a moment longer."

"Very well, then. So tell me; what is it I can do for you?"

As Gallowglass opened his mouth to speak, it seemed to Ulysses that he might burst into tears at any moment. And then everything came pouring out of him in a torrent of distressed recall.

"They took my daughter. They said that if I wanted to see her alive again then I must finish my work, see it through to the end. I was being blackmailed, I know that, but what could I do? She's all I have now, since... since my Mary..."

Gallowglass broke off, his lip quivering. Ulysses said nothing, giving the man the space he needed to continue.

Recovering himself, Gallowglass went on.

"Anyway, I agreed. Of course I did, and I almost had her back, she was almost safe again, but then that bastard, London's self-appointed caped crusader, interfered in it all and the locusts came and took her."

"The locusts?"

"And now, for all I know she could be..."

The wretched man broke off again, heavy tears splashing into his lap.

"It's alright." Ulysses reached out a comforting hand. "Tell me. Slowly."

Steeling himself again, the shaking man gathered the emotional strength to finish his story.

"That jack-a-knave, that bastard, Spring-Heeled Jack is planning a rescue operation."

"Spring-Heeled Jack?"

"He says he can get her back. I don't see what else I can do. Much as I hate the idea of him screwing everything up again, I don't see that there's any other way. But if that's how it's got to be I want someone else there with him every step of the way – someone I can trust. I want you to go with him, Quicksilver."

"But of course," Ulysses said. "And with me you get Nimrod, my manservant, too. He's a bit handy in a scuffle, you know?"

Gallowglass looked as though he were about to cry again. "It is such a relief to hear you say that. But time is pressing. You have to come now. That fool vigilante's meeting us within the hour."

"Now? But of course," Ulysses blustered. "Where are we meeting him? Where is this rescue attempt taking place?"

Gallowglass turned his mournful eyes on Ulysses once more.

"St Paul's. We're meeting him back at the St Paul's west wall."

Ulysses completely failed to stifle his gasp of horror.

"Oh, Victor. What have you got yourself mixed up in?"

CHAPTER THREE

Exterminator Salvation

It was not until just before dawn that Ulysses Quicksilver and his ever faithful manservant actually met up with Spring-Heeled Jack in the shadow of St Paul's.

Despite the fact that the locusts had returned to their lair the street was quiet. Since the Wormwood Catastrophe whole areas of London had become veritable no-go areas, contaminated, as they had been, by the mutagenic rain that had fallen on the capital, causing damage that would take years to put right.

Those who could afford to had vacated homes and business premises this close to the contamination zones. They preferred to stay well clear of the danger zones, no matter what propaganda the Government might put out. Public notices had informed the survivors of the Catastrophe that they had nothing to fear, as long as they were sensible and kept out of the contaminated areas. Nonetheless, the streets of London wouldn't be truly safe until the authorities got round to decontaminating the no-go zones, which was proving to be a painfully slow process in itself.

The blockades were only supposed to remain for as long as it took the over-stretched exterminators to get round to clearing those areas worst affected. Barricades and walls had been hastily erected around all of the deluge hotspots to contain them for the foreseeable future. Once the exterminators had been into this area, the barriers would come down. But for now, the streets surrounding St Paul's were strictly off limit.

At least the Upper City had remained mainly unaffected. Those who worked within the skyscraper office buildings had been shielded from the deadly downpour. But thank goodness that had been the case, Ulysses thought, for at least with the City and Government relatively unaffected by the Wormwood Catastrophe the globe-spanning empire of Magna Britannia was still able to continue to function as the leading world power, just as it had for the last 150 years.

"Long time no see," Ulysses said, looking the hulking vigilante up and down.

It had been a month since Ulysses had last had anything to do with the masked vigilante and, in that time, it looked as though he had made further improvements to his suit.

The cape was the same, as was the jet-pack harnessed to his back beneath it. His face was still hidden by an emotionless mask realised in black leather and brass, with red-lensed goggles built in. As far as Ulysses could tell, the most obvious enhancements that Jack had made were the addition of some sort of gas re-breather and the suit's gauntlets which were now equipped with scalpel-like blades.

In their turn, Ulysses and Nimrod were both attired in the finest leather, brass and treated rubber anti-contamination suits Robinson Heath's Adventurers' Emporium had to offer.

"Where's the doctor?" the vigilante asked.

"I sent him home. I think he's been through enough tonight already, don't you?

You haven't been frittering away your time I see," Ulysses said, regarding the steel talons.

"Well you know what they say," the vigilante replied, his voice a flat monotone, altered as it was by the mask's speaker-grille.

"What, no rest for the wicked?"

"That's not what I meant."

"The devil makes work for idle hands?" Nimrod suggested.

"No. I was thinking more along the lines of: 'Make hay while the sun shines'," Jack said, his monotone somehow managing to sound disgruntled. "And where have you two been? The Exterminators' Emporium's seconds sale?"

"I'll have you know that these are the best containment suits money can buy," Ulysses retorted. "But you're not far off."

"I prefer something of my own design." With that, the vigilante threw out his arms, the cape extending its broad bat-wings behind him.

"Yes, yes, put it away. We've seen it all before."

Jerking his arms back down, Spring-Heeled Jack folded his cape again.

He towered over the other two in his augmented suit and Ulysses had to admit – but only to himself – that he must make most two-bit criminals think twice when they came up against him. Fear must play its part in conquering those of the criminal fraternity Jack seemed to have now made it his life's work to eliminate, in his mission to keep London safe from the lawless.

"Enough of this macho posturing; we've a job to do. How long is it since the girl was taken?"

Spring-Heeled Jack glanced at his wrist-mounted chronometer. "Six hours."

It had taken that long for Victor Gallowglass to track down his old school friend to beg for his help. The rest of the time had been used in preparing for the hunt and, for Ulysses and Nimrod, that meant paying an out-of-hours visit to Robinson Heath's, to kit themselves out with the latest in personal anti-contamination protective gear.

The suits were all-encompassing conglomerations of leather and treated rubber, with reinforced steel toe-capped boots and fish-bowl helmets. Every piece was secured to every other with brass clasps and rubber seals.

Ulysses and Nimrod were each carrying the additional weight of a Smith and Winchester flame-thrower about their persons, the brass fuel tanks strapped to their backs. Ulysses had also rescued the grappling-gun he kept in the boot of his Silver Phantom Rolls, just in case. It now hung from a hook on the notched leather belt of his containment suit.

"So, we're all here," Ulysses said.

"Almost," Jack replied.

Looking towards the shadowed entrance of a narrow winding side-street, he pressed something on his wrist-mounted control panel.

As Ulysses peered expectantly at the shadows crowding the mouth of the alleyway, he thought he could see something like a steam-wagon parked there, back-end on to the main thoroughfare.

The relative peace and quiet of the empty street – nowhere in London ever being totally quiet, what with the movement of traffic through the capital and the ever-present clatter of the Overground, even in these days of curfews and security lock-downs – was broken by the rising hum of heavy machinery powering up. With a great clanking of piston limbs and the hiss of steam, something shouldered its way out of the back of the steam-wagon.

Eight feet tall and just as broad, a shape like a walking furnace strode out of the shadows and into the Smog-smothered pre-dawn light.

In that same instant the colour drained from Ulysses' cheeks.

"Oh my god, you have got to be kidding me!"

"It's alright. There's nothing to worry about," Spring-Heeled Jack reassured him.

"But that's..." Ulysses broke off as he stared into the glowing head-lamp eyes of the hulking search and rescue droid.

The monstrous machine looked down at him, its furnace maw opening in an exhalation of fiery heat.

And was it Ulysses' overwrought imagination playing tricks on him, or was the monstrous machine really regarding him with something like recognition.

Ulysses tried again. "But that's..."

"The Limehouse Golem. Yes, I – how shall I put this? – acquired it from the wreckage of the *Jupiter*, once it had been hauled out of the Thames."

"But I blew it to smithereens."

"That's right, you did. But don't worry, as well as rebuilding it, I also had the good sense to re-programme it."

Ulysses stared at the mechanised killer, mouth agape. He could see quite clearly now how the robot drudge had been welded back together, as well as the augmentations that had enhanced its frame. "Nimrod wasn't kidding when he said the Devil makes work for idle hands, was he?"

Jack relayed a command to the droid via a series of keystrokes on his control pad. With a grating of gears, the ape-like automaton leant forwards and reached out one massive crusher-claw hand towards the dandy, and then stopped, waiting.

"Go on, shake his hand," the vigilante said.

"*His* hand?"

"It's perfectly safe."

Ulysses took a cautious step forward and – his heart in his mouth – slowly stretched out his gloved hand.

"That is unless I decide to designate you as a target."

Ulysses hoped that the vigilante's words were supposed to have sounded ironic, but right at that moment he wouldn't have liked to place a bet on it.

"I'm joking," Jack said.

"Yes, yes. Of course you are," Ulysses blustered with forced good humour, but he quickly drew his hand out of reach of the droid.

"Very wise, sir," Nimrod commented, so that only his master could hear.

"It's only a tool, after all, and nothing to get het up about," Jack stated. "It will prove useful if we find ourselves having to clear any obstructions on our way through the ruins."

Ulysses turned and looked at the looming barricade behind them. Beyond it lay acres of burnt-out buildings and derelict streets, the legacy of Wormwood's bitter waters. "Do you really think she's still alive somewhere in there?"

"I have to hope she is," the vigilante said, "and if there is even the faintest glimmer of hope, I have to try to rescue her, otherwise..." His words trailed off.

"Indeed."

For a long moment none of them said anything.

"So, I've brought a droid," Jack said, breaking the tense silence at last. "What have you brought?"

"Don't start gloating," Ulysses warned. "We wouldn't be about to embark on this little sojourn into Locust London if it wasn't for you."

"A pair of Smith and Winchester flamer-throwers. Will that suffice?"

"Could come in handy."

The roar of Jack's jet-pack firing startled Ulysses and, in a cloud of rocket smoke, the vigilante propelled himself onto the top of the wall, thirty feet above them.

"What are you waiting for?" the vigilante called down to the dandy and his manservant.

Ulysses eyed the wall, with its 'Warning – No Entry' signs and barbed wire clad parapet, wondering how he and Nimrod were going to get to the top, never mind how they were going to fair once they were on the other side.

"You haven't seen a ladder lying around here, have you?"

CHAPTER FOUR

No Man's World

It was eerily quiet on the other side of the wall. There was the distant, yet ever-present, sound of the Overground. And there were the sounds of other Londoners doing their best to go about their business as normal – from the stevedores at the Wapping Docks to the steam-powered hansom cabs ferrying people across the city. But inside the exclusion zone, where the streets looked as though they had been subjected to the most terrible aerial bombardment, it was deathly quiet.

Cautiously moving their flame-throwers in sweeping arcs, Ulysses and Nimrod set off along the devastation of Cannon Street. As Spring-Heeled Jack led the way, they watched for any indication of movement from either side of the thoroughfare, the golem-droid keeping in step behind.

In the end there had been no need for Ulysses to find a ladder to scale the west wall; the golem had punched a hole through the reinforced concrete with its pile-driver fists, and they had simply walked through behind it. It had only taken the droid a moment to haul an abandoned goods lorry in front of the hole, effectively sealing it again.

Ulysses could see the dome of St Paul's ahead of them. The beautiful architecture of the dome – Sir Christopher Wren's legacy to London and the English Church – was marred by the presence of the Northern Overground line behind it. A bend in the track skirted right past the cupola and, a little further on, the base of a supporting pillar had been positioned just outside the cathedral churchyard.

St Paul's was probably no more than a couple of hundred yards away, but it might as well have been a couple of hundred miles when one took into consideration all the obstacles that would have to be negotiated to reach it. And God alone knew where they were supposed to start looking for the child. She could be anywhere within the vast warren of burnt out streets and partially-demolished buildings.

Blackened vehicles littered the streets, fallen omnibuses blocking the road as effectively as any government barricade. At more than one point, buildings had collapsed into the street. If they wanted to penetrate the exclusion zone as far as the cathedral, they were either going to have to clamber over these unsteady structures or enter the maze-like warren of side-streets made all the more labyrinthine by the magnitude of the disaster that had befallen this part of the city.

In the days directly following the Catastrophe, the armed forces had pushed back the seemingly endless tide of bugs swarming out of the St Paul's area, managing to stop the fires spreading beyond New Bridge Street to the west and Queen Street to the east. Industrial droids had helped to raise the thirty-foot tall barricade from prefabricated slabs of concrete and reinforced steel. Within less than a week, St Paul's had been cordoned off and any of the 'changed' that had slipped through the net had been quickly neutralised.

People couldn't bear the thought that the monsters that now plagued St Paul's after sunset had once been their fellow citizens. No, they might once have been people but they were people no longer. There was no hope for them now. They couldn't be changed back – or so the government-sponsored scientists claimed – and so it was best for all concerned to grieve, forget and move on. Let the authorities deal with London's pest infestation.

However, it soon became clear that the authority's chosen method of pest control was neither quick nor efficient.

Interestingly, from a scientific point of view, there were distinctive sub-species among the changed, although the most numerous appeared to be the cockroaches. These had fled into the sewers and abandoned Underground tunnels, feeding on the scraps left behind by the city-dwellers above and only really caused a problem when they burst through into run-down or derelict properties, infesting them as surely as their significantly smaller cousins.

Then there were the locusts. Six feet in length, these were great winged monsters that bore an uncanny resemblance to the people they had once been. That was apart from their totally alien, mantis-like heads, with their bulbous compound eyes and bone-breaking mandibles.

Observation stations posted at watch towers around the restricted zone reported that the 'changed' trapped within the confines of the St Paul's area had reverted to primitive insect instincts and had established a colony within the shell of the abandoned cathedral.

The rescue party halted in front of a vast wall of broken stone and twisted steel and regarded the unsafe structure; the golem-droid scanning it with lighthouse sweeps of its baleful eyes.

"So what now?" Ulysses said.

"Well, if it was just me, I could hop over this in an instant." Spring-Heeled Jack said.

"But it's not just you, is it?"

"It would take too long for the golem to clear a safe path through, if time is of the essence."

"Which it is."

"So, if you're not prepared to risk climbing over it, then I would suggest we find a way round it."

"Then we go round."

The three men and the robot turned left into Old Bailey Street and Ulysses was almost surprised to see the recognisable landmark of the ancient and venerable law courts ahead of them. But soon they were following side-streets and alleyways, negotiating the tunnels and rat-runs formed by the devastation.

They moved from streets open to the sky into the near-dark of the tunnels, from windswept corridors that lay between the towering shells of fire-twisted financial buildings into the damp, dripping depths of cellar underpasses. And they were always on the lookout for signs of life, fingers hooked around the triggers of their flame-throwers, the vigilante with a hand to his pocket mine dispenser, just in case.

The first of the monstrous insects came scuttling out of a collapsed alleyway. Each was roughly the size of a man, and each was a horrific hybrid of mantis and locust.

Ulysses gunned the trigger of his Smith and Winchester. A jet of liquid fire roared from the end of the weapon. One of the creatures fell shrieking from its precarious perch on the tunnel wall, landing on its back amidst the black puddles of fetid water, its legs frantically pawing the air.

A moment later, Nimrod's flame-thrower sprayed fire into the dark hole and another wall-crawler went tumbling to the ground. It ran past them, giving a high-pitched scream, and disappeared along the alleyway behind them, its chitinous shell aflame and trailing black smoke.

With a sound like a scream of rage, another locust launched itself at Spring-Heeled Jack, twisting its body in mid-air to meet him face on, mandibles snapping hungrily.

With a flick of his wrists, the vigilante activated his gauntlet-mounted claw-blades. As the locust made a grab for him, he crossed his arms and slashed the insect across its belly. Severed limbs went flying, trailing the disgusting green ichor that passed for blood among the changed. The creature splashed into a puddle at his feet. As it continued to wriggle helplessly he planted one heavy boot in the middle of its thorax and, with another sweep of his blades, delivered the killing blow.

Hearing a grinding of robotic servo-motors, Ulysses turned. The two-ton automaton was bearing down on him with clanking piston-strides.

Ulysses put his finger to the trigger of the flame-thrower, his first thought being that there had been a malfunction and the droid's former programming was reasserting itself. His second thought was that washing the golem with burning naphtha wasn't going to do the slightest bit of good, as much of the automaton's internal mechanisms were protected behind a shell of heat-resistant ceramic armour.

Ulysses could do nothing but stare into the malignant gaze of the Limehouse Golem's headlamp eyes as it reached one massive crushing hand towards him, and then snatched a mutant locust from the wall above him.

The golem closed its fingers, the insect's armoured body cracking open like a soft-boiled egg, foul-smelling goo spurting from between the cracks.

The scrabbling of insect limbs on brick echoed from the tunnels all around them.

Ulysses, Nimrod and the vigilante shot wary glances all around them; the droid's body rotating about its waist joint as it scanned the maze of collapsed alleyways, optical sensors scanning for body-heat signatures.

A horde of pale, chitinous bodies emerged from the gloom.

"Um, sir," Nimrod said, raising his flame-thrower. "I think we made them angry."

"Like pouring a kettle of boiling water on an ants' nest," Ulysses agreed.

Spring-Heeled Jack said nothing, but instead entered a code on his wrist-mounted control panel. The golem-droid immediately hunkered down, taking on a prize-fighter's stance, swaying from side to side, its huge steel fists bunched.

As he scanned the walls of the canyon above them, thick with massing insects, Ulysses' treacherous thoughts began to wonder if having the golem join the battle would be enough. When he had agreed to this mission he had known that they would meet resistance upon entering the insects' territory; he just hadn't expected anything on this scale.

"Give them hell!" Ulysses bellowed and pulled the trigger of his flame-gun.

The insects fell in their droves, the liquid fire washing over them in a torrent, but still they came.

Spring-Heeled Jack hacked and slashed, while the golem-droid tore the warrior insects from the walls and hurled them onto the ground where it crushed them beneath its massive feet, leaving nothing but a mess of slime and broken limbs behind.

Although they were giving a good account of themselves, Ulysses was not sure how long they could keep it up against such overwhelming odds. The flame-throwers' fuel was not inexhaustible, and if one of the horrors got close enough to rip open one of their containment suits then they would be exposed to the toxins in the atmosphere.

As another locust fell before him, its compound eyes sizzling and bursting as they burned, Ulysses became aware of a harsh grating sound, even over the shrieks and screams of the dying insects. He glimpsed movement out of the corner of his fishbowl helmet, and dared to turn his head.

At his feet a manhole cover had been raised and moved to one side. A grimy face peered up at him from the hole.

"If you want to live," said the man, in a rough East End accent, "come with me."

CHAPTER FIVE

The Eighth Plague

The manhole led into the crumbling sewer system that ran under St Paul's. After a fraught race through the stinking, claustrophobic tunnels, hot on the heels of their raggedy rescuers, they at last made for the surface again.

Climbing a corroded ladder they entered a subterranean chamber, watched over by what appeared to be beggars wielding rifles. And so it was that, under an armed guard, they at last entered the hallowed halls of the Old Bailey.

Ulysses, Nimrod and Spring-Heeled Jack stood at the centre of a high-roofed, echoing chamber. They had been forced to leave the golem-droid behind; its massive bulk was too big for the manhole. As he had ducked into the manhole himself, the last sight Ulysses had, as the cast-iron cover was pulled back into place over his head, was of the golem standing braced above him, covered in locusts, tearing the monstrous insects limb from limb.

Peering through the gloom, Ulysses took in their new surroundings. The three of them were surrounded by a rag-tag band of filthy, scruffily-dressed men and women – a dozen or so, Ulysses guessed, at a rough count. Beyond them the marble tiled floor was covered with make-shift beds.

Anxious faces watched them with wide-eyed fascination. There were men and women of all ages here, and even a few children.

Ulysses gasped. He had thought the contamination zones were deserted. But these people appeared to be unchanged. So why hadn't they tried to leave their hiding place and make it back over the wall?

But if they had been living here since the Catastrophe, and had remained unchanged, then...

Cautiously Ulysses undid the seal on his helmet and lifted the glass fishbowl from this head.

"What are you doing?" Spring-Heeled Jack hissed.

There was a lingering malignant odour in the air as of unwashed bodies and disease. For a moment, Ulysses considered putting his helmet back on, but then thought better of it.

Ulysses was relieved, but also surprised, to see that none of these refugees bore any obvious signs of mutation. They must have been among the lucky few to escape the *Jupiter* Station's toxic deluge, and the imbibing of that other vital chemical component that had laced Dr Feelgood's Tonic Stout. Supposedly the creation of an anonymous philanthropist, it had in fact been the product of another of disgraced former Prime Minister Uriah Wormwood's detestable schemes; engineered to force the globe-spanning empire of Magna Britannia to evolve beyond its Neo-Victorian bounds.

Although the three of them had been saved by the intervention of a number of those hiding out within the Old Bailey, Ulysses considered, they weren't safe yet. Too much had happened to these poor wretches in the last few weeks; they had seen too much to place their trust in strangers just yet. The dozen or so men and women now surrounding them were all armed – some with the most bizarre and antique firearms, others with cobbled together crossbows and knives. The dandy adventurer had seen a fair number of unusual weapons during his travels, but none quite like these before.

The three of them moved together so that they stood back to back, facing their possible saviours, keeping the whole ring of armed men and women in sight.

As Ulysses scanned the uncertain faces ranged before him, he saw a tall man, dressed in a grubby black cassock, rise from where he had been administering to an anxious-looking mother clutching a baby. The man turned and approached. He was lean, as well as tall, and his gaunt, aging face was framed by lank wisps of shoulder length white-grey hair. At his neck Ulysses saw the white flash of a dog collar and a heavy silver crucifix hung on a leather thong over the stained material of his robe.

The circle of guardians parted as he approached.

"And who do we have here? Three more lost sheep to join our growing flock, or more sinners in search of absolution?"

"'And the Lord said unto Moses, 'Stretch out thine hand over the land of Egypt for the locusts, that they may come up upon the land of Egypt, and eat every herb of the land, even all that the hail hath left. And Moses stretched forth his rod over the land of Egypt, and the Lord brought an east wind upon the land all that day, and all that night; and when it was morning, the east wind brought the locusts.'"

The Preacher's declamation was met with a chorus of amens and hallelujahs from the faithful, or the Children of the Catastrophe as they chose to call themselves.

"So let me get this straight. You think that the events of Valentine's Day are akin to the plagues of Egypt?"

"And you don't?" the Preacher railed.

"Put it in layman's terms for me," Ulysses suggested.

"Pestilence, hail, frogs, darkness," the Preacher checked the list off on his fingers, "all came in the wake of the launch of the *Jupiter* Station. A prime example of Man's hubris; an assault in the face of God. It could only ever go one way."

"But I was there." Hearing Ulysses' confession gasps went up from the crowd. "The Catastrophe was the work of one man – Uriah Wormwood, erstwhile Prime Minister of this great country of ours. It was not an act of God, or the Devil, for that matter."

"Does the Bible not say, 'The Lord moves in mysterious ways'?" This was met with more amens and exclamations in the name of great Jehovah. "And now we find ourselves beset by locusts.

"'For they covered the face of the whole earth, so that the land was darkened; and they did eat every herb of the land, and all the fruit of the trees which the hail had left: and there remained not any green thing in the trees, or in the herbs of the field, through all the land of Egypt.'"

"Praise the Lord!" came a euphoric cry.

"You know what?" Ulysses said, pointing. "A couple of hundred yards that way – if that – is a wall and a way out of this living hell. Why don't you just leave?"

"Because the Lord is testing us," the Preacher said, looking aghast at even the suggestion that they might escape from the purgatory in which they now dwelt. "On the other side of that self-same wall lies a modern day Sodom and Gomorrah. Here we are safe from the corruption and temptations of the city. Why would we want to leave?"

"But what about the children, you have trapped with you here? What about the old, the infirm? If you're not all sick already, they soon will be. It's unsanitary."

"There's nothing for us on the other side of the wall. Not for any of us. Our life in this world might be hard, but we shall have our reward in heaven."

Some might have had their faith tested by the events of recent times but with the Preacher it was more a case of that which doesn't kill you only makes you more committed. Ulysses considered that there was no reasoning with a man like that.

"I tell you now, God is not done with this new Babylon, this London!" the Preacher pronounced, his voice rising to a bellow. "London shall know God's wrath again. He shall not be content until every sinner has been made to account for his sins! Are you saved, sinner?"

"You tell me," Ulysses threw back. "No, hang on, don't bother. I think I can probably guess what your answer would be."

"Then you seek absolution."

"After a fashion, I suppose," Spring-Heeled Jack butted in.

The Preacher looked at him sourly. "You can take that off." He pointed at the vigilante's mask.

"I'd rather not, if you don't mind."

"What are you? You look like the Devil."

"Do you believe I am the Devil?" Jack challenged.

"Don't be ridiculous! I have encountered the spawn of Beelzebub, Lord of the Flies, and they are far more terrifying than you!"

"Her name's Miranda," Ulysses said.

"Miranda?" The Preacher was caught off-guard for a moment.

"His absolution. We're on a rescue mission," Ulysses added. "A young girl was taken by the locusts and carried over the wall into this no man's land of yours."

"A child you say?"

"She's only eleven years old," the vigilante said.

"Then you do seek absolution." The Preacher looked from Jack to Ulysses, and back again with a needling stare. "If the girl is still alive she will be in the hive."

"The hive?" Ulysses asked. "Where's that?"

"Why, within the desecrated house of our Lord, of course," the Preacher said, an unsettling smile spreading across his face.

"Then if that is where she is, we must be on our way," Ulysses said. "Now, if you'll just excuse us."

Nimrod rose to his feet, taking up his fishbowl helmet again.

"To enter the hive is to step through the gates of death," the Preacher told them.

"Right you are then," said Ulysses. "So, like I said, if you'd just like to point us to the nearest exit we'll be on our way."

"You're not going in there, just the three of you."

"Well, yes, as it happens." Ulysses was beginning to lose his patience with the priest. "Unless you're offering to come with us, that is."

"But of course."

"I thought not, so just point us to the-" Ulysses broke off. "You're what?"

"I am offering to come with you."

"But–"

"The road to salvation is long and hard," the Preacher explained, "and we are all of us sinners. A man can only earn the right to enter the kingdom of heaven by accomplishing good deeds and our place there is not yet assured." He took in his congregation with a sweeping gesture. "But, if it be the Lord's will, it will be soon."

"What do you mean?" Jack asked.

"We are being tested but the Lord has seen fit to provide us with the opportunity to redeem ourselves."

There was another shout of "Amen!" and weapons were raised and shaken in excited vindication.

"And with your coming into the wilderness the Lord has given us a sign. Tonight we strike back against the locusts, at the heart of the hive. And during our time in purgatory, on our own personal journey through the valley of the shadow of death, we have not been idle. We have been making ready, preparing the way of the Lord."

Ulysses shot anxious glances between the rabble-rousing fire and brimstone Preacher, his rabble-roused faithful flock and Nimrod and Jack.

"What precisely did you have in mind?"

"'Vengeance is mine,' saith the Lord.' And we have been truly blessed. For God has granted us the instrument of his vengeance."

"Instrument of his vengeance?" Ulysses looked at the Preacher with horror, but the priest seemed too caught up in his own rapturous vision to notice. "You mean you have a secret weapon?"

"There is nothing secret about it," the Preacher said, smiling as if he were addressing a simpleton. "And now you have brought us the means of delivering God's vengeance into the heart of the hive, the very pit of demons itself."

"We have?" Jack said.

Preternatural awareness flared at the back of Ulysses' brain, a split second before he heard the piston footstep of the droid.

He spun round, even though he already knew what he was going to see.

The Limehouse Golem loomed large before him. Ulysses wasn't sure whether he felt relieved or horrified to see the monstrous automaton. It bodywork was stained with a dried crust of goo and ichor and its ceramic armour bore the scars of its battle with the insects.

"You went back for it," Jack said, with almost fatherly concern, much to Ulysses' chagrin.

"No," the Preacher corrected him. "It found its own way here. It followed you home."

CHAPTER SIX

The New Queen of England

The rescue party and the Preacher's faithful flock stopped at the bottom of another rusted iron ladder.

Down here in the darkness Ulysses was glad of his helmet; it helped mask the effluent smell of the sewers, which brought back unpleasant memories of the wretched Professor Galapagos, the degenerating lizards and the trout-faced fishman.

He looked up into the gloom of the shaft above his head. "This is the place?"

"This is it," the Preacher confirmed.

"You're sure about that?"

The Preacher smiled broadly in the lamplight, the extremes of light and shadow giving him an almost demonic appearance. "Oh, I'm sure."

At the rear of the procession of the faithful, with a hiss of escaping steam, the golem-droid came to a halt. Ulysses noticed that it was carrying something; something large and spherical, covered by a tarpaulin.

They had not met anything on their way through the labyrinthine tunnels. It was certainly much safer moving around underground. If they had tried to approach the cathedral-hive from above ground, they would have had to contend with the full might of the hive's soldier caste.

It was incredible, really. Within the space of only a few weeks, creatures that had been created simultaneously from a whole cross-section of the populace living and working within the St Paul's area, had stabilized genetically. They had become a recognisable sub-species of giant insect, even forming into different castes very much as one would expect to see inside a termite nest.

As well as the highly aggressive soldier caste, made up of larger, and particularly lethal, wingless specimens, armed with viciously strong crushing mandibles, and the winged hunter caste, Ulysses supposed there must be a worker caste that maintained the hive. He found himself wondering what the queen of such a colony would be like.

Ulysses turned his gaze from the vertical shaft above him to the Preacher.

"After you," he said with a wave of his rubber-gloved hand.

If Ulysses hadn't already known that the nest had been constructed inside the church of St Paul's itself, he would have been hard-pressed to see that that was where they were now.

The longer he stared at the towering structures all around him, the more he could convince himself that it was just about recognisable as London's greatest church building, despite the locusts' desecration.

The Preacher had been as good as his word, leading the way from the sewers into the crypts beneath the cathedral. The first thing he had done on entering the mucus-encrusted walls of the catacombs was to take a machete from under his cassock and gut the first drone they ran into, taking it apart with savage glee. Then, splattered with the sticky white mess of the insect's innards, he had extracted some grotesquely quivering internal organ or other, the faithful taking it in turns to smear their clothes, and even their skin, with the vile stuff that oozed from the horrid receptacle.

"To mask our natural odour," he said as he passed the slime sac to Ulysses and his companions. "With this covering you the locusts will believe that you are one of their own."

And so, reluctantly, that was how they had penetrated the hive.

From the crypt they entered the main body of the church and it was there that they came upon the locust drones in greater numbers than ever before. They edged their way forwards, following the assured example of the God-fearing Preacher, who boldly led his flock where angels now feared to tread.

Ulysses' first instinct upon meeting the insects was to freeze, his second to turn his flame-thrower upon the drones and burn the lot of them within their sacrilegious nest. But they were right inside the hive now, and such a course of action would have been nothing less than suicidal. The locusts would have stripped the flesh from their bones, just as surely as their Biblical counterparts had devoured the crops of Egypt all those millennia before.

And so Ulysses, Nimrod and Spring-Heeled Jack had continued to follow the Preacher and his flock as they made their way deeper into the church, towards the heart of the hive.

The interior of the cathedral had been completely transformed by the gigantic insects. Sir Christopher Wren's remarkable, beautifully-wrought designs paled in comparison to the pillars and galleries raised by the locusts that buried the former beneath tons of compacted earth, chewed pews and saliva-gummed paper.

They passed countless worker drones, coming within only a few feet of them on more than one occasion as they crept slowly and silently forwards, always moving in the direction of the high altar. The insects were busily occupied with maintaining the structure of the hive and tending to the hundreds upon hundreds of soft white eggs that filled the twisting terraces and tunnels.

Ulysses gazed at the egg-filled hollows and galleries that rose up in tiers like the stalls of a choir before him. "There must be thousands of the things," he said, in an appalled whisper.

"There are," the Preacher confirmed. "'They covered the face of the whole earth, so that the land was darkened; and they did eat every herb of the land, and all the fruit of the trees which the hail had left: and there remained not any green thing in the trees, or in the herbs of the field, through all the land of Egypt.'"

The Preacher scanned the galleries of the cathedral-hive. "The queen must be nearby."

The Preacher beckoned them forwards, squeezing past a pillar plastered with regurgitated hymnals; the massive column one of the four great pillars that supported the cathedral's remarkable dome.

Ulysses looked at the Preacher suspiciously. "Have you been here before?"

The wild-haired cleric turned, his face contorted in silent anger, a callused finger on his lips. With his other hand he pointed dome-wards.

Ulysses, Jack and Nimrod looked up as one. The dandy was forced to swallow hard as he felt his gorge rise.

"Meet the new Queen of England," the Preacher said. "For if we fail in our endeavour this day that is surely what she will become."

The abomination filled the space that lay below Wren's desecrated dome. Lying atop a mound of excretion-glued church furniture, and what were undoubtedly human remains, hanging within a cradle of solidified mucus strings, the queen was little more than a massive egg-laying abdomen. The part of the creature that was recognisable as one of the 'changed' insects writhed, as if in pain, whilst being continually fed by an endless chain of her faithful subjects.

But by far the larger part was little more than a swollen sac of undulating, white, boneless flesh. As wide as a locomotive carriage and twice as long, the distended abdomen was coiled in on itself within the void beneath the dome. Even as the horrified rescuers watched, a new egg was pushed from the sagging sphincter of the ovipositor. It was immediately collected and carried away by a waiting drone, the worker setting off to find a safe resting place elsewhere within the hive; the next locust in line preparing to take the next egg.

An endless chain of locust drones waited on the queen at either end, an endless stream of slave-insects feeding her tasty morsels plucked from the ruins of St Paul's so that she might continue to lay more and more eggs, the whole process driven by the sole instinctive need to perpetuate the locust species.

"Sir," Nimrod whispered at Ulysses' shoulder, "if all those eggs hatch..."

"I know, the locusts will swarm and fall upon London in an apocalyptic re-enactment of the Eighth Plague of Egypt."

"Our purpose is clear," the Preacher suddenly declared. "The abomination and her unholy brood must burn in the purifying fires of God's holy retribution!"

"I agree!" Ulysses joined him in his rabble-rousing as the insects became aware of their presence within the hive. Unstrapping the Smith and Winchester from his back, he passed the flame-thrower to the priest. "Here, take this."

The Preacher accepted the proffered weapon with a quizzical expression on his face.

"Where are you going?"

"We have to find the girl. But you have your own holy work to be about, and that will give you a headstart. The queen must die. Long live the Queen!"

CHAPTER SEVEN

Revelation

"This way," Spring-Heeled Jack said and set off up the echoing stairs.

Ulysses tensed for the hundredth time, wondering if the sound would alert the locusts, despite the measures they had taken to mask their presence. He shot anxious glances both up and down the broad spiralling staircase that led from the ground floor of the cathedral to the Whispering Gallery at the bottom of St Paul's magnificent dome.

A worker drone suddenly appeared around the turn of the stair. Ulysses, Nimrod and the vigilante pressed their backs flat against the wall. The creature passed first Jack, then Ulysses, and then the three rescuers heard a fiery bellow as the Preacher unleashed the full fury of Ulysses' borrowed flame-thrower on the nest.

The drone halted abruptly. Its head arched back, antennae rippling as it sniffed the air. A pheromone warning had been sent informing every locust within the cathedral that the hive was under attack. And then the locust was gone, moving at a canter as it continued on its way down the spiralling staircase, moving as fast as a six-legged thoroughbred.

"Come on," Jack goaded the others as he began to take the steps two at a time, his cape flowing behind him, "there's no time to waste. We have to find the girl."

Taking several more striding steps, Ulysses found himself at the entrance to the world famous Whispering Gallery. Only it looked nothing like the interior of the dome that St Paul's was famous for. Now it was the locusts' larder.

The inside skin of the dome – that had once been adorned by the most marvellous paintings – was now plastered with more masticated paper, fabric, earth and mucus; all mixed together by the worker drones.

Locked within the mud and paper walls of the larder, like flies trapped in amber, were the insects' victims. There were cats and dogs and all manner of birdlife; the occasional flutter of a wing or pained yowl alerting the rescuers to the horrible truth that the locusts' queen obviously liked her prey to be served up warm.

But worst of all were the alcoves containing human beings. Everywhere Ulysses looked he saw pale, drawn faces, peering out from the cells of the prisons in which they had been secured.

"There!" Jack called out, pointing to the other side of the gallery. "There's the girl!"

Ulysses started moving, hurrying after the vigilante, Nimrod bringing up the rear. The vigilante had done well to recognise the child, given that her hair was plastered with hardened mucus and only her face was visible within the horrid crust.

The three rescuers made their way around the gallery ledge, the late afternoon sunlight pouring in through the high windows painting the faces of those trapped within the larder wall, giving them the appearance of cherubic angels.

The gallery was eerily deserted, the Preacher's attack on the hive obviously impelling the drones to rally against the enemy, instinct informing the insects that their priority was to safeguard the queen and her offspring, the blood royal, and, thereby, the future of the colony.

Ulysses glanced down over the railing of the walkway. He could see the queen, writhing as if in torment, as a host of drones came to her aid; swarming all over her, cutting through the concrete-hard mucus-strings holding her in place with scissoring mandibles. They were freeing her from her constraints, presumably to move her to safety.

Seeing the drones scuttling all over the queen body's only impressed upon Ulysses how big the locusts' monarch was. Even without the egg-producing sac she was still twice the size of even the largest of her soldier bodyguards. God alone knew what she had been before the transforming rain fell on London.

The orange glow of an explosion illuminated her monstrous majesty for a moment as the Preacher and his crusading soldiers of Christ set to work purging the hive. And was he imagining things, or could Ulysses really hear a bellowed exorcism taking place below them within the nave of the church?

"Help me get her down." Spring-Heeled Jack was struggling to free the child from the larder wall, tugging at the mucoid crust with his gauntleted hands. The vigilante extending his talon-blades with a flick of his wrists the dandy pulled away great pieces of the sticky crust.

And then Victor Gallowglass's daughter was free. She moaned softly as the vigilante lifted her down and laid her gently over his shoulder.

"Let's get out of here," he said.

"What about the others?" Nimrod asked.

"We leave them."

"We can't do that," Ulysses' manservant said in utter disbelief.

"I can, and I will," the vigilante declaimed. "I came for the girl, nothing more."

"Nimrod's right," Ulysses interjected. "You've got a lot to learn about being a hero if you're ready to leave these poor bastards to, what would appear to be, a fate worse than death."

Another explosion rocked the cathedral dome.

"Take the girl and leave, if you want. Victor Gallowglass will be grateful, I'm sure, but I for one – and Nimrod, for another – cannot simply leave everyone else to burn in the fires of hell that our new acquaintances are unleashing down there. Come on, old boy, let's get to work. We haven't got much time."

The vigilante watched, stunned into inaction, the girl limp over his shoulder, as the dandy and his manservant set about ripping down more of the hardened mucus shell, encasing the locusts' victims.

The crust was coming away more readily now, Nimrod helping those freed by Ulysses' exertions, clamber free onto the walkway of the gallery. The barely-conscious wretches seemed incapable of doing very much for themselves at all. Some mumbled their thanks, their words slurred as if they had only just woken from some interminable nightmare. Others began to cry. All of them huddled together helplessly, waiting to be told what to do.

"Nimrod, get these people downstairs," Ulysses instructed his manservant. "I'll finish off here."

Nimrod herded the helpless, disorientated prisoners of the locusts towards the staircase; taking his position at the front of the line, flame-thrower sweeping the stairwell in front of him.

Ulysses shot Jack a dark look as another portion of the larder wall gave way with a sticky crack.

"Still here? Decided what you're going to do yet?"

"Wh-What's going on?" came a half-conscious murmur from behind Ulysses before the vigilante could answer. The dandy turned and looked into the face of an unshaven, rough-looking rogue. The rogue looked at the dandy and the towering figure of Spring-Heeled Jack, his eyes taking time to focus. He screamed as cruel recollection returned and threatened to overwhelm his mind.

"Monsters!" he howled. "The monsters are coming!"

"Look, you're alright," Ulysses told the man, placing his hands firmly on his shoulders. "We're going to get you out of here."

"You!" the vigilante said suddenly, taking a step towards the wretch. "I know you."

The man's already drawn face suddenly turned even paler and he ceased his wailing.

"Is he a friend of yours?" Ulysses asked.

"No," the vigilante replied. He lent forwards, bringing his face closer so that the man could see the demonic visage of his mask quite clearly. "You were taken at the same time as the girl."

"What do you mean he was taken with the girl? Oh, I see," Ulysses said, as realisation dawned.

"If it hadn't been for you and your friends," Jack snarled, "we wouldn't be here now, especially not this poor child."

"Looks like it's your lucky day," Ulysses told the cowering kidnapper. "If Jack here had shared that little snippet of information before I pulled you free, I would have thought twice about saving you. As it is, you made your bed when you kidnapped my friend's daughter; now you can lie in it. Whether you make it out of here alive or not is up to you. And if you do, I suggest that as soon as you're clear, you start running – and don't stop."

Gunning the trigger of his Smith and Winchester, Nimrod doused the swooping locusts with another jet of burning naphtha. The giant insects made horribly shrill noises as they dropped to the ground, their wings weighed down with burning oil. Yelps of fear and shock came from the huddle of desperate wretches following him. But that last sweep of the flame-thrower had done the trick. It had cleared a way through to the Preacher and his party.

The bodies of workers crisped and blackened in the intense heat. Eggs blistered and popped.

Bringing up the end of the line, along with the vigilante and his precious cargo, Ulysses was momentarily taken aback to see the golem-droid standing there, amidst the rising flames, still carrying whatever it was it had brought here from the Old Bailey.

Ulysses stared into the soot-blackened face of the Preacher.

"We are ready," the cleric said, with something like triumph in his voice. He regarded the line of shuffling prisoners, with surprise shaping his features. "It would appear you have been busy doing the Lord's work too."

"Yes, we're ready to leave," Ulysses said.

"Oh no, we're not leaving." The Preacher sounded almost surprised that Ulysses should even suggest such a thing. There was an unnerving gleam in his eyes. Despite the flames raging all around him, Ulysses felt suddenly cold. "No, what I mean is that we are ready to bring God's divine retribution down upon the abominations."

"What precisely did you have in mind?" Ulysses asked, sure that he wasn't going to like the answer.

Amidst all the chaos, the smoke and the flames, the Preacher strode up to the towering two-ton automaton and put one hand to the tarpaulin.

"Behold the instrument of God's divine retribution, his bow of burning gold, his chariot of fire," the Preacher said and tugged the tarpaulin free.

Nimrod swore with uncustomary force.

Jack stared at the object. "Now that *is* impressive."

The Preacher raised his crucifix and kissed it.

Ulysses' face drained of colour. "Oh my God, no."

"Is that what I think it is, sir?" Nimrod said, not once taking his eyes from the iron sphere grasped in the golem's hands.

"Unless I'm very much mistaken," Ulysses said, "I rather fear it is."

The two men regarded the spiked sphere, that proudly bore the misspelt mantra 'Vengeance is mine sayeth the Lord' on its tarnished surface in bold strokes of red paint.

"I know a bomb when I see one, and that's one hell of a big bomb," Spring-Heeled Jack said. "But where did it come from?"

"It's one of the devices used by the Darwinian Dawn during their attack on the Tower of London on the night of the Queen's jubilee," Ulysses said, taking a step back. He felt numb. "If you detonate that in here, the cathedral will be filled with Professor Galapagos's gas and that which isn't destroyed by the subsequent inferno will be reduced to a state of protoplasmic slime."

"I know," the Preacher smiled.

No wonder he had been so happy for his Children of the Catastrophe to attack the nest directly, and thereby create a distraction so that Ulysses and the others might search for the girl.

This had never been about getting in and out again as quickly as possible, or alive for that matter. As far as the Preacher and his converts were concerned, this was a one-way suicide mission. They were martyrs to their twisted cause.

"We have to get out of here," Jack hissed, the unconscious girl still slung over his shoulder.

"You have never been more right." Ulysses regarded the anxious faces of the freed prisoners before him. "Back to the crypt, and quickly!"

As Ulysses, Nimrod and Spring-Heeled Jack made their way back to the underground vault by which they had first entered the cathedral – their rag-tag band of survivors in tow – they thankfully ran into no resistance from the hive's guardian whatsoever. Above them, the fire was spreading; setting light to banners and extravagantly ornamented woodwork alike with sacrilegious efficacy.

However, on reaching the crypt it was another matter entirely. Nimrod had barely descended the steps before a pair of soldiers – their chitin armour tougher, their mandibles larger – caught up with them.

Ulysses only just turned in time. He met the rearing charge of one with the grappling-gun held out before him. As the unnatural creature snapped at him, with jaws perfectly capable of removing his head with one bite, Ulysses clubbed the soldier around the head with the stock of the device. It reeled, recovered, and then leapt forward once more, determined to bring the dandy down this time. But before it could reach him, steel claws flashed before his face, and the locust's head dropped onto the despoiled stone flags of the cathedral floor. Its body followed a moment later, twitching spastically, ichor dribbling from the stump of its neck.

"Take her," Spring-Heeled Jack said, as he swung the catatonic child from his shoulder and passed her into

Nimrod's outstretched arms and then turned to face the second soldier.

The monster's mandibles snapped shut mere inches from his face, as Ulysses, using the grapple-gun like a cudgel now, brought the metal barrel of the thing down on the beast's abdomen. The dandy's quick-thinking gave Jack all the time he needed to counter the locust's attack.

He kicked at the soldier's head but the action didn't lay the creature out. Instead it seemed to provoke the locust. Hissing like a cockroach, the over-sized insect reared up on its hindquarters, the shearing claws of its forelimbs raised, and then dropped again, putting all its not inconsiderable weight behind the attack.

Jack slashed sideways with his left hand, his talons meeting the serrated edge of the monster's own mutated locust-form and snagging into the steel-hard chitin. At the same time, he brought his right-hand up, his fingers bunching into a fist, and punched the razor-sharp tips of his other set of claws into the beast's thorax.

Internal juices spurted from the ruptured body cavity and Jack twisted his hand round, pulling his ichor-drenched fist free as the warrior fell backwards, its body jerking in a macabre dance of death.

"Look out!" Ulysses yelled, suddenly barrelling into the vigilante and sending him flying into the splintered remains of a partially masticated pew.

With a clattering crash, a pile of timbers and an assortment of organ pipes hit the stone-flagged floor in a welter of flames and an explosion of sparks.

Picking himself up off the floor, Ulysses looked at the entrance to the crypt, now blocked by half a ton of burning wreckage and twisted metal. He could hear muffled screams over the hungry roar of the spreading flames.

"Nimrod?" he called. "Are you alright?"

"Yes, sir," came his valet's reply, from the other side of the crypt entrance. "No injuries sustained here. How are you?"

"Chipper old boy, most definitely chipper. You go on ahead and we'll catch you up as soon as." Ulysses turned to the vigilante. "Where's that droid of yours when we need it, eh? Should get this cleared in a jiffy, shouldn't it."

"No can do, I'm afraid," Jack said, already tapping at the control panel on his wrist.

"What do you mean?"

"It's offline."

"What?" Ulysses raged.

"The Preacher must have turned it off after it got here."

"What? How did he manage that?"

"I guess somebody else around here knows almost as much about automatons as I do."

"Well can you shift that little lot?" Ulysses asked, taking in the burning wreckage blocking the crypt steps.

"No. Can you?"

"So what you're saying is that we're trapped."

"That's how it looks to me." The vigilante regarded him with the pitiless stare of his red-lensed goggles. "So where do we go from here?"

"I have no idea," Ulysses admitted, "but we have to get as far from the blast radius of that bomb as possible."

"I have an idea," Jack suddenly announced. "Follow me."

CHAPTER EIGHT

Exodus

Sprinting up the stairs as fast as their suits would allow, Spring-Heeled Jack and Ulysses Quicksilver returned to the Whispering Gallery.

They burst through the doorway – Ulysses remembering that on the other side of the gallery lay the door that led to the roof – only to be confronted by the sight of the kidnapper, cowering on the curving walkway, as if paralysed by fear, as another burst of hot incendiary light lit up the vaulted space below.

"You still here?" Ulysses asked, surprised.

"You left me here!" he screamed.

"No, we left you with a choice. You chose not to come with us," Ulysses pointed out as he and the vigilante advanced towards the man.

"It was nothing more than you deserved," Spring-Heeled Jack added.

Below them the queen continued to squirm in fear as her subjects tried to gnaw her free of her cradle.

Spring-Heeled Jack simply stepped over the wretch. But as Ulysses passed the kidnapper, the man shot out a hand and grasped hold of his ankle.

"Help me, I beg of you. Please, take me with you!"

"That all depends," Ulysses told the man as he pulled his leg free.

"On what?"

"Do you think you can keep up?"

Fire spurted from the nozzle of the flame-thrower, bathing the advancing insects in the light of God's vengeance. The Preacher turned and worked the trigger again, hosing another giant locust with holy flame.

All around him his Children of the Catastrophe – their pitiful lives given new purpose now that they faced a martyr's death – took the fight to the enemy, each playing his or her part to rid God's house of Beelzebub's spawn.

But their success was already a foregone conclusion; the device had been primed and the countdown to Doomsday had begun. They were only marking time until God passed judgement on those damned souls who had been brought low by the apocalyptic deluge.

Behind them, the droid stood motionless, the timer attached to the iron sphere ticking itself towards destruction.

Thirty seconds remaining.

"'In the beginning God created the heaven and the earth.'"

Another insect fell shrieking, the tongues of fire, like the Holy Spirit coming upon the twelve apostles at Pentecost, reflecting from the automaton's glazed terracotta armour, making the droid look like God's own avenging angel.

Twenty seconds.

"'And the earth was without form, and void.'"

And then the fuel supply failed. His purging of the unclean had drained it completely. Shaking off the flame-thrower's shoulder straps he prepared to meet the oncoming enemy with his bare hands.

Ten.

"'And darkness was upon the face of the waters.'"

In a blur of buzzing wings a locust swept down from its perch within the vault of the cathedral roof. It hit the Preacher head on, with such force that it sent him flying backwards towards the droid. But before his body could hit the ground the insect snatched him from the air, holding him close with its claws.

Five.

"'And the Spirit of God moved upon the face of the waters!'"

Four.

The locust climbed higher, through the smoky miasma pervading the cathedral vault.

Three.

Spittle flying from his lips the Preacher bellowed his frustrated rage to the starry-painted heavens. "'And the Lord said–'"

Two.

"'Let there be light!'"

One.

A swelling ball of crimson flame spread throughout the church with a whirlwind roar. Stained glass windows blew out in myriad explosions of sparkling diamond shards. Hundreds of the giant insects died instantly, crumbling to ash before the apocalyptic onslaught. Thousands upon thousands of eggs and grotesque larvae roasted.

And after the fire came the gas, the flames carrying it higher and higher. Those among the hive not caught by the initial explosion succumbed to the toxic cloud, shrivelling and dissolving as each regressed still further down the evolutionary scale, until all that was left of them was a runny brown protoplasmic soup that fell onto the furious flames to boil away to nothing.

Spring-Heeled Jack and Ulysses, with the crippled kidnapper in tow, stumbled as the shockwave of the explosion shook the beleaguered structure of St Paul's.

They threw themselves through the door that led to the roof stairs, the desperate wretch staggering after them, tripping over the threshold.

After the brilliant intensity of the firestorm consuming the cathedral, it seemed unnaturally dark on the other side of the door.

With barely a moment's hesitation, the three fellow escapees set off up the rickety wooden stairs they found beyond.

Every step they took – every twisting, turning flight of the stair, every landing they achieved – brought them closer to the roof of the cathedral and a way out of the hive.

At last they threw open another door and emerged into the cool of the evening.

The ruins of St Paul's lay spread out beneath them, the dusky purple shadows of twilight giving way to the growing intensity of the flames consuming the building as the sun set behind the ever present pall of the Smog.

Ulysses slammed the roof door shut behind them, and then looked for something he could use to keep it that way.

Spring-Heeled Jack regarded the terrified kidnapper but didn't say a word.

The clattering rattle of an Overground train passing by only a few yards away abruptly reminded Ulysses of precisely where they were. The layout of this stretch of the Northern Line, that passed within only a few yards of the dome of St Paul's, was one of the worst architectural atrocities committed against the city. An appalling example of how the pace of progress could completely fail to consider the impact such an eyesore would have on one of London's most cherished landmarks.

Ulysses could feel the parapet shaking as the train passed by; the encroaching night illuminated by the windows beneath them, alive as they were with a flickering glow.

With a crash of a shattering brick and a rending scream of tearing metal the dome came apart behind them.

Trailing tiles, bricks and splintered spars of wood, the locust queen hauled herself from the ruins of the roof and into the fading twilight.

Ulysses and Jack made a dash for the far side of the parapet but the kidnapper was still turning to what it was that had burst through the dome as the monstrous monarch swept him up in her gigantic mantis-like claws. Raising his struggling body to her clicking mandibles, she pushed his head into her mouth and removed it with one clean bite.

Casting the dead man's twitching carcass aside, the mother of the hive stalked towards them.

CHAPTER NINE

The Female of the Species

Ulysses' mind was awhirl. What did the Queen want? Was there a human intelligence at work within that mantis head of hers? Did insects harbour feelings of anger and revenge?

Her monstrous majesty put her head on one side and regarded the dandy with the faceted spheres of her huge compound eyes.

Ulysses took another step backwards and felt the parapet of the windswept stone balcony at his back. The wail of the curfew sirens rose in the distance, accompanied by the clanging of church bells, warning the wary to get indoors before the locusts went hunting.

The queen had him cornered now, and the only thing Ulysses had about his person remotely resembling a weapon was the grappling gun slung across his back – the same compressed-gas gun that had served him so well in his race to catch up with the Darwinian Dawn's zeppelin on Queen Victoria's 160th jubilee celebrations.

He heard the *schlock* of the vigilante's talons unsheathing and, trying not to make any sudden movements, reached for the grappling gun.

"You think we can take it?" Jack hissed.

The creature jerked its head as if it was listening to what was being said.

"We have to try. Besides, do we have any other choice?"

The giant insect gave a banshee wail and Ulysses was reminded of the fact that the thing rearing before him had once been human.

But just as he thought the queen was going to attack, great wings unfurled from its back and, with an inhuman shriek, the monstrous thing launched itself into the sky.

The dandy and the vigilante looked at each other.

"We have to stop her," Ulysses gasped.

"Say no more. You ready for another aerial adventure?" Jack asked as he took hold of Ulysses firmly under his arms.

"As I'll ever be."

Ulysses heard the hiss of the jet-pack's pilot light as the vigilante activated the rocket engine he had strapped to his back.

A cone of blue flame and choking oily smoke jetting from its exhaust, Spring-Heeled Jack leapt into the air. With a boom the jet-pack ignited and then the vigilante and his passenger were rocketing into the gathering dusk, after the locust queen.

"There she is!" Ulysses yelled over the howling roar of the wind. He couldn't be sure that Spring-Heeled Jack had heard him, but the vigilante must have spotted the fleeing queen as well, as he directed their soaring flight path to pursue the monstrous bug.

The locust was still visible, despite the rapidly failing light, the lights of the city below reflecting from its iridescent wings. It was moving west, possibly following the course of the sluggish river two hundred feet below.

They were high above the criss-crossing Overground lines now; although Ulysses preferred to focus on the creature they were pursuing, rather than the distance between him and the ground.

They were higher than the fleeing queen; the huge locust-thing moving much more quickly than he would have expected of such a huge insect. But they were closing on it now, Ulysses fighting to keep his eyes open in the face of the cold wind buffeting him.

St Paul's was behind them. Ahead the dandy could just make out the shadows of the avenue of trees that bisected that, and beyond that, the twinkling lights of Buckingham Palace.

"What do we do now?" The vigilante's distorted voice sounded loud in Ulysses ear.

"Just get us above that thing!" Ulysses screamed back into the wind.

"Will do."

The two men hove in closer as the myriad maze of streets passed below them, amidst trailing columns of smoke and sooty clouds. And then the locust queen was directly below. It seemed oblivious to their presence, but that was a state of affairs that wouldn't last for much longer.

"Here goes nothing," Ulysses muttered under his breath, and then, clipping the grapple-gun to his belt again, shouted: "Let me go!"

There was a moment's hesitation – and then Ulysses felt the vigilante release his hold and the next thing he knew, the wind was rushing into his face even more furiously as he dropped like a stone through the agitated air.

He landed astride the locust between thorax and abdomen. As the surprised insect lurched beneath him, he grabbed hold of the first thing he could to stop himself from falling, which happened to be the bone-hard stubs of the queen's wings.

Ulysses' muscles tensed as he fought to control the blurred beat of the delicate wings, and then something gave with a cartilaginous crack. The locust dropped, its legs kicking in panic It felt like he was riding a bucking bronco, a wild rodeo mustang. The world rushed up to meet them. Lights whirled and spun. Trees flickered past. Ulysses felt sick.

A vast white facade was rapidly filling the space before Ulysses' eyes, and then he was hurtling past it, the locust still jerking beneath him.

The monstrous insect and its disorientated passenger slammed into the ground with the force of an omnibus crash. Chitinous limbs snapped and Ulysses was thrown free, landing in a carefully-clipped box hedge ten feet away.

Ulysses struggled to free himself of the shrubbery, his containment suit tearing on twigs as he did so, desperate eyes quickly finding the grounded locust again. Hissing violently, the queen struggled to rise and then flopped down on the tidy green sward of the lawn into which the collision had half buried it. Broken wings spasmed and the creature's mandibles scissored angrily.

The dandy staggered to his feet, unhooking the grappling gun from his belt. Confidently, he strode towards the monster as the queen struggled to rise once more.

"The queen is dead," he declared as he took aim with the device. "Long live the Queen!"

The grapple fired with a *whoosh* of compressed gas, the solid metal barbs punching through the carapace of the locust's thorax.

The giant mutated insect gave what sounded like a hissing scream and then crumpled, collapsing onto the lawn, sticky ichor oozing from the hole punched clean through its body, and didn't move again.

"Are you alright, sir?" a bewildered-looking footman asked as he hurried across the grass to Ulysses side, unable to take his eyes from the thing lying dead on the devastated lawn. And then, slowly, realisation dawned. "Oh my God," he gasped, and turned away sharply, a hand to his mouth.

"Yes, I think so. Nothing a glass of cognac wouldn't put right at any rate."

Ulysses turned from the cooling carcass of the locust queen to see a troop of guardsmen followed by more footmen hurrying from the palace and across the carefully-tended gardens to join them.

For a moment he thought he heard the roar of Spring-Heeled Jack's jet-pack above him, but then the sound faded into the distance again.

"If you can't stand the heat," he muttered under his breath.

The clatter of a rifle being raised and primed announced the arrival of the first of the guardsmen.

"What the hell's going on?" the man demanded, his gun pointing squarely at the dandy.

"Rather a long story," Ulysses mumbled. "How long have you got?"

"You're coming with me!" the guardsmen snapped.

"Really?" Ulysses countered. "I take it then that you have no idea who I am."

"Then perhaps you'd care to enlighten me, sir!"

"All in good time; all in good time. But how about that brandy first? Oh, and perhaps you'd like to pass on my deepest regrets to Her Majesty; it would appear that we have made a right royal mess of her croquet lawn."

CHAPTER TEN

Genesis

Victor Gallowglass flung open the door before Ulysses could knock. "Is there any news?"

He broke off almost immediately, frantically searching eyes settling on the one thing he wanted to see more than any other.

His daughter cowered between the dandy and his manservant, still in the nightdress she had been wearing the night she had been abducted. As soon as she saw her father, a certain sparkle returned to her sunken, hollow-eyed expression.

"Miranda?" Gallowglass's eyes were already brimming with tears as he stepped hesitantly over the threshold of his Belgravia townhouse, as if he couldn't quite believe that it was really her.

"Daddy," the child said, her voice barely more than a murmur, as if she was just waking from a dream.

And then father and daughter were reunited as Gallowglass dropped to his knees, there on the doormat. Parent and child threw their arms around each other, embracing in a hug that it seemed they never intended breaking. The girl's governess watched from the hallway behind, wringing her handkerchief in her hands.

Ulysses looked at his manservant. "Time to go, I think, don't you, Nimrod?"

"Very good, sir."

The two tired and filthy men turned and started to descend the steps of the Gallowglass family home.

Gallowglass looked up from where his face had been buried in his daughter's neck. "Where's the vigilante?"

Ulysses glanced up to where a smoky contrail described a curving path across the darkening sky.

"He had to fly," he said. "And so must we."

Back home in Mayfair, Ulysses collapsed into the leather armchair behind his desk, numb with shock.

He hadn't even bothered to remove his muck-encrusted boots before reading the letter that had been left for him by his brother. Now they were simply forgotten, along with the rest of his befouled condition.

He raised the handwritten letter and read it again.

Dear Ulysses,

By the time you read this, I'll be gone. I'm sorry I didn't say goodbye, but this letter will just have to do. I never was very good with farewells. Besides, I didn't want to hang around and give you the chance to dissuade me. This is something I should have done long ago.

Things are getting too hot for me round here. I'm an idiot, I know, but I've got myself in deeper than ever – than hopefully you'll ever know. So fate forced my hand, you might say, and it was time to leave.

I've gone off-world. Like I say, I should have done this long ago, rather than go and bring all my troubles to your door. As if you don't have enough of your own!

Anyway, don't try to come after me. After all, the empire needs you. And don't worry – I'll be alright.

We'll see each other again, when things have cooled down a little, I hope. But in the meantime, have a nice life.

Your brother,

B

P.S. – And if anyone comes looking for me, don't let on, there's a good chap.

* * *

Within the smouldering shell of St Paul's Cathedral, the fires had all but burnt themselves out.

And from the devastation left by the holy radiance of God's vengeance, the survivors congregated beneath the great shattered dome at the end of the nave, before the smouldering pulpit.

From his elevated position, the Preacher gazed down at his new congregation.

He had been a man once, a priest for a short while, and a husband and father before that. But that was a lifetime ago now – *two* lifetimes. Now he was something else altogether.

The left side of his face was a mess of crisped skin and blisters. The other side was something else entirely.

He looked down upon the Children of the Catastrophe with new eyes. They had all been reborn, each of them rising again from the ashes left by the purging fires of God's holy retribution; each like a phoenix rising from the flames, like Lazarus rising from the dead. Like the Son of God Himself rising to new life from the tomb.

His foot knocked against something heavy. He bent down and hefted it from the floor of the pulpit in his left hand. The chitinous claw that his right arm had become was of little use in that regard now.

It was a book; not some flimsy card and paper thing, but a weighty, leather-bound tome.

The Preacher studied the scorched leather tooling of the cover, his fingers tracing the shape of the cross worked into the dark, aged leather.

He opened the blackened Bible, letting the pages fall where they would. The good book open on the lectern in front of him, the Preacher looked again upon those gathered before him.

He had a new congregation now, more lost souls in need of spiritual succour and guidance than he had ever known before. There were those changed like himself but also the few remaining locusts, gathered now at the foot of the pulpit amidst the shrivelled larval forms and ruptured egg sacs.

Looking at the text before him, through one eye – red and irritated – he saw the word of God. Through the other a mind-numbing, sense-scrambling vision of God's word revealed itself to him. God's message leapt out at him from the page; the kaleidoscopic image repeating over and over again in a faceted visual cacophony, as he tried to adjust to seeing the world now through the compound eye of an insect.

He began to read.

"'And God said, Let there be light: and there was light. And God saw the light, that it was good: and God divided the light from the darkness. And God called the light Day, and the darkness he called Night. And the evening and the morning were the first day.'"

'And the locusts went up over all the land of Egypt, and rested in all the coasts of Egypt: very grievous were they; before them there were no such locusts as they, neither after them shall be such.' (Exodus ch.10 v.14)

ACT TWO

Something Wicked

March 1998

CHAPTER ELEVEN

The Great Game

It was uncomfortably warm within the darkened chamber, but then that was how he liked it. He felt the cold so. The lamps had been turned down. Shuttered with crimson shades, they bathed the room in a dim ruddy glow. That was how he liked it too. He found bright light... uncomfortable.

His breathing was rapid and shallow, and was drowned out by the respiratory sounds of the pump. This was the part he hated, more than any other. A shiver of sickness passed through his body, leaving him with a knot of nausea in his stomach. He was slick with clammy perspiration. In the gloom of the subterranean chamber his fish-white skin almost seemed to glow with an eerie, inner luminescence. Sitting there in the dark he looked just like a ghost.

Sometimes he felt as though he had died a hundred deaths already; that a little more of him died every time he had to endure the process. It felt as though it was killing him, and all because of the 'cure'. A cure, Grigori had told him, but what manner of cure was it that simply prolonged your death, rather than your life.

He hated being connected to the machine on a weekly basis, regular as the clockwork that ensured the transfusion device kept functioning. And yet, without it, he would have died long ago. Sometimes he wondered if that would have been such a bad thing. But he had suffered for too long, endured too much to give up now. Plain stubbornness was all that kept him going.

But it wouldn't be for much longer. Soon he would have the cure he had been seeking for all these years. Soon he would be free of the arcane machine.

The abrupt crackling hum of static broke through the asthmatic wheezing of the bellows, the ticking of the plasma exchange pump's regulator and the insistent *drip-drip-drip* of collected condensation dropping from the roof and hitting the stone-flagged floor.

Adjusting the chair in which he sat, operating the crank with his right hand, he brought the seat upright, pain lancing his body as the tubes inserted into his flesh pulled at the plug points.

Tapping a series of keys on the input keyboard in front of him he awoke his dormant Babbage engine. On the wall opposite a screen glowed into emerald life.

"This is London calling." The electronically-altered voice echoed from the walls of the room, sending spiking soundwaves crackling across the view screen. There was no way of telling whether it had been male or female before it became the mechanical automaton voice he now found himself listening to.

He activated a switch on the control panel.

"And how is London during these difficult times of transition?" His accent was pronounced, its inflections unmistakeably Russian. "Who's in charge these days?"

"Hello, Mother," the crackling basso voice replied. "Lord De Wynter is maintaining the status quo."

"Ah yes, of course. Your Prime Minister un-elect, as it were. So martial law prevails and the game continues. But enough of these pleasantries – what news?"

"It is my belief that the weapon has been successfully developed but we are not in possession of it yet."

"I see. Do you know what form it takes?"

"Not yet, Mother." The voice sounded nervous, uneasy.

"I see."

Bellows hissed and wheezed in the background, and somewhere, someone moaned in their restless sleep.

"Continue to keep a close eye on the subject. It is vital that we claim the weapon before anyone else does."

"Very good, Mother," the voice said, with something approaching coquettishness.

"Mother out."

"London out."

There was an electronic click as the ether-net call was terminated and the screen faded, leaving the albino gentleman alone in the ruddy darkness of his chamber once more.

Although now his skin was not quite so pale as it had been and his bones did not ache quite so much.

Soon, he thought. Soon he would have all that he needed to put the final stages of his plan into operation. Then victory would be his. He could taste his imminent success on the air, smell it on the wind, feel the truth of it coursing through his veins. He could feel it in his blood and his was the blood of kings and queens, princes and emperors; the blood of Saxe-Coburg. Blood royal.

CHAPTER TWELVE

Guilty Secrets

In the laboratory at his London home, Doctor Victor Gallowglass, the renowned haematologist, was busy about his own personal affairs.

He lifted his pen from the writing paper and paused to re-read what he had just written. His brow was furrowed in consternation. He did not believe he had ever written anything so important in his whole life.

A tear came to his eye as he read that last sentence again. He blinked it away. He could not afford to get sentimental about it now; it was too late for that. His purpose was clear. He had to remain detached, focus only on the immediate, see her as nothing more than a test subject. Otherwise he would never go through with it.

For as long as she could be connected to him, she would not be safe. He would deny them everything and cover his tracks as well as he could.

Returning the sheet to the blotter on his desk, the suffused light of his reading lamp reflecting from the glistening ink, he signed the hand-written letter.

A friend never in more need,

Victor

He folded the page carefully and neatly, and slipped it into a crisp white envelope.

On the front he wrote the addressee's name.

Ulysses L. Quicksilver, Esq.

Carefully placing the fountain pen in its gold and marble stand, he rose, and having dabbed his eyes dry, he left the study-cum-laboratory.

Slowly he walked downstairs. It felt like the longest, hardest walk of his life, as if he were walking to his execution or his own funeral. At the turn of the landing, before starting on the final flight down, Gallowglass halted abruptly, his breath catching in his throat.

Standing in the hall, wearing her eggshell blue woollen coat, was his daughter, Miranda. At that moment he felt as though he had never seen anything more beautiful and more precious. He fancied that she looked just like his late wife, even though that was impossible.

It had only been two weeks since her abduction and her ordeal within the locust hive, but she had come through it amazingly well. There was barely a mark on her now to bear witness to the nightmare she had lived through.

He felt so proud of her he was afraid he might burst into tears again.

Hearing his foot on the stair, she turned and looked up at him. Her innocent features knotted into a frown.

"Oh, Daddy, you're not ready," she said.

"No. I'm not coming with you."

"But you said –"

"I'm going to catch you up later," he lied. "I have some things to finish off here first." He passed the child's governess the letter. "See that you deliver this in person, Miss Wishart."

He knelt down in front of Miranda, helping her finish buttoning her coat. "I'll see you again soon."

She threw her arms about his neck and hugged him close.

"Don't leave me alone, Daddy."

"You won't be alone. Look, there's nothing to worry about. You'll have Miss Wishart with you." Miranda gave her governess a stern, appraising look. Miss Wishart smiled back, warmly.

"That's right, Miranda," she said. "I'll be with you at all times."

"And, besides, it won't be for long." Gallowglass lied again.

"But, Daddy, you still haven't told me where we're going."

"If I told you it wouldn't be a surprise now would it, my darling?"

A smile like sunshine after rain lit up her young face. She put her arms around his neck and pulled him close once more.

"Thank you, Daddy," she whispered in excited glee. This time he pulled her closer, kissing her on the cheek and burying his face in the hollow of her neck.

She pulled away from him suddenly. "Daddy, your beard's tickling me." She giggled.

"I'm sorry, my darling," he said, reluctantly letting her go. He got to his feet.

"Come, Miranda," the governess said, holding out her hand to the child.

The child, obedient as ever, did as she was bidden. Gallowglass stepped past both his daughter and her guardian and opened the door.

The three of them dutifully trooped out and down the steps to the street where Gallowglass hailed a cab.

As a horse-drawn hansom pulled up, Miranda gave her father one last beaming smile and, standing on tiptoes, stretched up to plant a kiss on his cheek.

"Now be good. And remember, I love you. *Always*. Now go. We mustn't keep Miss Wishart waiting any longer."

If he didn't do it now he would never let her go again and would never see this matter through to the end.

The child clambered up the step and into the cab after her governess. Gallowglass closed the door firmly behind them.

"Take them directly to 31 Charles Street, Mayfair," Gallowglass told the driver, pushing a crumpled five pound note into the delighted man's podgy hand.

A broad smile spread across the features half-hidden beneath the brim of the driver's pork pie hat. "Right you are, sir."

With a click of his tongue and a tug of the reins, the cabbie guided his team out and on their way.

"Bye-bye, Daddy," Miranda said, smiling from the window.

"Goodbye, my darling," he said, unable to hide the sadness in his smile now.

Gallowglass watched his daughter's suddenly uncertain face disappear into the Smog. Somewhere across town, the drone of the evening curfew chorus wound up to its siren wail.

Back inside, with the door to the street firmly closed, he gave in at last to his grief. But he didn't regret what he had done. He might never see her again, but she would be safe now – he'd made sure of that.

Returning to the first floor laboratory he paused to survey it for the last time. The enormity of the plan he had already put in motion struck him. His eyes lingered on the phials of blood samples, the microscopes, his Babbage unit, the sterile surfaces, his writing desk.

He took a deep breath to steady his nerves as he considered how many years of work were about to come to an end. But it was the only way.

A fire still smouldered in the grate. A prod with the poker roused it into crackling life, sending wisps of blackened paper spiralling away up the chimney.

Next to the writing materials on his desk, Gallowglass had left a tidy pile of paper files and Babbage engine print-outs. Beside these lay two carefully-placed packages, both the size and shape of cigar boxes, wrapped tightly in brown paper.

Gallowglass picked up the files and print-outs and approached the fireplace. He crouched down and methodically fed the sheets into the flames, watching as the formulae and test results crinkled and blackened. The culmination of a life's work, condensed down into a sheaf of papers, and now gone up in smoke.

His life's work destroyed, he returned to his desk. Taking up his doctor's bag, he opened it, exposing its red velvet lining. One by one he took a number of sealed phials of rich claret-red blood from a test tube rack and placed them carefully within the compartments of the carrying case.

His eyes glistening wetly, Gallowglass picked up the photograph of his late wife Marie that had always stood on his desk, kissed it and then put it back.

Taking a stoppered glass bottle from among a selection on the workbench, he placed it inside the carrying case and closed the bag.

Picking up another bottle, he studied the colourless liquid that sloshed inside it for a moment, before casually tossing it into the fire.

Then, with doctor's bag and the cigar box-shaped packages in hand, he left the laboratory and made his way downstairs. Once in the hall again, he took his hat and coat from the mahogany stand and put them on. Snatching up his cane from its resting place in an elephant foot stand, he opened the front door, turned out the lights, and left the house.

The curfew sirens were winding down. Smothered by the clinging fog, the streetlamps appeared like will-o'-the-wisps, tethered to the cast iron masts of the lampposts.

From the bottom of the steps he gave the Gallowglass family home one last look. The flicker of firelight was visible through the windows on the first floor.

And then he turned and set off into the deepening dusk.

There was a knock at the study door.

"Come in," Ulysses Quicksilver called, hastily hiding Barty's letter under that day's copy of *The Times*.

"I am sorry to disturb you, sir," his manservant began, on entering.

"That's alright, old chap," Ulysses said. "I wasn't doing anything special. No, just sitting here, reading the paper."

"It's just that you have visitors, sir."

"Visitors? After curfew? This is starting to become a bit of a habit."

Ulysses rose from his desk, his indefatigable curiosity having taken over from his brooding sense of melancholy at Barty's abrupt departure.

"A Miss Wishart," Nimrod called after him, as Ulysses headed for the front of the house, "and Miss –"

Grabbing the door jamb, Ulysses spun himself into the drawing room. His eyes opened wide in astonishment and a beaming smile formed.

"– Gallowglass," Nimrod finished.

"Uncle Ulysses!" the girl shouted in delight and ran from her place by her governess to throw her arms around her saviour and squeeze him tight.

"Miranda!" he beamed, returning the embrace. And then his smile darkened. "Where's your father?"

"Excuse me, Mr Quicksilver," the governess interrupted as politely as she could, handing him a crisp white envelope. "My employer asked me to give you this."

In Doctor Victor Gallowglass's study the liquid in the bottle lying in the fire began to boil and the glass cracked. A split second later, a fireball erupted from the fireplace, bathing the room in flames.

Hearing the boom of the explosion, Victor Gallowglass stopped and looked back. He watched as the flames blew out the windows on the first floor. Lights came on in houses all along the street, windows opened and servants were sent to the door to see what had happened. The fire was spreading quickly. Somewhere, far off, the wail of a fire engine could already be heard.

Silhouetted black against the blaze, Gallowglass turned from the burning building and disappeared into the night.

CHAPTER THIRTEEN

Cloak and Dagger

The sirens were louder now. London's noble fire brigade were on their way, but they would be too late. The neighbouring properties would be saved, but 14 Elizabeth Street would be gutted by the fire, just as he had planned. Then Victor Gallowglass could rest easy, certain at last that no-one would be able to resurrect his work after he was gone.

All that remained for him to do now was to put the last stages of his plan into action.

Over the wailing of the fire engines, the ever-present clatter of the Overground and the tapping of the soles of his shoes on the pavement, Gallowglass heard something else.

He shot a fearful glance at the rooftops to his left but didn't stop moving. He was being followed. He had rather suspected he would be. Tightening his grip on his bag and cane, he quickened his pace. He paused again only to pop his two carefully wrapped packages into a post box outside the Passport Office on Belgrave Road.

When he had put a fair few streets between himself and his home, he decided it was time he found himself another mode of transport and hailed the first cab he saw.

"You just come from there?" the cabbie asked as he climbed aboard, pointing back at where the Smog was coloured black and orange by the growing conflagration.

"The East End, and quickly."

"Right you are, sir. Missed the curfew, eh?" the man muttered, as he engaged the throttle and the steam-hansom chugged away.

Sat in the back of the jolting contraption, Gallowglass kept one eye on the tops of the buildings they passed, as the cab wound its way through the thinning traffic and Smog-choked thoroughfares. He kept both hands in his lap, one holding his cane, the other his bag.

The fog-blurred streets of Belgravia gave way to the mist-shrouded roads of Westminster; then Lambeth and on eastwards until Gallowglass recognised the dockside warehouses of Bermondsey and Wapping. He banged on the roof of the cab with his fist.

The cab rattled to a halt. "Will this do ya?" the driver called.

"This will do," Gallowglass said grimly, scanning the tops of crumbling tenements before alighting. Having paid the driver he set off again, this time following the lapping sounds of the waves against mouldering brickwork and the fog-horn cries of river traffic.

Guttering clattered above him and a shower of dislodged moss and brick chips cascaded down from the darkness above. Gallowglass quickened his pace.

He was nearly there. Only a few more steps and it would be as if he had never set foot on the path that had led him to the gates of perdition and brought him nothing but heartache.

The clattering sound came again, as if a horse were galloping over the tenement roofs above him.

Gallowglass began to run.

The galloping horse kept pace.

Panting for breath, Gallowglass turned into an alleyway that ran perpendicular to the route he had been following.

Deep down he knew it probably wouldn't make any difference in the end, but as long as he could keep his pursuer from catching up with him before his task was complete, that would be enough.

The clattering gallop suddenly stopped. Something landed heavily on top of an outhouse just metres from him.

A cascade of tiles crashed into the alley and Gallowglass ran.

His tail persisted, criss-crossing the alleyway above him whenever it met an obstruction. The doctor dared to glance upwards as he heard the thing take another bounding leap across the alleyway. He thought he saw something black – no more than a shadow – whip through the fog above him, its passage marked only by the coiling trails it left behind.

Gallowglass took a sharp left, throwing himself down a narrow rat-run, shoulders hitting the bulging bricks to either side of him. The sprinting hoof-beats quickened, were silenced and then crashed down again on the roof of a chandler's. There was a greasy quality to the air hereabouts. It was redolent with the lingering rancid smell of tallow and the honeyed aroma of hot beeswax.

And then there was the river ahead of him, the sluggish Thames, its thick black waters like treacle. Old Father Thames, the Big Stink, London's greatest sewer, and Victor Gallowglass's salvation.

The doctor burst from the alleyway onto a wharf-side jetty. The skeletal silhouette of a loading derrick rose out of the mist, looking like the ghost of the Tyburn tree, the net hanging from it completing the illusion that it was, in fact, a gibbet.

Gasping for breath, Gallowglass set out along the jetty, sprinting over the rattling boards and the murky river oozing beneath, his cane clutched tightly in his left hand, pulling back his right hand, and the carrying case held within it, ready to hurl it off the end of the pier and into the river.

With a tremendous crash something heavy hit the deck in front of him, landing like a spider, gangling limbs absorbing the force of the leap.

Gallowglass gave a stifled moan of surprise that was quickly snatched from his throat by the suffocating fog.

He lurched backwards, his feet slipping out from under him, as he attempted to pull back from the thing now rising to its feet.

His backside hit the jetty hard but he didn't pause for a second as he tried to scramble away, kicking at the rattling planks with his heels.

The thing rose, the long black cloak it wore falling around it to hide its unnatural lanky form, hanging like a shroud from its bony shoulders. Gallowglass saw now that there was a wide-brimmed black hat pulled down hard over a head that gleamed beneath the brim like polished steel. His assailant took a step forwards and Gallowglass got a glimpse of a limb as long and thin as a steel rod.

Staring up in horror, into the darkness beneath the brim of the hat, he was sure he saw the light reflected in the whites of the hunter's eyes.

Coming face-to-face with the grotesque horror that was trying to kill him snapped him out of his state of paralysing shock, and he had the good sense to bring his cane to bear.

Raising it in his left hand he pointed the end squarely at his assailant's chest and pulled the trigger concealed within the bone handle.

There was a loud crack and the gun-cane's single shot was spent. Gallowglass's assailant was hurled sideways across the jetty in a cloud of gunpowder, to clatter to the deck ten feet away.

Gallowglass was on his feet in a moment. Picking up his bag he started for the end of the wooden pier, sprinting past the flailing form of his attacker.

His pulse was pounding in his ears now. Behind him, he could hear the rattling sounds of the thing struggling to stand. After only a moment's pause, he heard the pounding impacts of its galloping run as it gave chase. He dared not look back. The end of the jetty and the river lay ahead; only a few more strides and he would have made it.

The galloping footfalls fell silent. Gallowglass kept running. He felt the breeze of his attacker's passing as it sailed over his head. He heard the whistle of the air passing through the spaces between its gangling limbs as its cloak streamed out behind it like devil wings.

In a blur his attacker landed with a crash on the planks in front of him. This time Gallowglass was ready.

He reached into the open bag swinging from his right hand and grasped the bottle within. Pulling back his arm he bowled it at the thing's face. It was a throw his Games Master at Eton would have been proud of.

The creature screeched as the bottle smashed and the hydrochloric acid ate into its flesh.

The scuttling thing recoiled, shaking its head as if that would somehow free it of the agonising pain, clawing at its face with the dagger points of its fingers.

Gallowglass was paralysed by a combination of fear and bewilderment.

The high-pitched screeching of his assailant changed, becoming an asthmatic whine and then it sounded like the thing was coughing, or barking, or –

– *laughing.*

Gallowglass had never heard anything so unpleasant or unsettling in his life. And then the thing spoke.

"Slice and dice, slice and dice," it chuckled, silvered finger-blades scissoring open and shut with a sound like a cut-throat razor being sharpened.

Gallowglass forced his body to move. He wasn't concerned with saving himself, he knew that wasn't an option – in fact it hadn't been an option since he had quit his Belgravia townhouse. As soon as he had set out that night he had known that he wouldn't be returning.

Pulling back his arm, he prepared to hurl the bag into the sludgy black waters of the Thames.

With a renewed burst of hysterical giggling, dripping blood and gore, the thing pounced.

Blood sprayed dark as port wine. The bag landed at the edge

of the jetty, its clasp open. And the phials of blood it contained tipped out of it.

"Slice and dice," the thing gurgled with macabre delight.

Gallowglass said nothing. Blood bubbled from the clean cut across his throat.

As the scissoring fingers opened him up and extracted his pancreas, Gallowglass saw not the hideous acid-etched, dagger-sliced flesh and steel face looming over him but the face of his wife Marie. He tried to call her name, but no sound other than a grim gurgle emerged from his mouth. And then his thoughts turned to his dear daughter Miranda and he knew then that, by his actions that night, he had made sure she was safe at last.

As the dissection of Doctor Victor Gallowglass continued, the phials of blood rolled away across the jetty. One rolled to the end of the pier and became lodged in between two boards, while the other two tumbled end over end into the river, there to be swallowed by the sludgy black waters.

CHAPTER FOURTEEN

The Blood's the Thing

The morning after, the Smog hung over London like a stale fart. The sky was grey, the pollutant cloud a faecal smudge above the city, the skyline a forest of barbed wire and hastily erected barricades. It wasn't the city Ulysses Quicksilver knew and loved anymore.

He climbed down from the cab and, having paid the driver, set off for the police cordon at the end of the road.

A number of police vehicles were pulled up across the end of the street in front the jetty, helping prevent the onlookers from getting onto the wharf and contaminating the crime scene. A pair of robo-peelers had been positioned on the nearside of the stretched tape to reinforce the point.

A slight sick feeling in the pit of his stomach as he considered what he might find awaiting him, Ulysses approached the police line. He had come along, having left Gallowglass's daughter in the company of her governess and Nimrod. The only company he had had on the journey had been his own musings concerning the contents of Gallowglass's letter. *Take care of the child*, it had said, *and trust no one.*

Even as the nearest automaton policeman was raising its truncheon to signal him to stop, the dandy investigator whipped out his leather cardholder and flipped it open.

"Good morning, Mr Quicksilver," the droid said in a tinny voice, having scanned his credentials.

Ulysses glanced at the name plate on the front of the droid. "Good morning, Gladstone. Is the Inspector around?"

"Inspector Allardyce is over there, sir," the robo-Bobbie replied, pointing towards the throng of people gathered at the end of the jetty.

Ulysses caught sight of a shock of ginger hair and clapped eyes on the trench-coated policeman for the first time since the two of them had worked together to defeat the crazed industrialist Josiah Umbridge. He also saw the dark brown stains of blood surrounding a sheet that was covering what was undoubtedly a body.

"If you would be so kind?" Ulysses indicated the tape.

"Of course, sir," the droid said, cheerily, lifting the tape.

Ulysses made his way over to the huddle of human policemen and the lab-coated forensic team.

He could see the shape of the body more clearly now. It was stretched out in a near cruciform shape beneath the peaks and troughs of the sheet. Whatever had done for the dead man had made a complete mess of him, that much was obvious. Blood had pooled around the body and run down between the boards of the deck over quite some area; so much so in fact that Ulysses wondered if there was any blood left within the body.

"Quicksilver," Inspector Allardyce said, with grudging politeness.

"Good morning, Inspector," Ulysses returned. Things had changed between them since their adventures on the moors of Ghestdale. "So, what do we have here then?"

"What does it look like?" the police inspector retorted.

"Ah, that's a relief," Ulysses said. "I was worried for a minute there that somebody had replaced the real Maurice Allardyce with an imposter, a mandrake perhaps."

"Very funny."

"But no, I see that all is right with the world."

"Not quite."

At a nod from the inspector, the white-coated, forensic-scientist still crouched beside the body pulled back the sheet.

Ulysses was unable to stifle his gasp of shock, his hand tightening his grip on the bloodstone-pommel of his sword-stick. He had seen such horrors before, but the obviously violent nature of the man's death wasn't what had drained the colour from his cheeks.

"I take it you know him."

"Yes," Ulysses said, in a small, quiet voice. "Yes, I know him. I mean, I knew him. His name's Gallowglass – Victor Gallowglass."

"An old friend of yours then."

"Yes. Something like that."

Myriad shocked thoughts crowded Ulysses' mind. Who could have done this? What was he going to tell Miranda? What would happen to the wretched child now? "I hadn't seen him for a while – a number of years, in fact – but he got back in touch again only recently."

"And why was that then?" Allardyce asked. "Why now?"

"He..." Ulysses caught himself. He couldn't trust anyone; that was what Gallowglass had written in his letter. The dandy's guard was back up in a second. "It was a personal matter."

"In trouble, was he?"

Ulysses was silent for only a moment as he marshalled his thoughts.

"What's all this about, inspector?"

"This here gentleman has been murdered."

Ulysses found himself unable to tear his eyes from the expression of terror frozen on Gallowglass's face. "You don't say."

Gallowglass's torso was a savage mess of open wounds and, without looking too closely, it appeared as though some of his internal organs had been removed.

For a moment Ulysses wondered if this killing had something to do with the locusts he had encountered in St Paul's, but he quickly dismissed that idea. The wounds were savage but clean-cut; they had been made with a blade of some kind, not a serrated claw.

"Have you found a murder weapon?"

"Looks like all sorts was used on him; flick-knife, scissors... All blades, but we haven't found any nearby. Made a nice mess of him."

"Yes, thank you, inspector, I can see that."

Had Gallowglass known that something like this might happen to him? Was that why he had given Miranda into Ulysses' care? Thinking of the child, he wondered how he could even begin to explain what had happened to her father.

"So," Allardyce said, "any ideas?"

"What?"

"Any ideas, who did it? You always seemed to have plenty of ideas about past cases and, I have to admit you've been right sometimes too. So, when I saw our friend here, I thought I'd get you in from the start to save time."

"Oh. I see," Ulysses said. He had not been expecting such a confession from a hardened member of the proletariat.

But there was something else going on here, more than simply Inspector Allardyce's change of attitude towards him. And Ulysses needed to find out what it was, if only for the little girl's sake. For, until he managed to fathom what was going on, he surely had to consider her at risk as well.

"Do you mind if I take a look around?" Ulysses asked.

"I wish you would," was Allardyce's blunt response.

Stepping past the body and the forensic examiner, Ulysses followed the trail of blood. That wasn't hard; there was so much of it. Well at least he knew he wasn't dealing with a vampire. He had never run into one himself, but he knew that such things existed on the continent. Although whether they were the supernatural monsters of legend some believed them to be, or the legacy of some dark experiment in the past, he didn't know. But he was confident that a blood-sucker was not responsible for Gallowglass's death just the same. A vampire would have taken as much blood as it could and not wasted a drop.

There were bloody marks all across the pier, like sticky footprints, but if that was indeed what they were, they were like no footprints Ulysses had seen. They were almost like hooves or the points of crab claws. A killer with hooves that cut up its victim with a blade. Ulysses knew of none like it, but he couldn't help recalling the memory of an article he had read in the paper only a matter of weeks ago.

He walked to the end of the jetty and gazed out over the sluggish Thames. What had driven Gallowglass to come here of all places? Ulysses looked from the coke-burning tugs moored across the river, to the wharf-side warehouses, to the grey shingle beach, to the boards of the pier.

He froze, eyes locked on the warped wood at his feet. There, lying wedged between a pair of planks was a test tube. It was sealed with a rubber bung and, as he bent down and gently worked it free of its resting place, Ulysses saw that it was filled with what looked like a sample of blood.

"What have you found there?" Allardyce asked, joining him at the end of the jetty.

"Take a look for yourself." Ulysses passed the inspector the stoppered glass tube.

"Blood?"

"That would be my guess, but of course we won't know for sure until it's been tested."

"I'll get the lab boys onto it."

"With all due respect," Ulysses said, "if we want the results before next week, I'd rather send it to an acquaintance of mine."

The inspector scowled.

"He is completely trustworthy, I can assure you."

Allardyce hesitated a moment longer, before cautiously handing the test tube back to Ulysses. "Just so long as you let me know whatever it is your acquaintance uncovers the instant you know."

The dandy smiled – "But of course, inspector." – and dropped the recovered piece of evidence into a jacket pocket.

Returning to the shrouded body, Ulysses said. "There's just one last thing I need to do before I'm done here."

"And what's that?" Allardyce asked.

"You don't happen to have a clean handkerchief on you, do you?"

"Of course, Mrs Allardyce insists on a clean handkerchief and a clean shirt every day."

"Well, that's good. Where would Magna Britannia be without standards? Lose those and we're no better than Mr Darwin's monkey's uncle. Can I borrow it?"

"I suppose so."

Ulysses took the proffered handkerchief and crouched down beside the body.

Lifting the corner of the sheet with one gloved hand, taking care not to reveal Gallowglass's rictus-locked grin, Ulysses selected a suitably deep cut and poked the balled handkerchief inside.

"Bloody hell! What do you think you're playing at?" Allardyce said.

"Taking samples."

"But the missus'll scream blue murder when she sees the bloodstains on that."

"If it will allay any marital discord, I'll buy you a new one. A new set, in fact."

"You could have warned me that's what you wanted it for."

"Look, if you didn't want my help, you shouldn't have asked for it." Placing the inspector's purloined handkerchief inside a clear plastic specimen bag, Ulysses got to his feet.

He turned and set off back along the blood-smeared jetty.

"I'll be in touch as soon as I have anything concrete," he said, giving the inspector a cheery wave. "But for the time being, I have an appointment with Dr Methuselah."

CHAPTER FIFTEEN

Bad Tidings

Standing at the door to the study, Nimrod watched as, holding the child's hands in his, his employer broke the news of Victor Gallowglass's death to the dead man's daughter. He saw the pale expression of shock shape her face. He saw the tears spring from her unblinking eyes. And he saw the wide open look of utter disbelief become an agonised grimace of abject grief.

She was, in some small measure, like the dandy adventurer himself. Her mother long dead, and now her father dead also, she too had become an orphan. The older man watched as the girl pulled her hands free of Ulysses' – withdrawing from the devil who had brought her such dire news, who had shattered her small world with his cruel revelation – and turned immediately to her governess for comfort, sobbing into the folds of the woman's skirts.

"I am so sorry, my dear," he heard his master say again. "So very, very sorry."

The scene was so familiar; it was as if the devoted family retainer was watching a moment being replayed from his past.

Another man, a younger man, crouched before two scared-looking boys, their hands in his, telling them that their father was dead. It had been all he could do at the time to hold his own emotions at bay as he watched the boys break down.

Nimrod turned away. He had seen too much of the grief of children.

His footsteps ringing from the tiled floor of the hallway, he returned to his own quarters below the back stairs.

Later that day there came a knock at the study door and, at Ulysses' behest, the child's governess entered.

"Miss Wishart," Ulysses said, smiling kindly and rising politely, inviting the woman to take a seat opposite him.

She sat uncomfortably at the edge of the chair, her hands in her lap, a balled up hankie in her hands, her eyes cast down.

"Thank you for coming to see me."

"It's the least I could do," Miss Wishart replied, obviously trying hard to put a brave face on things. "You have been such an accommodating host."

"How is she? How is Miranda?"

"She is sleeping now."

"Of course. Probably for the best."

An awkward silence descended between them.

"If there's nothing else..." Miss Wishart said, making to rise.

"This must be a very hard time for you too," Ulysses said. "First the business with the kidnap and now... this."

The woman's knuckles whitened as she tightened her grip on the damp cloth in her hands.

"Yes. Yes, it has." And then it all came pouring out of her, in a cathartic flood. "The poor child. She has been without a mother for so long. Dr Gallowglass was her only kin. She meant the world to him. And now this... I mean what's to become of the poor wretch? Where are we to live? Who will support us now? If I had known something like this might happen I would have begged him to come with us, on my knees!"

Miss Wishart suddenly looked up, meeting Ulysses' concerned gaze for the first time.

"I mean, what was he doing in the East End anyway?"

Ulysses studied her features, her almond eyes, her high cheekbones, her pursed rosebud lips, her dark hair, tied back in a tight bun, but highlighting her wonderful bone structure.

"That question has been troubling me too," Ulysses admitted. "Tell me, Miss Wishart, do you know what Dr Gallowglass was working on before he died?"

"I... I don't know," she replied, blinking in surprise. "I mean, obviously you know that he was a highly regarded haematologist but beyond that..."

"But you have no idea which particular mystery of the workings of the blood he was struggling with at the time?"

"No... None."

"Had anyone been to see him recently? Was he working for the government or a private client, or was he conducting his own research? What was so secret that even you, living under the same roof as him, wouldn't have any idea what he was working on?"

"Mr Quicksilver! Why would you presume that Dr Gallowglass would share his top secret research with his paid staff?"

"Of course. I apologise. I didn't mean to suggest that there had been any impropriety."

"Dr Gallowglass was a very private man," Miss Wishart said, stiffening. "And besides, it was not my place to pry. I'm sorry I can't be of more help."

"No, no. It's not your fault. I'm the one who should be sorry."

But it didn't change the fact that the old school friend he hadn't seen in years had been found savagely murdered half a city away from where he lived and worked, in a place that Ulysses wouldn't have imagined he would have been seen dead in. He only hoped Dr Methuselah's lab tests would give him some clue as to what it was that had led to the doctor's death.

He had one last thing to try.

"Miss Wishart, I am sorry to keep probing but do you know of anyone who might have wanted to cause Dr Gallowglass harm, or even, heaven forbid, want him dead?"

"No! Not a one. He was a kind and gentle man, a philanthropist who only sought to make the world a better place through hard work and dedication."

"But I would beg to disagree, Miss Wishart," Ulysses said, the smile gone from his face. "I would say that the recent kidnapping would suggest otherwise."

"No, I won't have it! Those damnable blackguards were mere opportunists, greedy wastrels who saw an opportunity and took it."

The woman's ire was up now; a red flush had come to her cheeks. Ulysses looked at her patiently and took a deep breath, before continuing.

"But Miss Wishart, there was no ransom demand, was there?"

The governess's shoulders sagged.

"No," she said.

"Then I would suggest someone was using the abduction of his daughter as leverage. Those kidnappers wanted something other than his money. They sought to influence his actions in some way, would you not agree?"

This time the governess said nothing at all.

"What was he working on? Do you have *any* ideas? This is very important"

Still she said nothing. Her bottom lip started to quiver.

"Had you noticed him behaving strangely of late?"

"But of course," the woman said, her back straightening. "I mean a man in his right mind would never have sent his daughter away to another man's house."

"You have a point, but were there any other signs leading up to that moment?"

"He wasn't quite himself again after the abduction, even when Miranda had been returned safe and sound."

"How do you mean?"

"I mean he hardly let her out of his sight and we certainly weren't allowed out of the house. That was what was so strange about the events of last night. Not only did he send us across town to here, but he did so without coming with us."

"I see."

"And then there was the time I walked in on him destroying his notes."

"He was destroying his notes?" Ulysses' face was suddenly alive with excitement.

"He didn't see me; I left before he noticed I was even there. He was burning them, in the grate in his laboratory."

"Why would he do that?" Ulysses asked, his mind working as fast as a Newcomen engine now.

"I didn't think it my place to ask," Miss Wishart said.

"No. No, of course you didn't."

"If there isn't anything else..."

"Of course, please feel free to go," Ulysses said.

The young woman rose and made for the study door.

"You're welcome to remain here as long as you need to," Ulysses added. "You and Miranda."

The governess paused and then turned back, regarding him with large, soulful eyes.

"But Mr Quicksilver, you have done more than enough for us already."

"I insist. And while we're at it," he said, flashing her a broad smile, "if you are to be my house guest, please call me Ulysses."

The governess blushed. "Very well."

Opening the study door, she paused at the threshold and looked back one last time.

"Good day to you, Ulysses."

Alone again, Ulysses took out Gallowglass's hand-written letter and re-read it for the umpteenth time.

In the light of that morning's gruesome revelation, it seemed obvious to him now that Gallowglass had feared something might happen to him. And yet it almost seemed that Gallowglass believed his daughter Miranda to be in danger too. Had his seemingly erratic behaviour been intended to divert attention away from her, eliminate the danger he foresaw coming her way? Had he gone knowingly to his death?

Ulysses resolved that if he was ever going to find out why his friend had been murdered, he had to know what he had been working on. Then he might be able to work out who had been behind the kidnap and the cajoling, and that in turn might lead to, if not the killer himself, then at least the individual that set the killer on Victor Gallowglass. And the only way he was going to be able to do that was if he paid a visit to the Gallowglass family home, to see if he might uncover any further clues.

CHAPTER SIXTEEN

After the Fire

The fire had completely gutted the upper storeys of the house and it had only been thanks to the sterling work of London's noble fire brigade that none of the surrounding buildings had in fact been damaged.

But within number 14 Elizabeth Street the fire had burnt fierce and strong. Even from outside the property, Ulysses could see how the fire must have started in the front corner room on the first floor. From there it had quickly spread to the second storey, the airy attic allowing the fire to seize hold within the roof space particularly effectively. As far as Ulysses could see, the ground floor remained intact but the roof and top storey had fallen into the rooms below.

Ulysses found himself wondering again at the state of Gallowglass's mind in those last hours of his life, that he could so rashly destroy not only his family's home but, by his actions, put his neighbours in danger.

With cautious steps, Ulysses ducked under the safety cordon, flashing the constable on duty his ID, and – ignoring the young officer's words of warning – approached the property. A hulking fire-suppression droid – not so unlike the indefatigable Limehouse Golem in form – squatted by the front steps, motionless, having been deactivated for the time being.

On the ground floor everything was coated in a sticky layer of wet soot and ash. The furnishings had been ruined by the drenching the fire brigade's hoses had given the burning building. Family portraits still dripped with water, while a large coat rack glistened with moisture. Ulysses wrinkled his nose at the smell of the place – an acrid combination of smoke and damp.

Watching where he trod and where he put his hands – as much to avoid ruining yet another suit, as anything else – he made his way upstairs.

At the top of the stairs, Ulysses found himself in the open air again, the filthy smear of Smog clouds the only roof above his head. Water dripped from the sodden rafters and what remained of the roof-beams. Ulysses grimaced as a sooty droplet of water splattered against the lapel of his jacket.

Ulysses had never visited Victor Gallowglass at his Belgravia home but Miss Wishart had been able to tell him all he needed to know to find the location of the doctor's lab. This fact only added credence to Ulysses' belief that Gallowglass had set the fire himself.

The door to the laboratory stood before him, its paintwork black with smoke damage, blistered and peeling. Ulysses put a cautious hand to the door handle. It had partially melted and was still warm. Beyond, he could see the scorched internal walls of the room; plaster cracked and flaking, the bricks exposed beneath, the wallpaper having burnt away.

The devastation within the lab was total. Everything was covered in the same cloying black mush, the once carpeted floor flooded with a soupy mixture of ash and water. The laboratory was open to the sky. He could distinguish the shapes of tables, stools, workbenches, scientific apparatus, even a Babbage engine, through the incomparable mess. As he advanced into the room, he cleared fallen pieces of timber from before him with his cane.

His heart sank. Finding anything amongst all this mess was going to be a challenge.

He picked his way through the smouldering ruins, heat radiating from the bricks of the walls that still stood, until he came to what was left of the house's central chimney stack. The top portion had collapsed under the stress of the fire, bringing down the floor of one of the rooms above. Ulysses poked at what he found within the grate but it was nothing more than black paper and grey ash. And yet, amidst all the devastation there *was* something, some rumour of an earlier intrusion. Someone else had been here since the fire had been brought under control.

Ulysses could feel his hackles rise, the familiar itch of prescience at the base of his skull. He shifted his weight onto his back foot, the mulch, paper and crumbling charcoal crunching uncomfortably loudly.

He froze. Had the sound he had just heard been him or something other?

Ears straining for any sound, Ulysses reached for his revolver. He made to leave the room, the sounds of his footsteps noisy in the mess of sludge that covered the floor.

When the other finally revealed itself, it made no sound but Ulysses sensed its presence nonetheless. He darted glances all about him. He sought the watcher in the reflections revealed in the dull mirrors of rippling grey puddles.

At that moment, giddy with adrenalin, a host of thoughts paraded themselves through Ulysses' agitated mind. There were a whole host of concerns regarding the child, her governess and even his brother Barty, but there was one thought his overwrought mind kept lingering on and that was the body on the pier and the nature of its killer.

Victor Gallowglass had been savagely slain with cruel efficiency. In fact, practically any one of the brutal wounds that had scored his flesh could have killed him but their proliferation suggested something else to Ulysses; that his assassin – and he was sure that Gallowglass's death had been an assassination and no mere random murder – had toyed with Gallowglass right until the end. The dead doctor's slaughter might have been sanctioned by another, but its perpetrator had taken great satisfaction in its gory work.

That same killer was watching him now with unflinching interest.

There came the skitter and scrape of metal claws on the beams above and a light shower of ash rained down.

Body tensed, Ulysses slowly looked up into the face of Gallowglass's murderer.

The devil smiled back at him.

"Slice and dice, little red bag," it gurgled. Scissors flashed. "Slice and dice."

And then, bladed fingers springing wide as gin-traps, the killer pounced.

CHAPTER SEVENTEEN

Ripper Jack

Foregoing his gun, Ulysses unsheathed his sword-stick and brought it to bear, putting his weight onto his back foot to absorb the shock of the assassin landing on top of him. But despite parrying its initial strike and preparing himself, it still felt as though he had been hit by a steam-wagon. Ulysses gave in to the crushing weight and, curling his body, rolled onto his back amidst the mess and the mulch covering the floor.

As he did so, the spider-thing's steel limbs arresting its fall as its hooves hit the filthy floorboards, Ulysses kicked upwards, the momentum of his roll pushing him up onto his shoulders as, thighs aching, he focused all his strength towards his feet. As he pushed upwards he unbalanced the thing, pitching it forwards so that it came crashing down in the mess of the fire and water-ravaged ruins.

But he had only earned himself a temporary respite. Even as he was struggling to his feet, so too was the assassin. However, the killer righted itself with much greater ease, flipping itself upright with a twist of its telescopic limbs.

It faced him on all fours now, its arms and legs projecting from either side of its cloak-draped body, splayed at right angles. It scampered towards him, grinning; its face the wrong way up.

As it scuttled towards him the head rotated owl-like about its distended neck joint, smiling all the while. And then it unfolded itself and leapt.

But Ulysses was already running. He knew that in the confines of the ruined house he didn't have a hope against the spider-like stalker. But if he could get clear, and lure it out into the open, then just maybe...

He flung himself through the door and slammed it shut after him, even as the arachnid assassin hauled itself over the top of the doorframe, pulling itself through the fire-weakened lathes of the wall.

Ulysses threw himself down the stairs, the spider thing landing on the top rail of the banister behind him. He didn't dare look back as he fled from the monster. In his mind's eye he could see it hauling itself along the rungs of the banisters, crawling down the stairwell.

Another scissoring kick took it to the final turn of the stair, only moments after Ulysses made it into the hallway. As he ran for the front door, he pulled the coat rack and hat stand over behind him. The furniture slowly toppled over like a felled tree, crashing into the wall opposite and creating an obstacle for the giggling killer.

The assassin leapt from the stairs directly onto the obstruction, squeezing itself through the triangle formed by the toppled stand, the wall behind it and the smoke-blackened ceiling, twisting its body into impossible shapes.

Ulysses stopped, looking back, watching the leering killer as it crawled from shadow to shadow in its relentless pursuit.

As long as they remained in the house, the assassin had the advantage. With that in mind, he pulled open the front door and threw himself down the front steps.

Hearing the crash of the front door and then Ulysses' sprinting heels, the on-duty policeman turned, rudely roused from a waking dream in which he was tucking into a plate of lamb chops, creamy mash and steaming onion gravy.

"Here, what's going on? You alright, sir?"

Hearing a second crash, the constable looked back towards the house and saw what it was that had just punched the same door from its hinges, and was now coming after him.

"Good lord!" he gasped, the colour draining from his cheeks.

"Get out of here!" Ulysses shouted, as he ducked under the police line and headed off up the street.

In the open at last, now he felt that he might actually have a chance against the relentless assassin. Ulysses sheathed his sword-stick and reached for his pistol.

"But, sir, my orders –"

"My advice would be bugger your orders. Get out of here now!"

The policeman gave Ulysses an appalled glance and then turned on his tail and ran, his helmet clattering onto the cobbles behind him.

Ulysses turned back to the house and, in the cold light of day, saw the killer properly for the first time.

It was moving like a dog or a wolf now, racing towards him, where before it had rearranged its body to move like a spider to negotiate the broken beams and other obstructions within the fire-ravaged house. Much of its body was hidden by the black cloth of its cape, which rippled behind it like the wings of some great bat.

Ulysses raised his pistol and fired.

There was the spang of metal on metal and the galloping killer stumbled. But the very next second it recovered itself and resumed its charge. Ulysses fired again. The bullet found its target, but the thing didn't even miss a pace.

Ulysses was reminded of the Limehouse Golem with its granite-hard carapace, utterly resistant to his bullets, and how it had taken a magnetic mine to bring it down. Even then the vigilante Spring-Heeled Jack had been able to re-build it.

Gallowglass's killer unfolded itself, rising on its backward jointed hind-legs. The fore-legs of the creature became arms and hands again as it brought its cruelly-sharp bladed-fingers to bear.

The thing now looked like a man who had suffered the attentions of some brutal medieval torture device and yet – no matter how impossible such a feat might seem – had survived. Every part of its spindly body was longer than it should be, its limbs made up of more joints than was natural, and atop a flexible, telescopic neck the leering face of a man smiled down at him. And it was only a face, stretched taut across the gleaming chrome dome of an artificial skull beneath.

As the killer continued to bear down on him, eating up the yards between the two of them, Ulysses holstered his pistol and unsheathed his rapier once more. If dead lead couldn't stop the thing, then he would have to resort to cold steel.

Ulysses saw the killer's hands were of soft human flesh, the slicing scalpel claws inserted into the necrotising tips of its fingers. He brought his blade up towards the killer's serpentine neck.

Metal rang on metal and Ulysses' nerve-endings burned as the jarring sensation rushed up his arms to his shoulders. It was all he could do not to drop the sword-stick.

The killer struck out with the five blades of one hand; Ulysses only just managing to parry the attack. His blade singing, he spun it in his hands and laid a counter-strike across his body, aiming at the thing's head.

The assassin was just as fast as he was, one arm folding impossibly at both elbow and shoulder so that another steel taloned hand might deflect the dandy's blow.

Metal rang as the two traded blows, but both were evenly matched. If they continued like this, Ulysses knew that it would be the one who's stamina lasted the longest would ultimately be the victor, and he didn't appreciate that realisation one bit. If he was going to best Gallowglass's killer he was going to have to try something else. The question was, what?

Ulysses put all his strength behind another thrust of his blade and, as the assassin pulled itself backwards to avoid the attack, the dandy turned and ran. Behind him the clockwork killer hissed and, in the very next instant, set off after him.

Adrenalin giving him the burst of speed he needed to put some distance between himself and the automaton, Ulysses suddenly found himself in the crowded confines of Buckingham Palace Road. But the bustling throng wouldn't save him now. Besides, he didn't want to complicate matters by having the blood of innocents on his hands.

"Get out of the way! Get out of here!" he screamed, waving his hands furiously. But the shambling masses merely looked at him with unimpressed or disgruntled expressions on their faces.

Then a woman screamed, and Ulysses knew that the killer had caught up with him again.

A man swore, his unabashed burst of expletives attracting Ulysses' attention. The moustachioed man was standing beside what appeared to be a Penny Farthing bicycle enhanced by the addition of a Trevithick steam engine. In three strides, the dandy had crossed the pavement, sheathed his blade, and mounted the contraption before the man could let fly with a second vitriolic tirade.

"Crown business!" Ulysses shouted to the man as he kicked the engine into life and activated the throttle with his right hand. "Queen and country, and all that. Report to the nearest police station and you'll be fully reimbursed in due course!"

The steam velocipede sped away up the road as the automaton bounded over the heads of the bewildered crowd and landed in the middle of the road with a clatter of iron-shod hooves.

Horses whinnied and shied. Children howled in terror and a trundling steam-wagon slewed to a halt across the road, narrowly avoiding a costermonger's barrow.

But Ulysses didn't stop; he didn't even dare look round. He simply gunned the throttle again, bracing himself, shoulders hunched, leaning low over the handlebars of the bicycle as the vehicle roared on up the road.

Even over the purr of the Trevithick, Ulysses could hear the clattering gallop of the unnatural thing chasing him up the street in broad daylight. Their passing provoked gasps of surprise and unadulterated horror from those going about their everyday business, and left stock-still, gawping statues in their wake.

His getaway by velocipede had only bought him temporary respite. The automaton was still in pursuit and still had to be dealt with, and Ulysses knew that to do that he would have to get off the road eventually.

Ulysses scanned the road and alley openings ahead of him, swerving to avoid a collision with an omnibus.

He was heading south, towards Chelsea Bridge Road. To his left, behind the tight-packed tenements lay the tracks leading out of Victoria station; if he could just lead the automaton onto the rails, just as a train was building up a head of steam as it left the platform...

Ulysses quickly dismissed that idea; it was far too risky, and could well put innocents at risk.

Reaching the end of Buckingham Palace Road, he steered the velocipede into a narrower, and much less busy, thoroughfare. If he kept going this way, he'd soon be at Chelsea Bridge and the Embankment. Perhaps if he could somehow trick the killer into following him into the river...

Ulysses had enjoyed more dips in the turgid Thames than was really healthy, but if that was what it took to stop the thing...

He was suddenly aware of the fact that the galloping automaton was no longer chasing after him. Where had it gone? Ulysses eased back on the throttle.

The clockwork killer landed with a crash on the road in front of him, in a tangle of telescoping limbs.

Ulysses reacted instantly, pulling sharply on the handlebars and throwing the velocipede into the nearest alleyway. The contraption rattled and jolted over the cobbles and collected detritus that strewed the way ahead, only travelling another ten yards before it hit a discarded hod of bricks.

Ulysses found himself flying unceremoniously through the air, the world spinning around him, as the velocipede's impact with the obstruction launched him out of the driver's seat. He landed on his back amidst a pile of what smelt like rotting cabbages, but was on his feet again in seconds.

Behind him the automaton scampered along the alleyway after him. He could hear it spitting in annoyance, its feet splashing through puddles of foetid water and the ring of its finger-blades as they slid across each other.

Unsheathing his sword-stick again, Ulysses turned to meet the assassin.

The alleyway ahead of him was empty.

"But not for long, I'm sure," the dandy muttered to himself.

Water dripped onto his forehead, startling him and making him look up.

Crawling down the damp, grey bricks of the wall next to him came the cyber-organic assassin.

"Slice and dice, Mr Scaredy-man," the killer burbled with glee.

Dropping to the floor of the alleyway, it scuttled towards him, forcing him further along the passage.

An insidious whirring of clockwork underlay its syrupy giggles. "Tick-tock! Tick-tock!"

It was toying with him. It could have pounced and finished him in an instant, but it was enjoying protracting the moment, wringing every last drop of fear from its victim; only it didn't know Ulysses Quicksilver that well.

Ulysses risked a glance behind him and saw the solid wall at the end of the passage not ten yards away. He had taken shelter within a dead-end. Rusted iron fire escapes clung to the sides of the buildings around him. If he could just lure the thing beneath one of them, leap up and pull the ladder down on top of it, he might at least be able to pin it down long enough to put his blade through whatever passed for its brain and be done with it.

As the semi-automaton, semi-human, and wholly sadistic, killer reared up again on its hind-legs, dagger-claws bared, Ulysses lashed out with his trusty blade.

It rang from the monster's metal limbs – the gleaming steel rods deadening the force of Ulysses' strikes – just as it did from the gleaming carapace of its robotic torso.

The hideously smiling, acid-etched face leaned in close and Ulysses could smell engine oil, sour meat and formaldehyde.

One clawed hand slammed against Ulysses' right wrist, pinning it to the wall. It exerted pressure against the joint, forcing his fingers open and the sword-stick fell from his grasp.

"Now, let's open you up and see what makes you tick," the creature giggled, reaching for him with its other hand, one claw extended, the tip of the stiletto blade mere inches from Ulysses' throat.

Ulysses stared into the creature's glassy eyes and, for a moment, saw himself reflected within the black oblivion of its dilated pupils.

Elsewhere, other interested eyes studied the face on the grainy monitor feed.

"Sir? It's locked on to another target."

The other was at the technician's side in a moment. His striking attire – green frock coat, silver-embroidered waistcoat, and gold silk cravat – were at odds with the lab-coated technicians clustered within the monitoring station.

"Quicksilver," he said, slapping an ebony cane into the palm of his hand. "When did he get involved?"

"He turned up at the house. The assassin had been instructed to wait there and see if anyone else turned up." The technician pointed at the face on the screen. "He turned up."

"Shit!"

"What shall we do?" The man turned anxious eyes on the steely face at his shoulder, the agent's greying hair slicked back from a pronounced widow's peak, giving him an even more sinister appearance.

"Call it off."

Ulysses took a deep breath, steeling himself.

And then, the killer froze. A frown stole the insane smile from its face and it shook its head, as if something had wormed its way inside its steel skull and was bothering it.

Hissing like an angry cat, it leapt clear of the alleyway, landed on the wall behind Ulysses and raced right up it, disappearing over the parapet twenty feet above.

And then it was gone, leaving Ulysses alone and in a state of shock.

CHAPTER EIGHTEEN

Proof Positive

Ulysses Quicksilver had come close to death on more occasions than he cared to remember, but he had never felt so helpless as he had at the moment when he stared into the soulless, smiling eyes of the cold-blooded killer.

Still shaking, he walked briskly away from the alleyway and into the bustle of Buckingham Palace Road. The steam-wagon was still there, rusty water still trickling from the guts of the ruptured boiler. An automaton-Peeler was trying to help the vehicle's shaken driver get the damaged truck out of the way of the traffic backing up behind it.

The thoroughfare was heaving as people began to make the mass exodus from their places of work before sunset and the swarmings.

No one noticed the dishevelled dandy as he picked up his pace, heading north along the crowded thoroughfare.

He might once have made regular appearances within the society pages of the popular press and, more recently, had his image broadcast across the nation, but out in the real world, the general masses barely gave well-known public figures a second glance. And besides, in his current condition, he would have had trouble recognising his reflection in a mirror.

His linen suit was streaked with black water, his hair was matted with soot and ash and his face smeared with dirt. He looked more like one of London's destitute than the man once voted Best Dressed Bachelor by *The Strand.*

As he passed beneath a broadcast screen on Victoria Street, a disembodied voice boomed from the speakers.

"Escape the rat race of the human race and start a new life on the Moon!" Ulysses paused and looked up to see an image of Earth's satellite swell to fill the screen above him. "You'll find incredible opportunities awaiting industrious individuals in the off-world colonies, on Earth's most popular emigration destination. Even if you're simply looking to get away from it all, at the Empire's most exclusive holiday resort, with weekly flights departing from the London spaceports, let us bring you the Moon in style!"

Ulysses had forgotten about Barty during his unnerving confrontation with the automaton assassin. Only a matter of days ago, his errant brother had quite literally taken off for the Moon, following untold others from around the world who seemed to think they could leave all their worries behind by escaping the planet.

But Ulysses had somebody else to think about, someone else's future to sort out now. The orphaned Miranda Gallowglass – eleven years old and not yet able to make her way in the world – was depending on him.

Barty would have to wait until he had resolved the current situation. Ulysses needed to find out who had set the crazed cyborg killer on the wretched Victor Gallowglass, yet spared the dandy.

Maintaining his pace, keeping one eye on the rooftops for any sign that the assassin had chosen to come after him again, Ulysses reached inside his ruined jacket and, catching sight of himself in the glass of a shop front as he passed by, looked aghast and muttered under his breath, "Another bloody suit ruined. I'm fast going to become my tailor's best customer at this rate."

He finished fishing in his inner pocket and pulled out his battered – but fortunately working – brass and teak personal communicator. Keying in a number he put the device to his ear and endured the buzzing ring at the other end of the line, his heart still pounding.

He needed to spend more time practising the consciousness-centring relaxation techniques the monks had taught him while he had recuperated within the legendary Shangri-La.

"Sir?" came his manservant's voice, as Nimrod answered.

"Are our houseguests still safe indoors?" he asked.

"Yes, sir. As per your instructions."

"Good. Then make sure they stay that way, will you, old chap? There's a good man."

"But of course, sir. Did you find what you were looking for?"

"No. I went looking for clues and found something else entirely."

"Would you like me to meet you with the Rolls, sir?"

"No. I want you to remain with the ladies. No one comes in or goes out without my say so, is that understood?"

"Yes, sir."

"And make sure your pistol's fully loaded, although all things considered, an electric cattle-prod or a phlogiston discharger might be a better idea, if only we had such a thing."

"A phlogiston discharger, sir?"

"Never mind. Just keep them safe, will you? And you'd best send Mrs Prufrock home while you're about it."

"Very good, sir. And might I enquire as to what you are doing now?"

"I have to see a man about an automaton assassin."

"Very good, sir. I shall expect you presently then," Nimrod replied.

"Is this right?" Inspector Maurice Allardyce asked, as he admitted Ulysses Quicksilver into his office at Scotland Yard.

"The desk sergeant said you wanted to see me."

"That's right," Ulysses said, tight-lipped, hovering awkwardly beside the chair in front of the inspector's desk. At least he assumed it was the man's desk; something had to be supporting the drifts of paper that were mounded before him.

Allardyce looked him up and down and smiled. The dandy was on edge; the man who was as happy mixing with royalty as he was passing the time of day with tramps obviously felt out of place at the police station. And Allardyce knew why. This was *his* territory, and the caddish rogue and agent of the crown knew it.

"Twice in one day? People will start to talk?"

Quicksilver flashed him a quick, unimpressed smile.

"Anyway, what happened to you? You look a mess."

"Do I really? Well thank you for pointing that out."

"So what can I do you for?"

"As it turns out, I've come here to ask you for a favour."

"Really?" Allardyce was intrigued now. "Won't you take a seat?"

Quicksilver looked from his sodden suit trousers to the leather-cushioned chair and back to the inspector.

"You're sure you don't mind?"

"As long as you don't bleed everywhere. You're not planning on bleeding everywhere, are you?"

"I'm not wounded, if that's what you mean, thanks for asking."

Allardyce smiled again. "Just your pride, eh?"

Quicksilver scowled through pursed lips.

"So, what's this favour you're after?"

"It's concerning the murdered prostitutes."

"Oh yes, friends of your –"

"Don't, Allardyce," the disgruntled dandy snapped. "Just don't, alright?"

"Alright. So, what do you want to know?"

"Tell me about the murders."

"Over Whitechapel way?"

"Yes."

Allardyce looked at the dandy, suspicion narrowing his eyes.

"What does this have to do with Galeglass, or Spyglass, or –"

"Gallowglass!"

"Yeah, so like I say, what has this got to do with what I let you in on this morning?"

"That's what I intend to find out."

"Very well."

Allardyce moved a teetering stack of card folders, bulging with everything from crime-scene snapshots to witness statements, making room amidst the paper drifts.

"How many have there been now?" Ulysses asked, eyeing the pile of case files.

"Four to date, at least that we know of. The first one was Mary Parks."

"I need details."

"Killed on the twenty-fourth of last month," Allardyce replied, opening the folder at the top of the pile and skimming the paperwork within, "found behind the ragged school off Commercial Road at 5.56am the next morning by a milkman doing his rounds. Time of death was put at between eleven and midnight the previous night."

"No, I need details. Tell me everything."

"There isn't much more. Twenty-three years old, a whore, worked the Shadwell Basin area normally."

"No, you idiot. I mean, how did she die?"

Allardyce gave Ulysses a disapproving look, but for once decided to keep his mouth shut.

"Her killer gutted her like a fish. Pathologist's report says that she had her liver, spleen, and half her intestines removed, along with her womb. We don't know what he did with them, they were never found. Quite possibly kept them as trophies. Could've eaten them for all I know. Take a look for yourself," he said, passing Ulysses the file. "Go mad. There's pictures too, if that's your thing."

"And the next?" Ulysses asked, studying a black and white photograph, a grim expression on his face.

"Elspeth Pritchard."

"And what did he do to her?"

"Slit her open from her gizzard to her navel, took her heart and her kidneys but left her lungs spread outside of her body for all to see."

Ulysses took the second file from Allardyce and began to peruse its contents.

"So, Allardyce, tell me. Ignoring everything else you suspect about this case, just going by our killer's peculiar... tastes – his *modus operandi* – if you were a betting man, who would you say killed these women?"

"Well, that's easy," the inspector began and then stopped.

"No, go on."

"Very well. Every copper worth his salt would say the same thing. These murders are textbook Ripper. But I know that's impossible."

"Jack the Ripper."

"Of course, bloody Jack the Ripper."

"That's what I thought you'd say," the dishevelled dandy said, smiling for the first time since entering the inspector's office.

"But I'm not an idiot, whatever you might think. What are you trying to get me to say, eh, Quicksilver? I know it can't be the Ripper. That would be impossible."

"Would it?"

The dandy detective rose from his chair and leant across Allardyce's desk, helping himself to another card-bound file.

"Here, do you mind?" the inspector challenged.

"I'm sorry?"

"And in case you hadn't noticed, you smell like something the cat threw up. Anyway, you never said what happened to you."

"Then let me tell you," Ulysses said, shaking off his sodden jacket and taking a seat.

To his credit, Allardyce didn't interrupt once as Quicksilver described the assassin that had attacked him, although he couldn't hide the scowl of mocking disbelief that formed on his incredulous face.

"So, in short," Quicksilver concluded, "I believe the bastard you're looking for is a semi-automaton assassin, between six and eight feet in height, dressed in a cloak, and with flick-knives, or something very like it, for fingers."

Allardyce looked at him, mocking derision writ large on his features.

"You have got to be bloody kidding me."

"No, I am not bloody kidding you," Quicksilver said with forced patience, in the tone of a man who has had enough and is trying *very* hard not to lose control, "and I would remind you of what we both witnessed in Whitby."

Allardyce's expression morphed from one of laughing disbelief to shameful embarrassment.

"And you think that your attacker is the same psycho who butchered those East End whores?"

"There is no doubt in my mind that the thing that attacked me, and Gallowglass's killer, are one and the same. And having seen what it did to the late doctor, and from what you've shown me this evening, I would say that it was our knife-fingered friend who did for them too."

"So you want me to circulate your automaton assassin's description."

"Semi-automaton. Cyber-organic, I believe. And no, I don't *want* you to. It's up to you whether you circulate its description, but I think it would probably be a good idea if you want to catch this villain."

"But why Gallowglass and a bunch of shilling whores? What could they possibly have in common, unless of course the good doctor sought a release from his worldly worries outside of the marital home."

"He was a widow."

"But doesn't he have a live in housekeeper."

"Governess," Quicksilver harrumphed, cheeks reddening. "And, of course, what you say is highly possible. Your Whitechapel whores met their ends not far from where Gallowglass died. However, his body was not found at a well-known pick-up spot, and his behaviour on the night in question does not suggest that he was looking for diverting entertainment. But I'll admit that it's possible. Why don't you stick some manpower on the case, and leave the leaps of logic to me."

"Well, you're the celebrity detective," Allardyce retorted.

"Indeed," the dandy said, his shark-like grin putting the police inspector in his place again, "I am."

CHAPTER NINETEEN

The Last Will and Testament of Victor Gallowglass

When Ulysses Quicksilver finally made it home – filthy, wet and cold – it was to find Dr Methuselah's analysis of the two blood samples waiting for him. But he decided that whatever it was that the cantankerous old coot had discovered could wait until after a hot bath and a change of attire. He did have house guests after all, and Inspector Allardyce's comments had brought it home to him that standards had to be maintained.

"Another one for the dustmen, don't you think, old boy?" Ulysses said as he handed his sodden and sooty jacket to his manservant, having barely got further than the threshold of his Mayfair home.

"Very good, sir," the immaculately turned out Nimrod responded, his nose wrinkling as he took the proffered garment and held it at arm's length.

"And run me a bath, would you? Nice and hot and plenty of bubbles. I have a need to be clean."

"Yes, sir."

"Where's the child? And her governess?"

"There are upstairs, sir, in the nursery."

"The nursery." A smile came to Ulysses' face as he remembered how he and Barty had played together there when they had been children, when their parents had still been alive. The smile faded. "I'm glad the old place is seeing some use again."

"Did you want to see them, sir?"

"No. I don't want to see anybody until after I've had that bath. Apart from you, of course, old chap."

"Of course, sir," Nimrod said with a sigh.

Later, as he luxuriated in the hot water – eyes closed, letting his thoughts drift with the curling clouds of pine-scented steam – Ulysses considered what he knew of the circumstances of Victor Gallowglass's death, the nature of his killer, even the events leading up to the kidnap of his daughter and how Miranda was mixed up in it all.

An hour later, now with more questions than answers on his mind, Ulysses dressed in a clean white shirt, gun metal grey silk and moleskin trews, then retired to his study to partake of a plate of shrimp and avocado, and study Dr Methuselah's analysis of the blood samples.

After all the waiting and the expectation it wasn't what he had been expecting. To be honest, he hadn't been certain what he had been expecting, but it certainly wasn't what the results were showing him.

There was absolutely nothing special about the blood sample Ulysses had rescued from the shattered test tube that had been brought to the pier. It was a perfect match for the other sample Ulysses had collected from the blood-drenched crime scene, from Gallowglass's body itself.

He threw the smudged Babbage printout onto the desk with a harrumph of annoyance.

But what had Victor Gallowglass been doing carrying a sample of his own blood all the way from Belgravia to the East End and a pier on the River Thames?

This mystery had its claws in him now and wouldn't let go.

There came a knock at the study door.

"Come!" Ulysses snapped, his irritation spilling over into his tone of voice.

The door opened. "Sir, this also came while you were out," Nimrod said, passing Ulysses an innocuous brown paper package, tied with string.

"Well, what have we got here then?" he mused. There was something unnervingly familiar about the tidy hand that had inscribed the address, it looked to be that of Gallowglass.

It was no bigger than a cigar box. Ulysses hurriedly pulled the string free and then paused. He picked the package up and put it to his ear, listening intently for a moment. He then shook it gently.

Nimrod, watching him all the while with hawkish interest, swallowed hard.

"Can't be too careful," Ulysses said, placing the package carefully on the desk. "Not after what happened last time. Well, here goes nothing."

He ripped the wrapping paper free, revealing, as he had suspected, a taped-up cigar box.

"So far so good," he said, reaching for a Sri Lankan ivory letter opener and running it along the seams of the box.

Throwing caution to the wind, Ulysses prised open the box. Ripping off the lid, he then set about carefully removing the wads of cotton wool filling it until the treasure it contained was revealed.

It was another sealed test tube full of what Ulysses presumed to be blood from its colour and viscosity. He took the phial in his fingers and carefully lifted it out of the box. It felt cold to the touch, the thick, near-black liquid moving sluggishly from one end of the tube to the other as it see-sawed between Ulysses' finger and thumb.

And there was something else, a piece of paper, frayed down one side as if it had been torn from a journal, bearing a note written in the same tidy hand.

This thing of darkness I acknowledge mine.

Nimrod's eyebrows arched as he peered across the desk in an attempt to read the note himself. Ulysses spun it round with a finger, for him to see.

"'This thing of darkness I acknowledge mine,'" he read. "Most intriguing."

"Not really, Nimrod. Classic Shakespeare. Third year, Chalky Chambers' English Literature class, last period before lunch on a Thursday, if I rightly recall. Gallowglass and I both endured the old beak's lectures about the Bard, but that was actually one play of his I did enjoy."

"Oh, I see," Nimrod said.

"No, old boy, I don't think you do. 'This thing of darkness I acknowledge mine' is a line straight out of *The Tempest*, when the magician Prospero talks of Caliban, his deformed and monstrous slave."

"I see, sir."

Ulysses' eyes narrowed as he leaned forwards, resting his elbows on the desk in front of him, his fingers steepling before his face.

Was this Victor Gallowglass's last will and testament, one phial of blood and a scrawled line from Shakespeare?

"You know what? I think I *would* like you to intrude upon our guests in the nursery."

"Mr Quicksilver? You wanted to see me again?" the governess asked, as she poked her head around the study door.

"Ah, Miss Wishart. Please, come in. I am sorry to trouble you again," he said, affecting his most ingratiating manner. "And do, call me Ulysses."

She blushed, but took a seat. "What did you want to see me about?"

"I am afraid that my continued badgering is in pursuit of the truth, as to who had Dr Gallowglass murdered. And so I must ask you again if you can recall anything – anything at all – that your employer might have said or done that might give us a clue as to what he had become mixed up in and that could have resulted in someone wanting him dead."

"We have gone over this before." The governess sounded on edge.

"I know, but there must have been something, no matter how insignificant you might consider it. Any clue at all."

"I did not pry into my employer's business," Miss Wishart said simply.

"Of course, I understand that, but that's not what I was implying," Ulysses coaxed. "I'm sorry if that's how my questioning came across, but is there anything – anything at all?"

"I was employed to look after and educate his daughter, Mr Quicksilver. I was not his housekeeper. In fact, I was not his keeper in any way, shape or form. I did not ask him what he was working on in his lab just as I did not ask him what transpired when he attended surgery at the Daedalus Clinic on Harley Street, or what business he had on the Isle of Wight."

"The Isle of Wight?" Ulysses repeated.

"On royal business, naturally," Miss Wishart said proudly, basking for a moment in the reflected glory of her employer's highly-regarded position. "It was Dr Gallowglass by royal appointment, in case you didn't know."

"Miss Wishart," Ulysses exclaimed, leaping up from his chair on the other side of the desk, "I could kiss you!"

"Mr Quicksilver! The impropriety!" the woman gasped, recoiling, but unable to hide her smile amidst her blushes.

"Nimrod!" Ulysses shouted, making for the study door. Before he could reach it, the door opened, Nimrod already waiting there at the threshold.

"You bellowed, sir?"

"Nimrod, pack a bag. It's time we got away from the Big Smoke for a couple of days, don't you think? A bit of sea air," he said, flashing the governess a devilish grin, "that's what we need."

CHAPTER TWENTY

The Isle of Wights

Gravel crunching noisily beneath its tyres, the Rolls Royce Mark IV Silver Phantom pulled up outside the main visitor's entrance to the grand, creamy stoned Italianate palazzo-style house.

Ulysses Quicksilver opened the passenger door and got out, marvelling at the grand facade, with its promenade balcony and belvedere tower, one of two possessed by the property. He then moved to the rear of the vehicle where he opened the door to let Miss Wishart and her charge out of the car.

The governess almost let her carefully composed guard down as she stepped out of the Rolls and saw the house for the first time. The child, however, had none of that foolish adult bravado to maintain.

"Isn't it wonderful, Miss Wishart?" she said as she gazed up at the entrance facade.

"It is a fine example of a mock Italian Renaissance palazzo, certainly," the governess replied, quickly recovering her composure.

"Yes, Miranda," Ulysses said, squatting down on his haunches in front of the child, "it is wonderful, isn't it? Shall we take a look inside?"

"Oh, yes please. Can we?"

"Of course you can, if that's what you'd like."

"Yes please, Uncle Ulysses."

"Come on then," he said, taking her by the hand and the two of them made for the pillared entrance at a gentle run, valet and governess following behind.

The ferry journey had been tolerable and, from the drop off point at Fishbourne, it had only been a short drive along hedgerow-bordered roads to the East Cowes promontory and the former royal residence.

Osborne House had stood on this spot for roughly 150 years, having been completed in 1851, built by the renowned London architect Thomas Cubitt to a design of the Prince Consort's.

Her Royal Highness Queen Victoria and Prince Albert had bought the house that once stood at the location as a summer house and rural retreat, somewhere they could go to, to escape the stresses and strains of life in London. The Queen harboured fond memories of childhood holidays, whilst the views of the Solent from the grounds reminded her husband of the Bay of Naples.

Of course the three storey Georgian house that stood on the site when they purchased the property soon proved too small for their burgeoning needs, unable, as it was, to cater for the needs of their growing family. Pulling down the old house and building anew was considered the only appropriate course of action. And it catered for the Queen's heirs still.

Only now it wasn't a holiday home; now it was a hospital. Although, if truth be told, it was more prison than hospital; a containment facility for those members of Queen Victoria's extended family too old and decrepit to look after themselves but too important to be allowed to end their days in peace.

It was only thanks to Ulysses' royal insignia-stamped ID that they had made it past the heavily fortified gates and the automaton sentries on duty there.

"Ah, Mr Quicksilver."

A portly, middle-aged woman in her late fifties, wearing the starched grey and white uniform of a royal nurse, trotted down the main stairs towards them, moving with all the vim and vigour of someone half her apparent age.

"I'm Matron Handy," the woman said, grasping Ulysses' hand in hers and giving it a vigorous shake. "Sorry to keep you waiting. Dr Quercus will be along shortly. He is just with one of their royal highnesses at the moment, you understand."

"Of course," Ulysses said.

"As it's such a pleasant day, perhaps you would prefer to wait in the gardens?"

The air contained within the hallway was sterile and pristine, just like the tiled floor and the clinical white interiors of the house. Travelling from the permanently Smog-shrouded Londinium Maximum to this place had been, quite literally, a breath of fresh air.

Ulysses suddenly longed to smell the pollen-scented air, the sea-salt tang of the coastal breezes and the scent of new life – green shoots, spring blossom and freshly mown grass.

"Yes," he said. "Why not?"

The grounds of Osborne House were as impressive as the house itself. They started with a series of terraced knot gardens that descended to a fountain, which had as its centrepiece a cherub apparently throttling a swan, and from there continued out towards the coast via the great lawns and a riding path.

Ulysses descended the steps behind the grand Pavilion with Matron Handy at his side and his manservant following a few respectful paces behind. Some way ahead, Miranda skipped over the lawns between the dwarf conifers, being pursued by her governess who seemed anxious not to lose sight of her charge, fussing after her like a mother hen.

Amongst the shrubberies and carefully-clipped box hedges, nurses and their automaton Nightingale unit counterparts pushed frail, near-skeletons in bath chairs around the grounds so that they might partake of the fresh sea air; or sat with them in the sun, parasols protecting them from the hazards of having too much of a good thing.

"So how many patients do you have here?" Ulysses asked the matron.

"Oh, not patients, Mr Quicksilver. Residents," the matron corrected him with the tone of a disappointed headmistress. He imagined that she used the same tone with her royal charges and ran a tight ship. He could guess who the real ruler was here.

"So,how many do you cater for here?"

"As many as is necessary."

"And were any under the care of Dr Gallowglass?"

"Oh, none," Matron Handy said.

"I'm sorry? But I understood he worked here?"

"Dr Gallowglass was an infrequent visitor."

"Now, now, Matron, I hope you're not boring our guests with trivial details," came a voice from behind them, as a gentleman as portly as Matron Handy – looking almost as immaculate as Ulysses' manservant, in his black frock coat and pin-striped trousers – scampered down the steps after them.

"Mr Quicksilver, I presume," the man said, extending a hand.

"You presume correctly." Ulysses took the man's hand and shook it, expertly hiding the revulsion he felt in response to the doctor's wet-fish grip. "And you are?"

"Dr Quercus, Chief Physician. So sorry to have kept you waiting. You should have rung ahead in advance and warned us that you were coming."

"Oh, you know how it is. We just happened to be in the area... Matron Handy was just telling me about Dr Gallowglass's involvement here at Osborne House."

"Ah yes, we were so sorry to hear of the good doctor's sad demise," Quercus said.

Matron Handy looked at the Chief Physician askance; obviously Dr Quercus had not seen fit to share that particular piece of news with her yet.

Ulysses was actually rather surprised to learn that the news had already reached the Isle of Wight, considering the current climate, especially if Gallowglass had only been an occasional visitor to heaven's waiting room.

"I'm surprised you heard so soon."

"We are not as cut-off out here as you might think." The Chief Physician smiled his simpering smile again, half-closing his eyes as he did so. The more Ulysses thought about it, the more he thought the Chief Physician resembled a self-satisfied toad; the expression on his amphibian features suggesting that he had recently enjoyed a satisfying meal of fat maggots and juicy flies. It was not an appealing look.

"But just the same... *The Times* only broke the story this morning and I rather suspect that we were on the same boat as shipped those papers to your island retreat."

"But of course, why wouldn't we know when his replacement, Dr Pavlov, arrived on the ferry last night," Quercus said.

"Dr Pavlov?" Ulysses repeated, struggling to mask his surprise. "Is he...?"

"A Russian gentleman, but very well-spoken. And, of course, he comes with the highest credentials."

"Of course he does," Ulysses said. "And the paperwork all checked out, I'm sure."

"But of course. Why wouldn't it?"

"And where is this Dr Pavlov now?"

As if on cue, the watch pinned to the front of Matron Handy's apron began to buzz with the urgency of an alarm clock, its face flashing with a pulsing red light.

"What is it matron?" Dr Quercus demanded.

"That's the call for the crash team," Matron Handy said, a look of growing horror in her eyes.

"You mean one of our residents is suffering a cardiac arrest, matron?"

Miss Wishart looked round anxiously as the siren sounded and even Miranda looked up, her childish curiosity distracting her from the game she was playing.

"Do now worry," the Chief Physician said. "Heart attacks, and strokes, and the like, are not uncommon with such an elderly populace. But thanks to our devoted ministrations most come through."

The matron's watch buzzed again. "Dr Quercus, there's been another one."

"Another one?" the Chief Physician exclaimed. "I find that highly unlikely. Two heart attacks? Within a minute of each other?"

The fateful watch chimed again, its face lit up like a Christmas tree.

"Better make that three," Ulysses said. "It sounds as though you have a crisis on your hands, Dr Quercus, and in a crisis, I'm your man!"

CHAPTER TWENTY-ONE

Doctor Death

Ulysses raced through the shuttered rooms of the house, following the spluttered directions of both Matron Handy and Dr Quercus as they panted after him and his manservant, struggling to keep up.

They passed from one hospital ward – the air thick with the smell of death, held at bay by disinfectant – to the next, and in each one, its occupants seemed more decrepit, more skeletal, and somehow less and less human. They passed more of the startled nursing staff, the incessant tannoy alarms setting their nerves on edge, and the statuesque Nightingale units that were making calmly for the epicentre of the emergency.

"And the first time you ever saw this Dr Pavlov was this morning?" Ulysses panted.

"Yes," Quercus gasped, barely able to catch his breath.

"Something tells me he wasn't intending to make a return visit."

Staggering up another twisting staircase, Ulysses flung himself at a pair of swing doors awaiting him there and crashed through into the near-darkness of the uppermost Pavilion ward.

Lying corpse-like within their tubular steel cots, oxygen tents and iron lungs, these residents were among the oldest of Victoria's surviving heirs. Like the Empress herself, they were not permitted to die but kept in a state of living death, just in case they, or their blood-matched organs, should be needed to perpetuate the royal gene-line.

At the end of the ward a number of beds had their curtains pulled shut around them, and, visible on the wall above each one, amber warning lights flashed as alarms rang, the rest of the room's occupants wailing in sympathy. From the curtained cubicles no one voiced any cries of distress; they were too far gone.

He half-expected to see the spider-like automaton assassin perched on the curtain rails above a bed, but there was nothing like that waiting for him here.

As Matron Handy sent the nursing staff scurrying to tend to the ailing ancients – the Nightingale units laying their electro-conductive hands on the fluttering chests of the dying royals, the sound of charging defibrillators filling the ward with a rising hum – Ulysses, with Nimrod following close behind, kept on for the curtained cubicles.

Reaching the furthest screened beds he yanked the curtains aside and suddenly he found himself confronted by a lean and wiry-looking individual, who was administering something to the emaciated body lying in the bed beside him.

The man turned. He was dressed in a white doctor's coat and had a pinched, tight-lipped expression of ruthless determination on his face. He wore a pair of round, wire-framed spectacles and his porcelain pale skin, along with his centre-parted lacquered hair, gave his face the appearance of a billiard ball. In one hand he was holding a scalpel, in the other a hypodermic needle.

"Doctor Pavlov, I presume," Ulysses said.

The man simply snarled before making a dancing lunge towards him, with the surprising balletic grace of a fencing master. Ulysses himself only just jerked his body back and out of reach of the scalpel. Its razor-sharp edge caught him on the sleeve, sending several buttons spinning to the polished hardwood floor.

"Not again!" Ulysses wailed in frustration at the destruction of his suit, and then took another dancing step backwards through the clinging curtains as the man came at him once more. This time the scalpel removed a button from Ulysses' silk waistcoat.

"Dr Pavlov!" Quercus spluttered.

The moon-faced man swore sharply in Russian.

And then Nimrod was there beside Ulysses, making a grab for the man, trying to wrap him up in the folds of the flapping curtain. But the mysterious Dr Pavlov was too quick for him. Dancing backwards, shifting his weight on to his back foot, he dodged out of reach of Nimrod's floundering lunge.

But it gave Ulysses all the time he needed. Making his own riposte, he thrust with his unsheathed rapier blade. Bravely, or perhaps foolishly, Dr Pavlov tried to parry the lunge with his scalpel but, in the end, such a gesture was futile. The blade went spinning from his bleeding hand and clattered onto the floor.

Now that he had the upper hand, Ulysses moved forwards again.

Ulysses led with his sword. But then Pavlov was spinning past him, avoiding his blade and coming at Ulysses with the hypodermic needle he was still holding in his other hand.

Ulysses tried to bat the hypodermic from Pavlov's hand before he could sink it into him. God alone knew what it contained. He fell against the foot of a steel-framed cot, desperately pulling his blade back once more, hoping against hope to deflect the hypodermic.

And then the butt of a pistol swept down through the swaying curtains, and struck the hand holding the needle hard. With a cry Pavlov drew back his hand as the needle went clattering to the floor.

In the next instant he turned and vanished between the swinging drapes. Scrambling to his feet, Ulysses set off after him.

Fighting his way clear of the persistent curtain, Ulysses was just in time to see Pavlov hurl a steel chair through a window. Ulysses heard the chair rattle and clang as it bounced off the side of the building. Pavlov was already following it, kicking some of the larger shards of glass still caught in the frame clear as he clambered through.

Ulysses threw himself after the assailant

He was just in time to see Pavlov launch himself from a precarious ledge and land heavily, with an audible, winded gasp, on the flat roof of another wing of the complex.

Ulysses hurled himself across the gap between the two buildings. He landed not far from where Pavlov had landed, his dive turning into a roll as he turned the momentum of his fall to his advantage. He came up out of his roll and onto his feet and immediately set off after the fleeing doctor.

Ahead of him the second belvedere tower rose four storeys above the roof. The daring doctor was already elbowing his way through a window and into the tower.

Ulysses pushed through after him only seconds later, missing the doctor's coat-tails by a whisper.

And then he was standing on the stone stair inside the tower, listening to the sounds of the fleeing doctor's footsteps receding above him, the agitated shouts of security guards rising from below.

Ulysses had no idea where Pavlov thought he could escape to by ascending the tower. Perhaps he hoped to hide from his pursuers and double-back after they had passed his hiding place, but with Ulysses so close on his tail, such an approach seemed doomed to failure.

At the top of the tower he saw Pavlov edging out onto the balcony beyond one of the tall arched windows.

Over the pounding of his heart, Ulysses fancied he could heard the purr of an engine somewhere above in the cloud dotted Solent sky.

"Give it up, Pavlov!" Ulysses shouted. "The game's up. There's nowhere left to run!" The bespectacled interloper shot him an angry glance and then turned his attention to the jutting parapet of the belvedere above him. Ulysses' heart skipped a beat as he realised what the man was intending to do.

Releasing his hold on the stones facing the tower wall, Pavlov reached for the parapet above – and jumped.

Fingers scrabbled at the cast mouldings and found a hand-hold, and then Dr Pavlov was hanging there, arms at full stretch, his feet kicking over the precipitous six storey drop below.

What was the man doing?

The sound of aero-engines was getting louder.

Swinging his body to increase his momentum, Pavlov suddenly jerked his arms upwards again, trying to grasp the ledge of the tower roof.

Fingers found hand-holds again and Ulysses watched, incredulously, as Dr Pavlov pulled himself up onto the top of the tower and out of sight.

Ulysses lent out of the window. The engine roar was deafening now and the downwash whipped through his hair, forcing him to half close his eyes.

And there, above him, its bloated whale-like silhouette blotting out the sun, was a dirigible. Ulysses watched as it cleared the top of the Belvedere and began to rise. Struggling to climb the rope ladder dangling beneath it was Dr Pavlov.

Unholstering his pistol, Ulysses took aim. But the wash of the dirigible's engines and the reappearance of the glaring sun from behind the airship conspired to spoil his aim. The *crack* of the pistol firing was followed by the *pang* of the bullet ricocheting harmlessly from an engine housing. And then Pavlov was disappearing inside the gondola, suspended beneath the sky leviathan as it climbed ever higher and further out of range.

"Security!" Ulysses bellowed back down the tower. What was needed here was a rifle and fast. "Get up here now!" But by the time the first puffing guard reached the top the dirigible was already a shrinking silhouette on the eastern horizon.

CHAPTER TWENTY-TWO

An Ending

Ulysses wallowed in the smoky fug of the Inferno Club, considering all that had befallen him and the wretched Victor Gallowglass of late, over a glass of cognac.

After his encounter with the mysterious Dr Pavlov on the Isle of Wight, and the Russian's dramatic aerial escape, he now had more questions than ever before and a significant lack of answers. He needed time to think, to plan his way forward. Whatever the real reason for Gallowglass's murder, it was only the tip of the iceberg.

Ulysses was roused from his reverie by a polite cough and he turned to see a liveried footman standing beside his armchair. In one hand he held a silver platter bearing a simple, gold-embossed card. Ulysses picked it up and examined it.

The crisp white card bore a curious symbol; it was a circle, surmounted by a crescent and with a cross descending beneath it. On the reverse there was nothing.

"Who gave you this?" Ulysses asked.

"If you'd like to come with me, sir," the footman said.

The dandy looked at him, eyebrows knitting quizzically. "Very well."

Ulysses rose from his place by the fire and followed as the footman led him out of the Quartermain Room, along a corridor, up a staircase, and finally stopped before a velvet-upholstered door. Opening it, he ushered Ulysses inside.

The room beyond was small, opulently decorated, but bore only two things of particular interest. Most of one wall was covered by a large, gilt mirror. In the middle of the room, facing the mirror was a padded leather armchair. Ulysses took a seat as the footman pulled the door closed behind him.

"Well, well, well. What have we here?" he wondered aloud.

"Good afternoon, Mr Quicksilver."

The voice had come from a speaker trumpet set into the wall beneath the mirror.

"It would appear that you have me at a disadvantage," Ulysses said, addressing the mirror, peering at it closely, but seeing nothing beyond the reflection of the room and his own curious expression.

"Names are not important," the tinny voice came again. Ulysses didn't believe that the distortion he heard was simply down to the quality of the audio-relay.

"*Au contraire*," he countered.

It was a moment or two before the voice spoke again. "You can call me Hermes."

"The winged messenger."

"You understand the reference."

"I do, and I'm intrigued. What message is it that you wish to deliver?"

"Dr Pavlov was not working alone."

"I guessed as much myself when he was rescued in the nick of time by a ruddy great zeppelin. But what was he doing offing ancient royals at Osborne House in the first place?"

"He was trying to recreate Dr Gallowglass's work."

"What work?"

"I think you know that already."

Ulysses mind raced. Gallowglass had destroyed his notes before he ever set them all on the path to chaos and death. And then he remembered the cigar box he had received through the post.

"Caliban."

"Precisely."

"But why would Pavlov take such risks?"

"Because he needed a sample."

"A blood sample?"

"Precisely."

Ulysses steepled his fingers before his face. "Where is he now? Do you know?"

"Make your way to Moscow. Once you are there, find the Firebird. She will help you on the next leg of your journey."

"And what about Gallowglass's killer?"

"Do not worry about the Ripper. It will not trouble you again."

"How can you be so sure?"

"Trust me."

Ulysses continued to stare intently at the unyielding mirror.

"Why should I? I mean, why are you telling me all this?"

"Because it is in our mutual interest that you get to the bottom of this mystery."

"But what do you want from me? After all, there's no such thing as a free lunch."

This time there was no reply.

"Hello? I said, what do you want from me?"

Still nothing.

"Very well. Have it your own way." And with that Ulysses left the room.

In contradiction to the rules of pathetic fallacy, it didn't rain the day Victor Gallowglass was buried.

Not many came to the funeral. Other than himself, Miss Wishart, Miranda and the vicar, Ulysses counted only seven others. Most were strangers to him, but Matron Handy was there, along with Dr Quercus. He had half-expected an impromptu school reunion at the grave side, but it seemed that

Victor Gallowglass had been just as bad as Ulysses in keeping in touch with his old classmates.

One person Ulysses hadn't expected to see there was the head of Department Q, and leader of the government during the current state of emergency, the imposing Lord Octavius De Wynter.

He stood a little way from the rest of the funeral party in mourning black, a black-suited aide at his side.

As the Reverend Smedley droned on – like so many men of the cloth, finding himself having to speak with heartfelt conviction about a man he had never known – Ulysses glanced from the grimacing De Wynter, down the sloping sward of the cemetery to where Nimrod awaited him in the Rolls.

The droning of bees, the smell of the fresh cut grass and the distant call of a spring cuckoo carried Ulysses back to another time and another place; where another Ulysses had stood at another graveside, holding his sobbing younger brother's hand for comfort, Nimrod's hands on his own shoulders giving him the strength to be brave for the both of them.

And then Ulysses was roused from his reverie, aware that an uneasy silence had descended over the funeral party. Miss Wishart nudged him in the ribs and Ulysses saw that the vicar was beckoning them forwards, so that they might say their own farewells.

Miranda – wearing a black coat, tights, gloves and beret – knelt down at the graveside and, taking a handful of loose soil, cast it into the hole with the words, "Bye-bye, Daddy."

Miss Wishart was next. She said nothing but only sniffed and dabbed at her eyes with a balled up handkerchief.

Then it was Ulysses' turn.

Taking a handful of earth, he stood there at the graveside for a moment, not knowing what to say.

"Don't worry, Victor old boy," he muttered. "I'll look after her."

He scattered the crumbled earth into the hole, the soil rattling dryly on the lid of the coffin and the polished brass plaque bearing Victor's name.

Ulysses strode away from the hole in the ground as a shovelling sexton-droid, painted a matt funereal black, set about filling the grave.

The party broke up, people moving off in groups of two or three at a respectfully slow pace. As Ulysses gazed out across the sunlit cemetery to Nimrod, waiting as rigid and as still as a royal guardsman on duty at the Palace, his wandering eye caught De Wynter's own imperious gaze.

"If you'll just excuse me, ladies," Ulysses said and strode purposefully over to his superior.

"I understand you paid a visit to the Isle of Wight," De Wynter said as Ulysses reached him, his tone sharp.

"Yes, I did."

"Can I ask *what* you were doing there?"

"You can."

"Then what *were* you doing there?"

"I was following up a lead regarding a case I am working on."

"Would that be the Gallowglass murder, by any chance?"

"It would."

"And has the good doctor's killer been apprehended?"

"Not yet, but I'm sure it will only be a matter of time. The Metropolitan Police are on the case."

"Then it sounds as if your part in this case is over," De Wynter said. "Doesn't it?"

"There is one last lead I would like to follow up." Ulysses said.

"I would advise you not to bother," De Wynter said.

"Not bother?"

"You said it yourself; the police have the matter in hand and I am sure that whatever help you were able to offer them was gratefully received, but now it need tax your tenacious, enquiring mind no longer." De Wynter fixed Ulysses with a penetrating stare. "Do I make myself clear?"

"As crystal."

"I also understand you have new responsibilities now," De Wynter went on. "London's hardly the place to bring up a child at present, wouldn't you say? And you deserve a rest yourself, after all you've been through in the last – what is it now – six months?"

"Seven," Ulysses corrected, "but who's counting?"

"Seven months," De Wynter said. "Why don't you enjoy some time away from the capital? At that country pad of yours, perhaps, or maybe go further afield. I hear that there is nothing quite like Paris in the springtime."

"Yes, why not? Like you say, I have been... over-doing it a bit, lately."

De Wynter's slate grey eyes softened and his grim-set expression relaxed a little.

"Very good. I'm glad we understand one another."

"Perfectly," said Ulysses, a smile flashing onto his face, although his eyes remained hard and cold.

"Then I bid good day to you, Quicksilver."

"Good day to you, sir," Ulysses said, with a curt nod of his head.

Dismissed, Ulysses followed the governess and her ward as the two of them ambled along between the gravestones, reading the epitaphs inscribed upon them.

"Ladies," he said, offering Miss Wishart his arm as they walked. She accepted it willingly, flashing him a brief smile.

"Uncle Ulysses?"

"Yes, Miranda, my dear?" he said, giving her a broad smile.

"Is everything going to be alright now?"

Ulysses didn't answer but stared off into the middle distance for a moment. He thought he heard something; the scrape of a metal digit on a tomb, the rattle of gravel on a grave. He shot anxious glances in every direction but saw nothing, and then all he could hear was the rustle of leaves in the breeze. A shiver passed down his spine and a weird sensation, like pins and needles, pricked his thumbs.

"You know what?" he said, looking at each of them in turn. "I think we could all do with a holiday, don't you?"

Elsewhere orange hazard lights bathed the bricks of the sepulchral lair in strobing light, as the eighteen inch thick steel door of the vault closed with a groan. The technician then set about spinning the wheel-lock to secure it.

"Vault secure, sir," he said, addressing the other standing behind him.

The observer tapped a palm with the ebony cane he carried.

"I hope so. We don't want any more little accidents do we?"

"It won't be going anywhere, Mr Sixsmith, I can assure you of that."

"I hope so, Hollingsworth. I hope so."

"The door is tempered steel, eighteen inches thick."

"Eighteen inches? Really?" Xavier Sixsmith said, giving the door a tap with his cane. "Let's see you get out of there, you bastard," he growled.

Turning on his heel he made his way back up the brick-lined tunnel, the technician scampering to keep up with his purposeful strides.

"Come on Hollingsworth. Time to report in and see what the big man has to say."

On the other side of the steel door, suspended in its cradle of nutrient-feed tubes and power cables, bathed in a ruddy electric glow, the assassin slept in a fug of formaldehyde gas.

The chains supporting the harness rattled as the cyber-organic creation twitched and jerked, its resting mind reliving past crimes.

Silvered finger-blades scissoring unconsciously, it dreamed its dreams of murder and mayhem, and, satisfied smile spread across its acid-etched face.

I love my work and want to start again. You will soon hear of me with my funny little games... The next job I do I shall clip the lady's ears off and send to the police officers just for jolly wouldn't you... My knife's so nice and sharp I want to get to work right away if I get a chance. Good luck. Yours truly, Jack the Ripper.

ACT THREE

Blood Royal

April 1998

CHAPTER TWENTY-THREE

The Russian Connection

The air was clean and crisp, so unlike London, Moscow seemed like a city that should, by rights, belong to a different age, rather than just one from another country. It had its heavy industrial centres, of course, but these were well away from the old city itself and were nothing on the scale of those found within the capital of the Workshop of the World.

Fashions, Ulysses had noted, were not far behind the Neo-Victorian mores of the day that had, admittedly, been of more interest in the weeks before the Wormwood Catastrophe. Indeed, had Moscow's civic leaders been fully aware of the ongoing issues surrounding the aftermath of the Wormwood Catastrophe, they might have realised that, with the twenty-first century on their doorstep, here was an unrivalled opportunity for London to be supplanted as 'de facto' capital of the world.

But Moscow – and, Ulysses assumed, the rest of Russia – was still behind Britain. Whereas in London it sometimes seemed as though there was a broadcast screen on every street corner, here Ulysses had only come across them outside the Cathedral of Christ the Saviour and the Circus on Tsvetnoy Boulevard, and they had only been showing looped newsreel footage of the Tsarina Anastasia III, Queen Victoria's great-great-great-granddaughter, at official state functions, there being particular excitement surrounding her planned visit to the Czech capital in a few short weeks.

Perhaps the satellite states of Magna Britannia were not as well-connected as he – and the rest of the Magna Britannian populace – had been led to believe.

On this particular morning, Ulysses was accompanying Miss Wishart and Miranda on a gentle constitutional through Tsar Nicholas Park, named after the great-grandfather of the current Tsarina. It was now the second day since they had decamped to the Russian capital, Ulysses taking a suite at the St Petersburg Hotel where his manservant Nimrod was, even now, making sure that everything was just as his master liked it.

Ulysses and the governess were walking arm in arm as Miranda skipped along the path before them, chasing the butterflies that rose from the shrubberies and flowering buddleia as she passed by. At that moment, it seemed to Ulysses that she didn't have a care in the world. She was a hardy soul, he had to give her that.

The trees, wearing their coats of lush greenery hid the spires and domes of the city's Krymsky Val district, the fountains and clipped rhododendrons making it feel as if they were enjoying the environs of some pleasant country estate. For a moment Ulysses could almost believe that he had left all his worries a thousand miles behind.

"So, Mr Quicksilver," the governess said, "are you going to tell me why we've really come all the way to Moscow to 'get away from it all'?"

"Miss Wishart," he said, "do you mean to tell me that you think I have an ulterior motive for bringing you and the young Miss Gallowglass to this most marvellous city of shining cultural delights? And please, call me Ulysses."

"Yes, I do," she said. "I mean Moscow in April is hardly the most inspiring of holiday destinations. And if you insist on me calling you by your first name, then you had better call me Lillian."

"Lillian?"

"What's so funny about that?"

"Forgive me, it's just that I never took you for a Lillian."

"Oh? And what are Lillians supposed to look like pray tell?"

"Well, more..."

"Go on."

"Just, not like you."

"Whereas you look like exactly what you are."

"You can read me like a book, Lillian," Ulysses said.

"From cover to cover," Lillian replied and laughed.

"Very well then, seeing as how you've found me out..." Ulysses said. "We're here following up a lead."

"But I thought you said your superior said you weren't to," she said, her cheeks flushing in excitement at the suggestion that they might be caught up in something even just a little illicit.

"He did, that's right. But he also told me to take a holiday. Practically ordered me as it happens."

"Is your man really back at the hotel making things ready?"

"Now that would be telling, wouldn't it?" Ulysses said. "Let's just say that Nimrod had a life before that of gentleman's valet and that he still maintains certain contacts."

The governess turned to watch the child skipping ahead of them through the park.

"I do hope you are taking your new responsibilities seriously, Ulysses," she said. "I hope that you would not be doing anything to put the life of my charge at risk, especially after all her poor father went through to keep her safe."

"And she couldn't be safer than in the care of three adults as capable as you, me and Nimrod. She's a good girl and I believe she is more capable than you give her credit for."

"Well, we shall just have to see about that shan't we?"

For a moment there was nothing but an awkward silence between them.

"So, what happens now?" Miss Wishart said.

"I thought a trip to the ballet might be in order. This evening? How about it?"

"The ballet?"

"Yes, at The Bolshoi Theatre. It's quite the done thing, you know. And the Firebird herself is said to be performing tonight."

"The Firebird? The prima ballerina of the Bolshoi ballet?"

"Indeed."

"For all of us?" she said, her gaze taking in the child.

"Well, to be honest, I thought Nimrod might wait outside for us in the lobby, but other than that..."

"Well I suppose a trip to the ballet can't hurt, can it? Actually, I think it would be a very pleasant way to spend the evening. What will they be performing tonight?"

"Swan Lake, I believe," Ulysses replied, trying to recall what had been printed on the tickets that had been delivered to his hotel suite the night before. They had arrived in an envelope bearing the image of a phoenix rising from a nest of flames.

Miss Wishart suddenly pulled back and gave him a measured look of critical appraisal.

"And this has nothing to do with what happened to Dr Gallowglass or what happened at Osborne House?" she asked, as if somehow party to the minutiae of his thoughts.

He flashed her another devil-may-care grin. "Now I didn't say that, did I?"

CHAPTER TWENTY-FOUR

The Firebird

There was only one word for it: mesmerizing.

That was how Ulysses felt about the Firebird's performance. As he watched her pirouette about the stage, he barely blinked once, utterly transfixed as he was.

He wasn't a fan of opera and he hadn't considered himself a fan of ballet either, until that night, but he was definitely a fan of the prima ballerina of the Bolshoi – Natasha Alina Eltsina, the Firebird – who was dancing the role of the swan princess Odette. He didn't fall for her, however, until the fourth act and the scene where Odette and her lover Siegfried cast themselves into the eponymous Swan Lake to drown together, rather than be parted forever. Her portrayal of the dying swan had him utterly entranced, while Miranda and Miss Wishart remained enraptured.

And from his seat in the stalls he felt as if he could have reached out and touched her, had he so desired. He would never have chosen a life on the stage for himself, but at that moment he wished that he were the taut-muscled, chisel-featured Adonis with his arms encircling her.

As the music soared, so did his heart.

Reaching into his jacket pocket, he took out the gold-embossed tickets again and the note that had arrived with them.

It read simply:

Meet me in my dressing room, after the performance.

And was signed:

Firebird

Much as Ulysses might have liked to fantasise that she had sent him the missive with amorous intention, the Firebird, he reasoned, was an agent like himself, although who she was working for he couldn't be sure – not just yet. And he knew he had to tread warily from here on in, since he knew even less about the mysterious Hermes, who had set him on the Russian connection, as he did about the prima ballerina herself.

As the crowd rose and gave a standing ovation, Ulysses made his excuses – leaving Miss Wishart and Miranda applauding furiously – and headed for the nearest exit, hoping to beat the rush.

Ulysses made his way towards the back-stage area and through a velvet-clad door.

A chorus of trotting ballerinas scampered past him, shooting him appraising looks, giggling to each other behind their hands. Their comments lost on him, Ulysses simply did what he did best and smiled back, which only provoked more wide-eyed expressions of delight.

Ulysses signalled for the attention of a stage-hand, sitting on a crate and smoking a cigarette

"I'm looking for the Firebird." Ulysses said, speaking in that pronounced, rather-too-loud register that Englishmen abroad everywhere tended to employ.

The stagehand grunted and muttered something incomprehensible. "Natasha Alina Eltsina?"

The stagehand made a noise that sounded like "Ahh" and hooked a thumb over his shoulder, following it up with a set of directions that he attempted to deliver via a combination of Russian and complicated hand gestures.

At long last, after wandering the rat-runs for what was probably only five minutes but felt like longer, in a quiet corner behind the stage, set apart from the hubbub of the junior ballerinas' changing area, he came upon a door painted red and bearing a modest gold star at its centre.

The door was ajar. Ulysses knocked, but his report was met with silence. Of course it was possible that the Firebird had not yet made it back from the stage; he had made his move as soon as the performance had ended after all. Perhaps she was entertaining fans at the stage door. He did not even know if the dressing room was hers, but who else – out of all those he had seen on stage that night – would warrant a gold star and their own private dressing room?

Cautiously he pushed at the door and immediately met with some resistance. Giving it a good shove, he succeeded in pushing it open fully at last, clearing the pile of clothes that had fallen down behind it.

The room was a mess and, for a moment, Ulysses was tempted to put the state of the place down to its occupant having an untidy, yet creative, soul. But on closer inspection he had to accept that the room had been ransacked.

He took a step into the dressing room, taking care not to tread on the dazzling and expensive-looking clothes that had been dumped onto the floor.

Where his hand touched the door it came away sticky and red.

The pile of clothes stirred and groaned weakly.

Ulysses was down on his knees in an instant, tugging gowns and boas clear of the pile to reveal the prone form of the Firebird.

The prima ballerina was still wearing the costume she had worn in her role as the swan princess. It hung in scissor-sliced lengths from her semi-naked body, saturated and sticky with her blood.

Realising that nothing he could do could save her now, her took her in his arms, cradling her head on his lap and rocking her gently, as he might a sleepy infant.

And then the Firebird spoke. Ulysses started as he realised that her words were in English. "Shhh, rest easy. It's going to be alright," he said.

"My knight in silver armour," she answered. "Tsarskoye Selo."

"What?"

"Go to Tsarskoye Selo."

"Tsarskoye Selo?" he repeated dumbly, still having no idea what she was talking about.

"Yes, Tsarskoye Selo. It lies south of St Petersburg. Take what lies in the devil's tomb... In Rasputin's tomb."

And then she was gone.

It took a moment for him to register the sound of the woman's screams behind him.

He turned and looked up into the terrified, youthful face of a ballerina on the cusp of adulthood, and his own face fell as she screamed again.

CHAPTER TWENTY-FIVE

Red Handed

"No, wait. You don't understand!" Ulysses cried out as the ballerina turned and fled.

Cursing, he gently laid the dead prima ballerina down amongst the swathes of strewn outfits, before springing to his feet.

The killer might have fled, but it would have left indications of its passing and, besides, Ulysses already knew who it was that had gutted the Firebird. For here he was in Moscow, thousands of miles from Londinium Maximum, while the Metropolitan Police hunted the self-same killer there.

Out in the corridor he could hear the young ballerina's cries, joined now by gasps of horror and shouts of confusion. Ignoring them for the moment, Ulysses left the dressing room and glanced about him. There had been a steady stream of people moving around backstage when Natasha Eltsina had been killed and so it was likely that there were people who had witnessed the killer's escape, and yet the shout of "Murder!" had not yet gone up

Ulysses looked up and noticed the marks left by the gouging steel claws of the monster as it had made its escape. He set off in pursuit at once, his heart pounding in his chest. He bustled his way past flustered stagehands and then he saw it, scuttling along the ceiling.

As Ulysses sprinted after it, it scuttled through a doorway.

Following, Ulysses suddenly found himself in darkness, the shadowy cut-outs of sets crowding around him, and realised he was on the stage itself. The house lights had been turned down. A sliver of gold and red appeared ahead of him, as something pushed its way through the closed curtains and out into the cavernous space of the auditorium.

With pistol in hand, Ulysses burst through the weighted curtains and after the killer.

Row upon row of empty, red-upholstered seats greeted him. And nothing else.

The curtains rippled behind him and Ulysses looked up.

The Ripper was clawing its way up the plush red curtains. Knowing that he wouldn't be able to do the same, the dandy ran through the high-roofed space of the theatre auditorium as the cyborg made its escape above him. Reaching the pelmet, the horrific thing launching itself at a box at the edge of the upper circle, and from there flung itself sideways to land amidst the seats beyond

Ulysses ran back across the stage and leapt over a parapet into the box that was side on to the stage itself. He was aware of figures moving towards him along the aisles between the seats. Somebody shouted something in Russian and then he heard the clear pronouncement "Stop!" in heavily-accented English.

Ignoring the command, he made his way to the back of the box, wrenched open the door and bounded through. It was imperative that he now found a up through the building.

He opened another narrow door and found himself on an even narrower landing with stairs leading both up and down. Without a second thought he flung himself up the stairs taking them two at a time, the sound of pounding footsteps on the stairs below him spurring him onwards.

Ulysses kicked open the door to the roof and dashed through, letting it bang shut behind him.

The reality of the situation he now found himself in hit him like a punch to the gut and he tensed as the cyber-organic assassin turned like a cornered tiger and flexed its blades.

Recognition seemed to flash in its eyes as it faced its pursuer. It hissed, lips pulling back from pearly white teeth, the grimace lending its acid-etched features an even more grotesquely-demonic aspect.

"No, no, no, little red bag. Not this time, not this time," it gibbered.

Seeing it waver, Ulysses felt a sudden rush of rage as the desire for revenge boiled within him; the image of the Firebird's savaged corpse fresh in his mind. He raised his gun. Surely a shot between the eyes would end this monster's reign of terror.

Slowly he pulled back the trigger. But then the rational part of his psyche and his deep-seated need for answers overrode his anger and his finger froze.

"Why?" he demanded. "Why did you do it? Why kill her? Who sent you?"

"No, no, no, *mustn't* say," the Ripper gabbled. "*Cannot* say. No, no, no, *will* not say."

Ulysses took a step forwards. The automaton assassin backed away from him.

"*Who sent you?*"

The cyborg's steel toes tapped and scraped on the stony surface of the theatre roof.

"WHO SENT YOU!" Ulysses screamed.

Hearing the door to the roof crash open again, Ulysses ducked and spun, his pistol whipping round to meet the black-clothed figures pouring through it. Ulysses recognised special forces police when they were pointing their guns at him.

Hearing a frantic scrabbling behind him, Ulysses turned and was just in time to see the killer scramble head-first over the edge of the roof and down the front of the theatre.

"Put the gun down!"

He turned back to see a striking blond-haired woman step from between the gunmen, wearing knee-length black boots and a black trench coat. Her blonde hair was whipping about her face in the wind. She was stunningly attractive, with high sculptural cheekbones and a delicate mouth, her skin like translucent porcelain, her lips full and red.

"So, Mr Quicksilver, we meet again," she said, a smile playing about her lips.

"We do?"

"Well we will, Ulysses, and as a result, I would advise that you trust me and do exactly as I say."

"Trust you?"

He began to lower his gun and then stopped himself, blinking.

Ulysses scanned the rooftop, looking for any possible way off it without having to resort to surrendering to the blonde-haired agent and her gun-toting henchmen, or having to go through them.

There was always the option of following the Ripper off the roof and, at that moment, Ulysses didn't see that he had any other choice.

He cautiously backed towards the edge with slow, shuffling steps, keeping one wary eye on the guns being pointed at him.

"Stop, Ulysses!" the woman called.

And then he heard a shout from below and glanced down. There, on the steps of the Bolshoi Theatre beneath him, was Nimrod. In his hands he held the trailing edge of one of the banners that were currently adorning the facade of the building, promoting the production of Swan Lake. As he backed away, pulling the banner from the front of the building, a vertiginous slide formed, the fabric rippling as it was caught by the breeze. That night's audience watched with confused and disapproving glances, but none of them moved to stop him.

There was no time to think, only to act.

Visions of a death-defying fall through a blizzard above the snow-clad peaks of Mount Manaslu replaying through his mind, Ulysses stepped off the edge.

There was a stomach-lurching moment of freefall and then the fabric of the banner went taut around him, slowing his descent, but only a little. And then he was skidding at speed.

He flew off the end of the improvised slide and into the arms of his manservant, knocking Nimrod to the ground.

"Sorry about that, old boy," he apologised, his face mere inches from the older man's.

"Don't mention it, sir," Nimrod replied, his cheeks reddening uncharacteristically.

As the two men disentangled themselves, Ulysses caught sight of a line of irritated and disbelieving faces peering over the lip of the theatre roof, the blonde-haired woman among them.

"This way, sir," Nimrod called breathlessly.

"How did you know?" Ulysses asked. "How did you know I was up there?"

"Let's just say, we heard a commotion and put two and two together."

"Are Miss Wishart and Miranda with you?"

"They're waiting in the car."

"The car? What car?"

It was then that Ulysses saw the Zil limousine pulled up beside the kerb, the faces of the woman and the child peering out anxiously through the glass of the rear passenger window.

"That car, sir."

"Where did you get the wheels, Nimrod?" Ulysses asked as he climbed into the passenger seat.

"I think it's best if I don't say, sir," his manservant replied as he took his place behind the wheel.

"How come?"

"Culpable deniability, sir. Now buckle up because this is going to be tight."

Its engine growling like a great Russian bear, the car screeched away from the kerb and sped off into the traffic, hurtling away along the Teatralnaya Ploshchad.

CHAPTER TWENTY-SIX

Tomb Raiders

While Nimrod drove through the night, Miranda and her governess slept. They hadn't dared return to their hotel. With his contact dead and the Russians on their tail, it would have been the first place anybody coming after them would have looked. And as long as the child and Miss Wishart were with him, he could keep a close eye on them.

During the journey Ulysses only dozed. On the rare occasions when he did drop off for more than a few head-jerking moments, his dreams were full of knife-fingered killers and a hundred dead Firebirds.

It was in this manner that they came at dawn the next day to Tsarskoye Selo.

The Tsar's Village, as was the name of the place when translated into English, lay sixteen miles south of the St Petersburg, and was one of the official royal residences of the Russian royal family; although the current ruler – Tsarina Anastasia III – made little use of either the baroque Catherine Palace or the neoclassical

Alexander Palace, preferring to base herself at the Peterhof, also known as the Russian Versailles.

But Natasha Eltsina's dying words hadn't sent them racing across the oblast, in an attempt to evade the authorities in Moscow, on a site-seeing tour of the royal palaces. They had come here for the famed royal cemetery, in search of the final resting place of the most infamous individual in recent Russian history.

"Go to Tsarskoye Selo," the Firebird had told Ulysses with her dying breath. "Take what lies in the devil's tomb... In Rasputin's tomb."

Nimrod brought the purloined limousine to a halt beside the cemetery wall, looking no worse for wear in spite of having driven all night.

"This is the place, sir."

"Indeed," Ulysses said, peering out of his window through the April morning mist at the cemetery wall and the roofs of the tombs beyond.

"Best you two stay here," he said to Miranda and her governess. "Nimrod will leave you the keys just in case, but should anyone turn up sound the horn immediately. Meanwhile, Nimrod and I will take a look around. Shouldn't be too long."

Miranda smiled at him. The governess, looking both bleary-eyed and anxious, merely nodded.

"Righty-ho then," Ulysses said, turning back to his butler sat behind the wheel of the Zil. "Let's go."

Despite the fact that it was April, it was cold in the graveyard. The two men strode slowly yet purposefully between the marble tombs and white headstones, attempting to decipher the Cyrillic script of the epitaphs and find what they were looking for.

"I don't mean to be impolite, sir," Nimrod said, "but do you know which is Rasputin's tomb?"

"Course I do, old boy," the dandy blustered. He stopped and smiled weakly at his manservant. "I had hoped it would stand out rather, being referred to as the tomb of a devil and all that."

"I see," Nimrod said.

"I mean, wasn't he involved with some cult or other?"

"You mean, the *khlysty*, sir?"

"That's the one. Don't they have some sort of cult symbol or other?"

"You mean like that one, sir?" Nimrod asked, pointing at the facia of a near-black tomb behind Ulysses.

Ulysses turned, and looked up at the symbol inscribed there. Beneath it, amongst all the Cyrillic script was a date: 16.12.1916.

Over eighty years before, Rasputin – the mad monk –had been murdered by a group of conspirators concerned that he had gained undue influence over the Russian royal family.

At the time it had looked like the outrage might lead to full scale revolution, until Queen Victoria – or at least the nation of Magna Britannia – had stepped in to quell the rising rebellion.

The Tsarevna Anastasia had survived and gone on to rule a Russia that was now, in reality, no more than a princeling state of Magna Britannia.

The rebel leaders made one last defiant stand in the middle of Moscow and were gunned down by landsknecht war machines, bathing the stones of the plaza in the blood of Lenin, Trotsky, Dybenko and Kerensky. The place had been known as Red Square ever since in fearful memory of how close Russia had come to falling to communism.

But the Marxist philosophy had not gone away and had found a home in the burgeoning United States of America, a nation kept in check by British foreign policy and unable to feed its own populace. The propaganda and ideals of the Russian Bolsheviks found favour there, and the concept of the American Dream was born. The last president of the United States, Woodrow Wilson, had been assassinated by a communist sympathiser in 1920 and the United States had been re-invented as the United Soviet States of America, or USSA.

"I told you it would be around here somewhere," Ulysses said.

Approaching the impregnable-looking stone door he tested it with a push of his hand. It didn't even give.

Nimrod joined him. "Would you like a hand, sir?"

"A hand would be... very handy," Ulysses said, and the two men now both put their shoulders to the door and pushed.

Still nothing.

"I believe the door may be locked, sir," Nimrod said.

"And we don't have a key."

"Just give me a minute, sir." Nimrod crouched down, a bundle of lock picks suddenly in his hand. Only a few seconds later there was a distinctive click and, at a push, the door ground open.

The grating of stone on stone was loud in the silent vault, the sound echoing away from them into the distant darkness of the crypt.

Ulysses rummaged in a jacket pocket for a moment – finding an old train ticket to Yorkshire, a comb and the tooth of a cave bear – before his fingers settled on the solid cylindrical shape of the flashlight. Flicking the switch, Ulysses aimed the torch-beam into the darkness beyond that had not been disturbed for God knew how many decades.

"After you, old boy," Ulysses offered generously.

"Will you look at that?" Ulysses said, drawing his manservant's attention to the curious markings on the wall above them, partially obscured by thick cobwebs and shadows. "What do you make of them? Some sort of cult signs or symbols? Possibly slightly out of the ordinary for a tomb, wouldn't you say?"

"I would, sir. And isn't it also more usually the case to find a body inside a tomb?"

"Indeed." The slab standing in the middle of the dank chamber was empty.

Ulysses played his torch over the stone, picking out the edges of the plinth, looking for any signs of where a body might once have lain, or any joins that might suggest that what they were looking at was a sarcophagus.

Ulysses and Nimrod crouched down, trying to find some way to move the slab on top of the plinth

Doubts started to worry at Ulysses' mind then. Perhaps this wasn't Rasputin's tomb. He had heard legends of what had been done to the miracle-worker's body after his death, but most accounts claimed that his body had ultimately been returned to this very vault, and the devil sealed inside for all eternity.

"Come on, Nimrod, this is no good," Ulysses puffed. "If this is a sarcophagus then I'm Tsarina Anastasia."

He took a step back and surveyed the slab once more. In the darkness, his foot brushed against something. Crouching, he sought it by torchlight. And then there it was, at the foot of the slab, amidst the bones of rats and putrid black fungal blooms.

It was a book, about the size of a notebook or journal.

Training his torch on it, Ulysses opened the covers.

There, on the page before him, was what at first appeared to be nothing but gobbledygook, but it was not unfamiliar gobbledygook, for it was written in the tight, tidy hand of the late Dr Victor Gallowglass.

CHAPTER TWENTY-SEVEN

The Enemy of My Enemy

Outside the tomb, the sun was struggling to penetrate the stubborn ground mist that shrouded the burial plots and wound between the stones with something like animal intelligence.

Ulysses took another look at Gallowglass's notebook now that they were out in the daylight. As he flicked through the well-thumbed journal thoughts poured through his mind. How had the haematologist's precious notebook ended up not only in Russia, but inside the empty tomb of Rasputin? And how had Natasha Eltsina known it was there?

"So, is this the Russian connection you were looking for?" Nimrod asked, nodding at the battered notebook.

"I suppose, actually, it is. Although I didn't realise this was what we should be looking for when we came to this country."

"But someone did."

"Yes," Ulysses mused.

Ulysses stopped abruptly in his tracks, putting a hand to Nimrod to stop him too, whilst slipping Gallowglass's notebook into an inside jacket pocket and swapping it for his pistol.

Six familiar black-clad figures stepped out from between the crowding tombs, guns trained on the two gentlemen.

Last to emerge was the blonde-haired woman, only now she was wearing a pair of dark glasses and much of her face was swathed by a black scarf.

"Mr Quicksilver," the woman said in accented, yet faultless, English, "or can I call you Ulysses? Please, put the gun down."

"Who are you and how do you know who I am?" Ulysses challenged.

"But of course, you won't remember yet. Let us just say that it is my business to know when an agent of the British throne is visiting my country," she said. "As to who *I* am, my designation is Agent Katarina Kharkova, or simply Agent K, if you prefer. Although you can call me Katarina."

"Agent K, eh? And who do you work for?"

"I am an agent of the throne of Imperial Russia. Whichever way you look at it, we're on the same side."

Ulysses regarded the six gunmen. "And which side would that be?"

"Now, now, Ulysses, you really are hard work, aren't you? Do you really want to talk politics or shall we – how do you say? – cut to the chase?"

"I would love do," Ulysses replied, "but before we do, if I am to co-operate with you, then you need to co-operate with me."

"I am sorry? In what way?"

"We pool our knowledge. *Quid pro quo*."

"But I am the one holding all the cards."

"Was the Firebird on your side too?"

Agent K said nothing, a smile barely hiding her growing irritation.

"Very good. Have it your way. And now I have a question for you."

"Go on."

"Natasha Eltsina sent you here, didn't she?"

Ulysses opened his mouth to speak, but then thought better of it and said nothing.

"What was it she sent you to find?"

"Isn't it possible that we are here simply to take a look around one of Russia's greatest Imperial monuments?"

"Not when it's eight a.m. on a misty April morning, no. Ulysses, I hate to do this to you," the woman said, "but perhaps now would be an appropriate time to tell you that I have an agent watching your car."

Ulysses frowned. There had been no warning hoot from Miss Wishart.

"Are you threatening me, Agent K?"

Agent K removed her glasses, wincing in the morning sunlight.

"I could have you arrested and the cemetery searched, along with you and your manservant. You could save yourself the trouble if you were to simply give me what we both know you have."

Ulysses said nothing.

"You do not need to be fighting me, Ulysses."

Ulysses relaxed, feeling the tension and stress of the moment easing. She was right, of course. There were six gunmen trained on the two of them and, for all he knew, she really was on his side.

Slowly, resigned to the fact that he was about to be relieved of his secret burden, Ulysses put a hand in his jacket pocket.

It was then that he heard the *scritch-scratch* of steel-claws on stone.

Following Ulysses' gaze, Agent K shot a glance behind her, even as the spider-legged automaton appeared over the top of a tomb.

"Tick-tock, tick-tock, tick-tock," it gibbered to itself.

Before any of them really knew what was going on, the cyber-organic killer had pounced from its perch and cut down one of the gunmen.

"Run!" Ulysses hissed at Nimrod.

They didn't look back, not once, not even when the screaming started and the ring of slicing blades quickly silenced the thunderous roar of heavy arms-fire.

"What in hell's name is going on, sir?" Nimrod puffed as the two of them sprinted away, heading for the entrance.

"Who knows," his master replied, "but ours is not to reason why."

"Ours is but to do and die," his manservant finished for him.

"I was actually thinking more along the lines of, the enemy of my enemy..."

Ulysses' mind was awhirl as he and Nimrod ran for the cemetery gates. He barely had a handle on what was going on. First the Ripper-thing had hunted him down before breaking off its attack. Then, to his amazement, it had followed him all the way to Russia and prevented him meeting with the Firebird. And now, here it was, apparently saving his bacon. But he wasn't going to worry about the details now; there would be time for that later.

At the gates to the cemetery was a nervous-looking guard glancing from the Zil limousine, to them and then the graveyard beyond, as the sound of gunfire echoed strangely from the avenues of burial houses.

Ulysses paused as the muzzle of the gun turned on him and stayed pointed at his chest.

"Your friends are back there and they're in a whole heap of trouble. Now you could stay here and wait for the fuss to die down and stop us from leaving, or you could go back there," – Ulysses hoicked a thumb over his shoulder – "and save Kharkova."

"Kharkova?" the big Russian repeated, reaching for the personal communicator attached to the lapel of his trench coat.

"That's right, your boss. The one who's in a whole heap of trouble. You could help her or you could walk away and we can all get on with our business, or, I suppose, you could simply shoot me."

Ulysses could see sweat beading on the gunman's head now as his eyes darted backwards and forwards. His gun was shaking in his hand.

Ulysses was only a few feet from him. His own hands wavered at his side, ready to go for either his gun, his sword-stick or simply to deliver a karate neck chop.

"And I've just realised that you probably can't understand a word I'm saying."

Glancing between Ulysses and his manservant one last time, tightening his grip on the gun the guard suddenly dashed away into the cemetery, leaving them alone with the car and its occupants.

Ulysses saw the anxious faces of Miranda and her governess pressed against the glass, their breath misting the window.

"What now, sir?" Nimrod asked, as the two of them scrambled inside.

"Drive!"

The engine revving loudly, the Zil tore up black mud and gravel and Nimrod directed it back onto the road and away from the cemetery.

Ulysses glanced past Miss Wishart and Miranda, out of the rear window, at the collection of black cars parked up outside the cemetery. There was no sign of anyone attempting to follow them.

"So where to, sir?" Nimrod asked, his penetrating sapphire stare locked on the empty road ahead as he pushed the accelerator pedal to the floor.

A road sign flashed past on Ulysses' side. "St Petersburg."

"St Petersburg?" the governess shrieked, probably more loudly than she had intended, from the seat behind him. "What in God's name for?"

"Sign says it's only fifteen miles from here to the centre of the city. And you know what begins its journey from St Petersburg, don't you?"

"What?" Miss Wishart asked.

Ulysses flashed Miss Wishart a wicked smile. "Let's just say we have a train to catch."

CHAPTER TWENTY-EIGHT

Prospero's Book

Taking a sip of the claret, Ulysses let it sit awhile in his mouth, savouring the rich notes of the wine before finally letting it slip, like warm syrup, down his throat. Placing the glass back on the table he took the book from his jacket pocket and regarded its cover with fascinated anticipation.

Here it was, the thing that he, and probably a fair number of other interested parties, had believed to have been destroyed in the house fire at number 14 Elizabeth Street; the culmination of Victor Gallowglass's life's work.

With something almost like reverence, Ulysses opened the leather-bound notebook, savouring the satisfying crack of the book's spine and the rustle of its bound vellum leaves as he did so.

There, on the very first page, written in Victor Gallowglass's now unmistakable tidy hand, was what at first appeared to be the utter gobbledygook Ulysses had observed on first opening the journal. But it was a form of gobbledygook that probably only three people left alive in the globe-spanning empire of Magna Britannia today would have recognised, and one of those people was Ulysses Quicksilver.

Warm memories of happier, simpler times came rushing into Ulysses' mind, his ears flushing hotly in excitement, as if warmed by the sun that had always shone during those fine summers of his childhood.

Victor Gallowglass's notebook had been written entirely in code; a code that Victor, Ulysses and the rest of their close-knit band – which included Piggy Hoggett and Digby Lovelace-Smythe – had created during the summer term of their first year at Eton.

Ulysses couldn't remember the last time he had used the language, or Babel as they had called it. He had thought he had put away such childish things after the death of his father.

Babel was not a language with its own unique grammar, syntax and vocabulary; rather a coded way of writing their mother tongue, English. As such anything could be represented by the code.

But what made the code a bugger to crack was that it was not merely a case of simple letter substitution. Some symbols stood for single letters or digits, but they could also represent whole words.

Equally, sometimes what looked like whole words, or even phrases, actually stood for individual letters. It was all very confusing, if you weren't in the know. It had been Digby's creation most of all, and when Ulysses had read in *The Times,* some years ago, that the man was now something in analytical engines, he hadn't been at all surprised.

And so, starting with Gallowglass's carefully-inscribed frontispiece, Ulysses tentatively began to trawl his memory for everything he could remember of the whimsical language.

An hour later, feeling that he deserved a break, Ulysses found himself gazing distractedly out of the dining car, observing the world whizzing by, not really seeing the pine forests and mountain villages flicking past his reflection.

They had been on the train now for approximately six hours, since making it to the Moskovsky Vokzal Station in St Petersburg and onto the Trans-Siberian Express.

The grand architecture of Moskovsky Vokzal and St Petersburg itself had soon given way to dull, grey industrial zones, which in turn gave out to acre after rolling acre of bleak-looking farmland. Now, hours later, the train was making the climb into the snow-clad foothills of the Ural Mountains.

Even here, thousands of miles from home, Ulysses' ID had worked its magic and he had been able to score four tickets to Vladivostock and a pair of adjoining berths; one for Miss Wishart and Miranda, the other to be shared by him and Nimrod, despite the older man's protestations that he would happily bunk down in the postal car if Ulysses preferred.

Feeling a delicate hand on his shoulder Ulysses started suddenly, lost in his drowsy reverie.

"Oh, I'm sorry. Did I disturb you?" Miss Wishart asked, taking a seat across the table.

"No, don't worry. I was away with the fairies, that's all." Ulysses' eyes strayed to the book, facedown on the tablecloth, and he reached for his wineglass. "To be honest I could do with a break. Would you like a glass?" he asked, nodding towards the half-empty bottle.

"Not for me, thank you," the governess replied, possibly just a little too hastily. Her eyes strayed to the journal. "May I? It's just that having been obviously so ill-informed about my employer's work while he was alive..." She trailed off. "Just out of curiosity... Because I'm nosey."

"Please. Be my guest."

"Oh," she said as she scanned the page in front of her. She turned to another, and another. "It's all nonsense."

"I know."

"But you've been here studying it for hours."

"Fortunately, as it turns out, I'm fluent in gobbledygook. Where's Miranda's, by the way?"

"I've just got her settled. She's exhausted, poor dear. She's been through more in the last few days and weeks than most adults have to put up with in a lifetime."

Ulysses nodded, gazing out of the window, noticing how the sky had purpled almost to black.

"I wonder where Nimrod has got to, fussy old soul that he is."

"I shouldn't complain, being waited on hand and foot like that."

"He does get paid, you know?"

"Just the same."

"Just like it's your job to look after Miranda."

"Well!" Miss Wishart harrumphed. "I don't know what you're doing wasting your time with the hired help here then. I suppose I'd better leave you to get on with whatever it is you're doing."

"Now come on, I didn't mean it like that."

"How did you mean it then?"

"It's just that... Well... Look, why don't we discuss it over a little dinner? You must be famished."

The governess rose sharply.

"Good evening, Mr Quicksilver," she said. "Oh and, since you asked, Nimrod is kindly keeping an eye on Miranda. Good evening." And with that she departed the dining car.

Picking up his wineglass Ulysses took another swig. It was going to be a long evening.

Their first night on the train, despite the hours spent trying to decipher his old friend's notebook and the wine, he'd barely slept, sure that the Agent K and her men would make an appearance as the train passed over the Urals. When he had slept, he had found himself running through the labyrinthine avenues of a graveyard, leading a sobbing Miranda by the hand, as they were pursued by a colossal, dagger-fingered monster and its army of over-grown, half-human locusts.

He woke as the train had juddered to a halt to take on water in the early hours of the morning, thinking that the stop meant they had been discovered, but nobody came for them.

Days later, with still no sign that the authorities were hunting them, Ulysses almost began to enjoy the journey. The days of enforced incarceration had meant that he had been able to translate much of Gallowglass's journal. And there had been another unexpected benefit as well; after days of asking, he had finally managed to wear Miss Wishart down and she had accepted his offer of dinner.

Ulysses rose as he watched Miss Wishart walk the length of the dining car towards him. She wore a slinky, low-cut black dress and Ulysses stiffened as he noticed how it flattered her hourglass figure. It was the first time he had ever seen her wear her hair down and it suited her.

Over dinner, the conversation returned to the subject of Victor Gallowglass's notebook and the mysterious nature of his work.

"So," Miss Wishart said, "what have you discovered?"

"Well, it makes for fascinating reading; if you're a geneticist or haematologist, I'm sure. I couldn't even understand half what I was able to decode, but what I can tell you is that he was working on something big."

"Really?" Miss Wishart said.

Ulysses' gaze lingered on the plunging neckline of her dress. "Let's consider the evidence," he said, placing his knife and fork on his plate. "First we have Gallowglass's notes, with all the details of what it was he was working on these last however many months."

Putting a hand into another pocket, Ulysses took out the phial of blood that had come in the cigar box with the hand-written note.

"What's that?" Miss Wishart asked.

"To be honest, I'm not yet certain."

"And what does this mean? 'This thing of darkness I acknowledge mine'?"

"It's from *The Tempest*. It's spoken by Prospero in reference to his slave, Caliban. So here we have Caliban and Prospero's book and then there's the girl."

"Miranda," Miss Wishart said.

"Precisely – Prospero's daughter."

"You think there's a connection?"

"You think it's a coincidence?"

"Well, I suppose Dr Gallowglass could have been inspired to use *The Tempest* for codenames for the project he was working on."

"Or..."

"You... You can't mean... You mean, you don't believe... Surely you can't mean that Miranda was another project of his, like this Caliban thing?"

"What I do know is that there's something special about the child. Did I tell you how stunning you look, by the way?"

She coyly reached across the table and stroked the soft skin of his left hand.

"Shall... Shall I get the bill?" Ulysses said.

CHAPTER TWENTY-NINE

Murder on the
Trans-Siberian Express

Later that night, Ulysses was woken by a terrible howling. The berth was dark, but bars of moonlight flickered across the ceiling, the silvery luminescence penetrating the pine trees crowding the railway as it passed through the rocky uplands of the Kuzneckij Mountains.

The blood-curdling howl came again.

Ulysses tensed, feeling his flesh goose-pimpling, the hairs on the back of his neck rising. He had faced all manner of horrors, but there was something about the howling of wolves that spoke to some primal part of his psyche, an inherited genetic memory of fear.

Sitting up, the naked woman lying beside him moaning softly as she stirred in her sleep, Ulysses turned and peered out of the window.

The wolves were running. He could see them quite clearly now, haring through the forest between the pines, attempting to keep up with the train. They were big and black, stark against the silvery snow.

"Good God," Ulysses gasped. He had never seen wolves like these before; never so large, never so heavily-muscled, never so possessed of such a malign intellect. He had certainly never known wolves to pursue a train.

Ulysses slipped out of bed and started to pull on his clothes.

"Mm... What is it?" Miss Wishart murmured.

The howl came again. It was as if it was coming from right outside the carriage now.

"Was that a wolf?" Miss Wishart whispered.

"Shh!" Ulysses hushed. He paused, his shirt half on, listening intently.

Was he imagining things? Had that last jolt been the train bumping over a join in the rails or the thud of something landing on its roof?

And then there was the dull itch at the back of his brain, getting more intense with every passing second, his body tensing in response.

"Stay here," he told the woman.

He finished buttoning his shirt, did up the belt of his trousers and pulled on his jacket; the phial in one pocket, the notebook in another.

"I'll do no such thing," she said, climbing out of bed after Ulysses, dropping the sheet and starting to pull on her own discarded clothes. "I shall see to my charge."

"Very well. But don't open the door to anyone until I return."

He picked up his pistol and strapped it on, checking the load at the same time.

Pulling on his crumpled jacket, sword-cane in hand, Ulysses stepped out into the low-lit corridor.

The next door along opened and a bleary-eyed, and only slightly bewildered-looking Nimrod peered out.

"Are you alright, sir? I heard wolves."

"Yes, I'm fine, old boy," Ulysses said, parting the curtains pulled across a carriage window and peering out.

He could see black walls of rock closing in as the train entered a defile.

Ulysses started, hearing a thud as something heavy landed on the roof.

The two men looked up, watching the rattling lampshades, pistols trained on the ceiling. Whatever it was that was now on the roof was moving ahead of them towards the front of the train. They followed, the carpeted floor deadening their footsteps.

Lights were starting to come on inside other berths now as their occupants were roused by the howling of the wolves.

As Nimrod and Ulysses moved warily down the corridor, a bitingly cold breeze stirred the curtains.

A cold, clear scream cut through the sleep-befuddled stillness of the carriage. Ulysses was unable to determine whether it had been made by a man or a woman, so soul-rending was the sound.

"Come on," he hissed, "this way."

The door into the next carriage was open and banging against the wood-panelling as the train jolted on its way through the tunnel.

Steeling himself, Ulysses stepped into the next coach.

Something moved in the shadows at the end of the corridor. Ulysses tensed, raising his gun and then relaxed again. It was a man that was approaching them.

At least it had the gait and silhouette of a man. But it was too tall to be a man, surely, its shoulders too broad, and that wasn't a fur coat he was wearing, but a pelt.

And then the shape stepped into the faint pool of light cast by an electric-lamp.

"Oh my," Ulysses gasped. "What big teeth you have."

The creature paused, ears flicking forwards, a low rumbling growl rising from within its great barrel chest. Blood, red and hot, steamed from its jaws while the horror regarded them with unsettlingly human eyes.

In one paw it carried a man's head, the wretched bastard's last expression of horrified surprise etched onto his face, his signalman's hat slanted at an almost jaunty angle. Of the rest of his body there was no sign.

The beast had to be seven feet tall at least, its head almost brushing against the carriage roof.

Dropping the signalman's head, the werewolf threw back its head and gave a howl that set the glass shades of the electric-lamps rattling.

Ulysses was aware of more lights going on inside sleeping compartments and a few doors opened, bleary-eyed passengers looking out of them for only a moment before ducking back inside. Muffled screams could now be heard along the length of the carriage.

Ulysses raised his pistol and fired at the very same moment that the monster sprang.

The bullet grazed the animal's side. At the same time, the werewolf's leap brought it down on top of Ulysses as the dandy hurled himself against a sleeping berth door, the lock giving way under the sudden impact. Ulysses fell into the cabin as the elderly couple occupying it sat up in bed in shocked surprise. He met their terrified stares as they clutched each other in fear.

"Begging your pardon," he said, scrambling to his feet again.

In the corridor there was the sound of Nimrod's pistol discharging and Ulysses turned as the werewolf yelped and staggered backwards, the hall carpet rumpling beneath its feet. However, the shot had barely slowed the monster's rapid advance, let alone floored it.

The narrow confines of the corridor did not make a good fighting arena. There was barely room to swing a cat, let alone a finely-balanced rapier. Ulysses turned and tried to run, Nimrod assisting him, dragging him clear.

A great claw tore the walnut panelling clear of the wall beside them. Stumbling back through an open carriage door, Ulysses slammed it shut. A second later it was ripped from its hinges.

Pulling its huge bulk through the doorway, the monster fixed Ulysses with the black pits of its horribly human eyes and another blood-chilling growl bubbled from within.

"Nimrod," Ulysses said in a low voice as the werewolf stalked closer, "we're going to hit it with everything we've got. Understood?"

"Understood, sir."

"Then let's do it!" Ulysses screamed and they both opened fire, sending a hail of bullets in the monster's direction until their pistols clicked empty. But as the gun-smoke cleared, Ulysses could see nothing but the wreckage of the broken door and dull electric light reflecting back from the myriad diamond crumbs of glass.

"Where's it gone?"

"Did we get it, sir?" Nimrod asked. There were glistening spots of black amidst the diamond shards littering the carpet at his feet.

"We hit it, but did we do more than that? That's the question."

Gunfire echoed along the passageway from elsewhere on the train. Startled shouts and anguished cries joined the choir of snarling, howling lupine voices.

Ulysses warily stuck his head around the jamb of the ruined door and saw the bodies strewing the passageway. He wondered how many had been slain in the brief attack.

He scoured the passageway with anxious eyes as he strode back along the corridor towards his berth, fearing that at any moment he might see Miranda amongst those lying there, arms and legs at unnatural angles; or Miss Wishart's dead eyes staring up at him accusingly.

With an ear-splitting crash, the hulking werewolf re-entered the carriage, feet-first, through a window.

As it landed in the passageway between Ulysses and his manservant, Nimrod turned, his gun already trained on the monster, even though there wasn't a chambered round ready within the breach. The monster reacted just as swiftly, lashing out with a clawed hand that smacked the useless weapon from Nimrod's grasp.

But Nimrod had bought Ulysses the time he needed to get in a counter-attack of his own.

Rapier blade in hand, he leapt in under the werewolf's guard, a massive paw striking his chest, lifting him off his feet and sending him crashing through a broken compartment door. Yet, the tip of his blade had found its mark.

Yowling in pain, putting a paw to its eye socket, the werewolf sprang and hurled itself back out through the shattered window, bowling into the tight-packed drifts of snow.

As soon as he could pick himself up from amongst the wreckage of the cabin, Ulysses was there at the window, peering out after the lithe shape as it bounded away.

The train had left the narrow pass and was now heading towards a ravine, spanned by a rickety-looking bridge. To one side of the train, the black wall of a cliff face rose up into the darkness, while on the other the snow-covered ground fell away to the white water that tumbled through the gorge beneath.

With the dull crump of an explosion, fire blossomed in the darkness, bathing the train and the snowy crags in hungry orange flame as the bridge exploded.

Pulling his head back inside the carriage he turned to Nimrod, eyes wide. "We have to get off this train!"

He didn't wait for a response but turned on his heel at once and scrambled on along the corridor, past the bodies of those slaughtered by the wolves. The offal smell of an abattoir had taken hold, the stink of death now permeating the place.

In no time he was at the door to the compartment shared by the child and her governess.

The claw-marks gouged into the walls, the splashes of blood on the covers of the bed and the curtains flapping in the night wind blowing through the glassless window told him all he needed to know.

Miss Wishart and the child were gone.

Ulysses was at the window in a second. He could see other wolf-like shapes running from the train through the darkness, disappearing between the trees. Two of the fleeing monsters were running on their hind-legs only, each one carrying a body in its arms.

"There they are!" Ulysses yelled.

He was preparing to climb out of the window as, eight carriages away, the locomotive – its driver and fireman already dead – powered off the end of the severed track and plummeted into the gaping chasm beyond.

CHAPTER THIRTY

The Company of Wolves

As the steam engine left the track, Ulysses and Nimrod found themselves thrown together, and then they were falling. The floor became the wall, the wall became the ceiling, and Ulysses and Nimrod crashed down amidst slivers of broken glass and rags of shredded curtain.

Picking himself up as quickly as he could Ulysses offered Nimrod his hand.

"Quick!" he said. "Give me a leg up, will you?"

Putting one booted foot in the stirrup offered by Nimrod's hands, Ulysses pushed himself up and grabbed the doorframe above him, before pulling himself into the crawl space of the passenger corridor.

The carriage continued to judder and vibrate as it ground inexorably along the rails towards the precipice.

Ulysses reached down into the cabin and pulled Nimrod clear of the devastated sleeping compartment.

Between the two of them, they managed to manoeuvre Nimrod into a position whereby the older man could grab hold of the lip of the door. From there – still possessing the same upper body strength he had enjoyed during his days as a bare-knuckle prize-fighter – Nimrod was able to haul himself up into the inverted passageway.

They made their way back along the corridor, heading towards the rear of the train at a crouching run.

Emerging from the broken window ahead of Nimrod, a kick of adrenalin gave Ulysses the last ounce of strength he needed to pull himself out of the train as he saw the edge of the precipice rapidly approaching. The carriage suddenly slewed sideways as it caught on a twisted rail.

"Go, sir!" Nimrod shouted.

Ulysses didn't need to be told twice. Flinging himself from the train, he landed hard on compacted snow the impact and the shock of cold leaving him breathless.

A second later he heard the thud of Nimrod hitting the ground to his left, as the carriage upended and dropped into the frothing waters of the cascading river.

Ulysses lay where he had landed, listening to the hollow, booming sound of the last few carriages plunging into the stygian depths of the ravine.

Hearing someone shuffling through the snow towards him, Ulysses opened his eyes as his manservant shook him by the shoulder. "Sir? Are you alright?"

Ulysses became aware of the dull throbbing around his right temple and put a cautious hand to the tender spot. His fingers came back smeared with blood.

"As I'm ever likely to be. Besides," he said, wincing as he smiled, "could have been worse."

"But what of Miss Wishart and the child?" Nimrod asked.

"They're alright, for the time being at least. After all, they're alive."

"But how can you be so sure they'll stay that way?"

"Because those monsters weren't messing around. I didn't see that anyone else had been taken. They came here with a malign purpose of their own. If the wolves had wanted them dead, they would have torn out their throats on the train and left it at that. No, there was something strangely coordinated about their attack. And the bridge blowing like that was hardly a coincidence either, was it?"

"No, sir."

Ulysses looked at Nimrod darkly. "But what would werewolves want with prisoners of any kind? More especially, what would they want with a little girl?"

Ulysses staggered over to the edge of the precipice, as close as he dared, and stared down into the abyss at the steaming wreck far below.

"No one else was meant to survive that," he said.

"But what could be so important about Miss Wishart and the child, that someone would go to all this trouble and commit mass murder, just to cover up their kidnap?" Nimrod asked, joining his master at the edge of the gulf.

"I'm beginning to think that my suspicions were correct," Ulysses muttered as he considered what he had learnt so far from his study of Gallowglass's journal.

"Sir?"

"Come on, old boy," Ulysses said, turning from the precipice and striding back along the length of the track. It was strewn with all manner of detritus from the wreck – packing cases, clothes, lampshades and shreds of cabin furnishings – that had been thrown from the carriages as the train slewed off the end of the broken bridge into oblivion. "The hunt is on!"

The two men moved at a steady pace as they trudged on through the snow, wrapped in furs that they had managed to recover from the train wreck. Their shoes and socks were sodden, their feet numb.

"What are they waiting for?" Nimrod hissed, shooting wary glances to left and right, seeing the moonlight reflecting red from the eyes of the circling wolves.

"Who knows? Maybe they're waiting for the cold to finish us off."

Ulysses had heard tales told of the skin-changers of the European heartlands. They had been practically hunted to extinction in many areas during the witch-hunts of the 16th and 17th centuries, but it was claimed that there had been a resurgence in numbers as a result of the 1914-18 War and Hitler's punitive action two decades later during the Second European War of 1939-45, when the German powers had capitalised on the lycanthropes' natural abilities, deploying them as the perfect shock troops and undercover infiltrators.

Once considered supernatural monsters, demons in another form, current thinking had it that the extreme form of lycanthropy that wrought such a change within the host at a physiological level, like true vampirism, was actually an inherited genetic mutation. Having become stable long ago, a sufferer was able to infect another via a transfer of bodily fluids.

Considering how the beast they had encountered on the train had seemed to shrug off the damage done by their bullets, Ulysses found himself wondering whether werewolves really were resistant to bullets, as folklore claimed – unless they were silver ones, of course – or whether it was simply that their unnatural constitutions and accelerated metabolisms allowed them to recover more quickly from injuries that would drop a man.

Following the tracks left by the pack had been straightforward enough. In places there were signs that the animals had been moving on all fours, but in others the clawed footprints of a wolf took on the marked stride of something that moved on two legs.

Before they knew it, their roles had been reversed. The hunters had become the hunted and the wolves had revealed themselves..

With the wolves still circling, herding them through the snow-blanketed forests, they came at last to a natural bowl in the landscape, utterly devoid of trees, a white arena bathed in moonlight.

It was here that the wolves made their move. As the huge animals slunk from between the trees, Ulysses and Nimrod moved to stand back to back. Nimrod's numb fingers unholstered and primed his pistol while Ulysses unsheathed his rapier in one fluid motion, the tempered steel singing as it slipped free of its scabbard.

"If this is it, sir, there's something you should know," Nimrod stammered through rattling teeth.

"Don't worry, old boy, it's not going to be the end."

"But if it is, sir..."

"This is *not* the end, Nimrod. Quicksilver and Nimrod deserve a less ignominious end than this. We deserve to go out in a blaze of glory, you and I, not as a frozen meal for a pack of mangy dogs!"

"But, sir, our situation is truly desperate."

And Nimrod was absolutely right; there was no arguing with that fact.

One werewolf had been bad enough. Against a whole the situation did appear to be unsalvageable.

"A blaze of glory it is then."

CHAPTER THIRTY-ONE

Battleship Potemkin

"Do you hear that, sir?" Nimrod hissed.

As he stared into hungry red eyes, Ulysses heard the thrumming purr of approaching aero-engines.

The wolves had heard it too. They tensed and glanced upwards, some even taking slinking steps back towards the tree-line.

Gliding into view over the spear-tipped tops of the trees, the dirigible looked like some great whale, a black shadow against the midnight blue, blotting out the stars as it passed over the clearing. Ulysses was reminded of the vessel that had rescued the murderous Dr Pavlov from his clutches, just in the nick of time.

The pitch of the engines changed and the airship came to a halt over the clearing. With a rattling clatter, a rope ladder unrolled, swinging wildly.

Ulysses wondered who their rescuer could be, but no matter who it was, it seemed better to make the most of the opportunity and worry about such minor details later. As the trailing end of the ladder came within reach, he grabbed hold.

"Nimrod, go!" he commanded.

Nimrod did as he was ordered, keeping hold of his pistol as he began to ascend the wobbling ladder.

Realising that they were about to lose their prey, the wolves made their move, the alpha male launching himself out of the pack.

The rifle-shot rang out across the clearing and the leaping beast tumbled to the ground a few feet shy of Ulysses. It lay there, its chest heaving as blood oozed black upon the snow. For a moment nothing – no man, nor wolf – moved.

Then another of the huge black beasts threw back its head and howled before charging the dandy.

Ulysses hurled himself up the ladder after his companion. He tried to ignore the snarls and scuffling sounds of wolves snapping at his heels as they tried to leap up after him.

Then a sudden weight pulled the ladder taut, almost throwing him off.

Ulysses forced himself to keep climbing despite the biting cold that was, even now, leeching the strength from his body.

A shot rang out and the ladder went slack. With that, the airship began to climb, the frustrated snarling and barking of the wolves receding below him. Ulysses climbed the rest of the way up and struggled over the lip of the gondola door, hauling himself into the cabin. He remained where he was for a moment, paralysed by cold, until Nimrod helped him to his feet.

At the wheel of the dirigible stood a figure lost in the depths of a thick fur coat.

"Agent K, I presume?" Ulysses said.

The pilot spun the wheel to port, steering the zeppelin away from the clearing and setting it on an easterly bearing before turning to greet her passengers.

She lifted the thick-lensed flying goggles from her face and regarded Ulysses with those familiar aquamarine eyes, as a stray tress of blonde hair caressed her cheek.

"Greetings, Mr Quicksilver, if we're going to be formal about things," Katarina Kharkova said. "Welcome to the Potemkin."

"You saved us, why?"

"Come now," Agent K chided. "I thought that manners were what made an Englishman."

"Very well. Thank you Agent Kharkova for saving our bacon. So, what I want to know now is why, on this occasion, you have chosen to save us, rather than leave us to die."

"As I told you before, we are on the same side. But you are right, I could have just as easily left you to die considering that is how you treated me and my men at Tsarskoye Selo."

"Then it would appear that I must apologise."

"Apology accepted," she said, fixing him with those piercing eyes of hers once more. "Mr Quicksilver, you are a man who knows all about duty, are you not?"

"Of course."

"Then you will also understand where I am coming from. I am an agent of the Russian Imperial Crown and I too am a patriot. And it is because I love my country that I was tasked with watching the Firebird."

"But why? Wasn't she one of yours?"

"Because, as I am sure you already know, she was not all she appeared to be. She was not only a prima ballerina, she was also in the pay of one of our own blue bloods who was trying to get his hands on a biological weapon."

"Get his hands on what?" Ulysses thought again of the notebook and the phial secreted in a jacket pocket, not two inches from his nervously beating heart.

"His power and wealth is – it would appear – not enough. Like many of those granted great power his hunger for more is insatiable. This individual is prepared to go to great lengths to get what he wants."

"And the Firebird was working for him?"

"Yes."

"You're sure?"

"Which is why I was so surprised to find you making contact with her.

Katarina distractedly brushed the loose strand of hair from her cheek and Ulysses noticed the thin scar that had not been there the last time he had run into her.

"What happened to your friends, by the way?" he asked.

"The machine-man–"

"That'll do."

"– killed them all."

"And where is this machine-man now?"

"I do not know."

"How do I know that you're telling me the truth?"

"Because I did not hypnotise you this time to make you believe me," she said with a sigh. "Or put it this way; you don't. But would it not pay to play along with me for the time being? It would appear to me that you have little other option."

"Nimrod and I could take control of this vessel. We outnumber you," Ulysses said.

"Yes, you are probably right," Katarina conceded, "except that you won't."

"And what makes you so sure of that?"

"Because, right at this moment, we are pursuing the creatures that abducted the child and the woman from the train." Unable to help himself, his heart racing, Ulysses ran to a window and peered out into the night, thinking that he might see the wolves below them, but he could make out nothing. "Because you want to rescue your women from the wolves, and because I want their master."

CHAPTER THIRTY-TWO

The Land That Time Forgot

They continued to climb until the dwindling peaks of the mountains receded behind them.

Within only a matter of hours the curve of the horizon ahead purpled and became tinged with orange. A golden line of fire ignited the horizon, presaging the coming dawn and, not long after, the sun rose. However, Agent K insisted on drawing the drapes, that she might not be blinded by the light, saying that the dazzle would distract her while piloting.

That day they made steady progress. They picked up the pack again as it left the higher wooded slopes and moved east. Sometimes they saw the wolves themselves; lean black shapes moving at a gallop across the frozen tundra. Sometimes, only the tracks they had left.

Agent Kharkova rested during the day, retiring to her aft cabin and letting Nimrod and Ulysses take control of the airship.

As well as taking his post at the wheel Ulysses spent much of each day continuing to try to fathom Victor Gallowglass's coded notes; translating page after page of chemical equations, blood analyses and gene-codes, which were almost as baffling to him as the code itself had initially been.

During their time aboard the airship, Agent K saw fit to reveal a little more about the man she was hunting. His name was Prince Vladimir of Bratsk, a nobleman whose ancestral lands were located at the eastern-most limits of Siberia. But that was all she would tell them, for the time being at least, and Ulysses was left to reconcile what he had learned of Gallowglass's work from the dead man's journal with what the mysterious Hermes, and now the Russian agent, had told him. Whichever way he looked at it, the mystery only deepened, and he was now in it right up to his neck.

"I know where we are," Ulysses stated, stumbling from his cabin just after dawn on the fourth day of their journey. They had been heading north-east for the last day and a half and had reached the very limits of the seemingly endless lands of Mother Russia.

"You do?" Katarina said, eyebrows arching at Ulysses in surprise from behind her dark glasses.

"The Central Siberian Plateau," he said with something like awed reverence in his voice. "We must be close to the borders of Mongolia."

Ulysses gazed down at the crumpled contours of hills, mountains and winding river valleys beneath, the plateau casting a long shadow which disappeared into the horizon behind them.

Mongolia was a wild and desolate land, as well Ulysses knew. The scrub was home to the barbarian tribes that were the bastard descendants of the great Genghis Khan's mighty Golden Horde. The bleak rocky uplands and deep, glacier-scoured valleys were home to primeval monsters once thought to have been extinct, but which were now husbanded and herded by the Mongol people.

"But, begging your pardon, sir," Nimrod interjected. "If this is Mongolia then surely we have travelled too far. Agent Kharkova said that this nobleman's demesne lay within Russia."

"On the Russian border," Katarina corrected him.

"And how close are we to his lands?"

"Not far," she said, hastily consulting her airship's navigation instruments.

"What's that?" Nimrod said, wincing against the brightness of the crisp morning light.

"An airship!" Agent Kharkova exclaimed, pulling the ship hard to port, forcing the two men to grab hold of anything they could to stop themselves careening across the cabin. "And heading north."

Ulysses had a clear view of the vessel himself now, and although one zeppelin looked a lot like another, there was something disconcertingly familiar about this one. He was reminded of Dr Pavlov's last minute escape once again.

"And what happens when we catch up with this vessel?" Ulysses asked.

"Oh, don't worry about that, the Potemkin can look after itself." Agent K said, smiling.

"Alright, so this thing packs a bit of a punch, does it? Very good, but what about –"

His words were abruptly cut off as something slammed into the side of the airship; a deafening, reptilian squawk reverberating throughout the Potemkin.

Ulysses was the first to recover. As a result he was the first to catch sight of the rending claws and great leathery wings of the beast.

With great beats of its wings, the gigantic pterosaur disappeared from view as it climbed.

There was a sound like the rending of metal, another sound like sail-cloth being torn and then a loud bang. The Potemkin lurched and began to lose height.

Ulysses turned to see a second creature flying directly towards the gondola with a fur-clad Mongol, holding a set of rough reins, saddled on its back.

A second later the Potemkin was smashed round from the rear as the giant pterosaur rammed it from behind. The force of the attack sent the airship spinning as the high-pitched whine of a failing engine turbine filled the cabin.

The view through the cockpit spun. The spearing points of treetops rushed to meet them.

"Brace yourselves!" Katarina screamed. "We're going down!"

CHAPTER THIRTY-THREE

The Khan

Ulysses, Nimrod and Agent K stood before the vast triceratops-hide tent, hands tied behind their backs with rough hemp-rope, all of them tired and sore after their forced march.

To call the mass of tents and temporary wooden corrals a camp was to do the Khan and his horde a disservice, for this was no mere Cub Scout jamboree.

Where the hills dropped down to the expansive flatlands, where the sparkling sapphire waters of a broad, slow-moving river snaked its way across the steppes, the Mongol encampment was laid out more like a mobile town than a simple caravan. Acres of tent-cloth and animal-hide covered the steppes for as far as the eye could see. Rudimentary roads criss-crossed the network of yurts and huts. The smoke from a hundred cooking fires rose lazily into the crisp morning air; the smell of roasting meat making Ulysses salivate in hungry expectation.

As well as pavilions and marquees, there were also numerous animal pens housing everything from yaks and mammoths to styracosaurs and pterosaurs, and even sabre-toothed hunting cats.

Spread out along the river bank for half a mile or more, the tribe's women-folk laundered clothes, collected water in dino-leather buckets and led their goats to the cool, clear glacial run-off to drink.

A polyphony of noises drifted across the meadows; the sounds of armourers' hammers, weapons being put to the whetstone, the bleat of goats, the grumble and fart of the saurian herbivores, the shouts and laughter of children, the prattle of the womenfolk and the boasts and jeers of men.

Ulysses, Nimrod and Katarina had been prodded and poked all the way through this warren of tented habitations and animal pens, the Mongols having left their saurian steeds at a corral on the edge of the camp. And then they had come before the battle-khan's tent at last – a grand conglomeration of several tents erected together.

The hairy brute that had brought them this far gestured towards the open tent flap with his axe, as he barked something in Mongolian.

"He wants us to enter the tent," Katarina translated. She looked especially weary. The trek across the steppes had weakened her more than it had either of the men. Ulysses put it down to the fact that she had barely slept over the past few days.

"Well here goes nothing," Ulysses said, and ducked inside.

The opulence on show inside was not what Ulysses had been expecting. Fine Chinese silks, painted with willow pattern designs, as well as red and gold dragons adorned the space within, while dozens of the finest Persian rugs had been scattered across the floor. Shuttered, fretwork lanterns hung from tent-poles and cushions embroidered with gold thread formed islands of comfort, while a smouldering brazier filled the pavilion with warmth as well as the aroma of frankincense.

But more than these, Ulysses was taken aback by the other – incongruous – items scattered around the tent.

There was a Spode teapot (complete with knitted tea cosy), being kept warm on a cook-stove, while a King George table had been laid with a very English-looking Royal Doulton tea service. To his right, Ulysses saw a de-commissioned British Army Wellington-class war-droid and a wooden mannequin wearing the garb of a Scots Guardsman, complete with bagpipes and kilt. There was even a Union Jack – the flag rather threadbare now, its ancient dyes faded – but nonetheless displayed proudly, strung as it was between two poles behind the khan's throne.

Considering the peculiar decorations, Ulysses would not have been surprised to find himself faced by a leather-faced Oriental gentleman wearing the latest in Savile Row fashion and spats, but the figure seated upon the throne fitted Ulysses' imagined idea of how a Mongol warlord should look perfectly.

He was dressed in furs, a tunic and yak-hair trews. On his head was a fur hat and his legs were wrapped with leather bindings. And he was fat. He sat slumped within his darkwood throne, his belly bulging. His face looked like a bag of billiards balls and his corpulent chin was covered with thick stubble. His hair was dark, almost black, his skin, what they could see of it, like tanned leather. His moustache was full and followed the Oriental fashion, but was as unkempt as the rest of him. Ulysses could see crumbs of food caught within the grease-matted whiskers.

The only thing that obviously connected the Khan to the eclectic decor of the pavilion was a strip of medals that were pinned to the breast of his goatskin tunic, and which Ulysses found it hard to believe had been won fighting campaigns on behalf of the Magna Britannian army in far flung, foreign climes.

In a stand next to his throne stood his sabre and hunting spear, and on another tailor's dummy rested the khan's helmet and lacquered armour. His throne was adorned with intricate carvings of predatory dinosaurs.

"Good day to you, sirs and lady," the khan said, bowing his head. "How do you do?"

"And a good day to you, sir," Ulysses said.

"How wonderful," the warlord said, suddenly clapping his hands together, a boyish twinkle in his eye. "A proper pair of

English gentlemen," he said, not even bothering to shoot the Russian agent a glance. "Be welcome, gentlemen, welcome. Can I offer you a cup of tea?"

Introductions over, the Khan had the ropes on their wrists cut and then invited them to sit with him while they partook of tea, accompanied by a curious yak dish, that was as chewy and as strongly flavoured as shoe leather.

Targutai Khan – or Targutai Khan, Khagan of the Golden Horde, to give him his full title – was, or so he asserted, heir to the lands and hereditary titles that the legendary Genghis Khan had once claimed as his. The fact that much of the thirteenth-century warlord's Asia-spanning domain was now shared between Russia, China and Eastern Europe was dismissed as merely an inconvenience, a situation that he tolerated, knowing that, by the will of his ancestors, they really belonged to him.

"Although I am the heir to Genghis Khan's noble legacy," the Khan said as he tucked into the meal, "I also consider myself a man of the modern age and there is no finer example of all that evolution has achieved than the modern English gentleman. What do you think of my collection; it has taken me some thirty years to collect."

"Tawdry," Nimrod muttered under his breath.

"A marvel, khan," Ulysses said, a little too loudly as he nudged Nimrod in the ribs.

"The Mongols might have conquered the world," Targutai went on, "but the character of the English gentleman is unsurpassed. With your Oxford University, your Buckingham Palace, your polo and your aristocracy; there is something for everyone to aspire to, don't you think?" The Khan took another sip of tea, the little finger of his right hand protruding accordingly.

"If you say so, khan, if you say so."

"And it is with that in mind that I must apologise for the rough way in which my riders treated you. But you have to understand that these are wild lands and you cannot be too careful. However, that said, I shall nonetheless have them flogged."

"Oh no, khan, not on our account please." Ulysses said.

"What about my airship?" Katarina muttered.

Ulysses shot her a disapproving scowl and hissed, "Not now." Turning to Targutai again he added, "I must say, khan, that your English is excellent. Have you spent some time on English soil? Did you study at Oxford yourself?"

The big man laughed and blushed. "You flatter me, sir. No, I have never seen your glorious sceptred isle for myself and yet I wish to travel there, in the guise of a proper English gentleman, and meet your Queen for myself. That is my dream."

Ulysses wondered what the real reason was for the Khan never having visited England, if he was so keen. Surely a man of his power and wealth would have made it happen already, if he had really wanted to.

"Now then, drink up, what-what?" the Khan badgered them, putting his own teacup down on a bronto-foot table beside his throne. "You must excuse me, but I am impatient to introduce you formally to the rest of my golden horde. Besides, you do not want to face the customary trial by combat on a full stomach. There will be time for feasting later."

The cup stopped inches from Ulysses' lips. "Trial by combat? Khan, I thought we were friends."

"And we will be, we will be, I am sure of it. But my warriors found you straying into my territories without so much as a by-your-leave. Why, for all I know you could be spies," he laughed.

"What? But –"

"Think of it as an ancient custom. I know how much you English love your traditions. Come."

Targutai rose to his feet and Ulysses realised, for the first time, that the warlord's great mass was as much about muscle as it was middle-aged spread brought on by good living and yak butter.

"Besides, nothing works up an appetite quite like a good fight, don't you think? What?"

CHAPTER THIRTY-FOUR

Blood Brothers

Ulysses, Nimrod and their Russian accomplice had their hands tied again and were led, under armed guard, to a cleared circle of dusty ground at the centre of the encampment. Targutai Khan, an attendant party of slave-girls and yak-butter greased warriors went before them. Ulysses noticed that every single man, woman and child they passed acknowledged their khan by averting their eyes and bowing their head.

A large crowd had already gathered around the ring, word having travelled quickly throughout the camp that there would be a show worth watching that day, one that would be spoken of around the campfires for years to come.

An awning almost as grand as the khan's tent offered shade from the sun that blazed down on these high altitudes, without the interruption of cloud of any sort.

Targutai Khan took his heavy-bladed sabre from a cowering slave and approached Ulysses. Spinning the weapon around a supple wrist, in a dramatic demonstration of his swordsmanship, he raised the edge before him and then brought it down with one sharp twist, slicing through the leather thongs binding Ulysses' wrists.

Was this match to be fought with sabres? Ulysses wondered, and found himself pining for his own sword-cane, still lost somewhere in the wreckage of the Potemkin. And if blades were the chosen weapon, was it to be a duel to the death or merely first blood?

Ulysses didn't fancy facing the warlord with an unfamiliar weapon, but then Targutai executed another couple of whirling windmill strokes before returning the sabre to his underling. Turning, he strode over to the dino-hide panoply, where, Ulysses noticed, Katarina was already taking shelter from the sun, and took his seat upon a backless chair among his harem. He clapped his hands together, barking something in Mongolian.

In response, the crowd began to hoot and cheer.

"And now we fight," Targutai said. "My champion! My bastard son, Chuluun!"

This brought another wave of cheering and hand-waving from the assembled Mongols. The crowd of eager spectators was growing all the time, no one wanting to miss the spectacle.

And then something rather more akin to the snowbeast Ulysses had wrestled within the smoky halls of Shangri-La than a man, shouldered its way into the ring.

The giant had to be a head taller than Ulysses at least. From the waist down he wore mammoth-hide trews, his legs were bound with leather thongs, and on his feet he wore yak-skin boots.

"Your champion? Ah, your champion. Of course, I see," Ulysses said with a sigh of relief, tensed muscles relaxing at the realisation that he wasn't going to have to fight the Khan himself. "Then let me introduce my champion," Ulysses announced with all the gusto of a showman.

"Your champion?" Targutai laughed.

"Yes, my champion, noble khan."

"Alright then, why not? What?"

Ulysses turned to his manservant. "Nimrod?"

"Yes, sir?"

"Do the honours, would you?"

"Yes, sir."

"Your butler?" the Khan said.

"I'd be lost without him."

"Very well then," the khan agreed, nodding to his men to cut Nimrod's bonds.

Before entering the ring, Nimrod removed his jacket, offering it to a bewildered-looking Mongol that he might hold it for him.

"Tally ho, what?" the khan said, excitedly. "Let the fight begin."

A huge cheer went up from the crowd as the butler strode into the ring and the heavily-muscled man-mountain assumed a fighter's stance.

A transformation came over Nimrod as he assumed his light-footed prize-fighter's stance. Constantly shifting his weight from one leg to the other, and back again, he never stayed still for a second, barely even blinking as he fixed Targutai's champion with a gaze as sharp and penetrating as sapphires .

A bemused expression gripped the Mongol's features as he regarded the butler hopping from foot to foot before him. And then his bewildered expression morphed into one of annoyance and he lunged at the smaller man, but Ulysses' manservant agilely side-stepped the clumsy, swiping blow.

The bigger man swung at Nimrod again. Again he missed, as Nimrod's upper body twisted, describing an arc that took his head out of reach of the Mongol's fist.

Chuluun swung again, the fingers of both hands locked together to produce a clubbing sledgehammer swipe designed to knock the other man out of the circle. But again he missed.

Snarling in anger, the brute came at Nimrod with a flurry of blows, taking swipe after swipe at the ducking and dodging butler, the exertion starting to show on his face, in his panting breaths and the glistening sheen of moisture now covering his body.

Nimrod didn't appear to have even broken a sweat.

The crowd were behind the bigger man but it didn't seem to be making any difference.

Suddenly bellowing like a mammoth, the Mongol charged at Nimrod, making a lunge for him, apparently intending to encircle him in his muscular arms and trap him in a crushing embrace.

One minute Ulysses' manservant was there in front of him, the next he was rolling under the Mongol's flailing arms and rising to his feet again in one fluid movement, putting all the momentum of his springing ascent into his rising right-arm.

His fist connected with the Mongol's jaw hard enough that everyone heard the crack of bone. Ulysses winced.

Chuluun's head jerked backwards, blood spraying from his mouth. There was the sound of bone snapping with whiplash force, a grimace of pain and shock knotting the big brute's features, before his eyes rolled up into his head. Chuluun staggered and crashed down on his back in the dust like a felled oak.

Silence descended over the crowd.

A lone round of applause broke the silence. "Well done, old boy. Bravo!" Ulysses called, a broad grin splitting his face.

Nimrod smiled in return and bowed to the khan and his attendants.

Ulysses turned to Targutai Khan, who looked back at him with an expression of slack-jawed disappointed disbelief.

"Well, you know what they say about an Englishman's valet; you should never leave home without one. I rather think that's round one to us, don't you?"

The khan's displeasure at his champion losing was only momentary and by the time he and his guests were tucking into a feast of suckling pig and triceratops – all except for the sneering Katarina, who was actually grimacing at the smell of roast meat that permeated the camp – Targutai seemed delighted that Chuluun had lost the match. He saw Nimrod's win as simply another example of the superior quality of an English upbringing.

And so, Ulysses and his prize-fighting manservant were being lauded as guests of honour and under suspicion of being spies no longer.

The khan insisted that he and Ulysses become blood brothers, having not given up all of his Mongol tribesman's ways in his study of the English gent.

Ulysses knew better than to protest and, having emptied another sack of fermented mare's milk, endured the ritual cutting of palms. Targutai grasped Ulysses' hand in his own great paw with a triumphant "Yaah!" and then, in calmer tones added, "You and I are now bonded close as brothers, my friend."

"Pleased to hear it," Ulysses replied. His hand throbbed, but at least it had been his left hand and not the right, which he favoured for sword play. "Well, if we're brothers now, you'd best call me Ulysses."

"And you must call me Targutai Khan!" the warlord bellowed, the liquor putting fire in his heart.

"Very well," Ulysses conceded.

The slap Targutai laid on his back almost sent Ulysses tumbling out of his seat. "I'm only joking, brother!" he guffawed. "What has happened to your robust English sense of humour? What-what?"

And so the evening dragged on as the festivities continued with raucous singing, wild dancing, arm-wrestling competitions, and enthusiastic, good-natured carousing.

"You know what you need, khan?" Ulysses said later, over a shared sack of liquor.

"And what is that, brother?"

"A Rolls Royce. Silver Phantom, Mark IV."

"A Rolls Royce?" Targutai gasped, his eyes lighting up in delight. "Could you get me one?"

"In fact, I'll have one sent over for you the very minute I get back to England."

"You could do that for me?"

"I could, khan, and I will. After all, you know what they say – one good turn deserves another." Ulysses flashed the warlord a shark-like smile.

"I love you English," Targutai exulted, "with your Rolls Royce, your cricket on the green, your cream teas and your boiled sweets!"

"I'll throw in a bag of mint imperials, too."

"A Rolls Royce? Finest automobiles in the world."

"I drive one, you know?" Ulysses threw in casually. "Although usually it's Nimrod that does most of the actual driving. But it's my car."

"And I love this butler of yours too," Targutai said, slapping Nimrod soundly on the shoulder. "You should stay here with me, Nimrod!"

"Uh-uh, he's spoken for," Ulysses said.

"More's the pity."

"I think he likes you, old boy," the dandy said, nudging his scowling manservant in the ribs.

"I never apologised for intruding on your lands and putting your men to all that trouble with the pterosaurs," Ulysses slurred, some hours later.

"Think nothing of it," Targutai said. "No, in fact think of it as a happy accident that has brought us together. I would not now have had it any other way. But Ulysses, my brother, you still haven't told me what you are doing so far from England. What matter is it that has brought you to these wild, desolate lands." The khan broke off and starting sucking noisily at a drumstick the size of a cured ham.

"Well, Targutai, old boy," Ulysses began, "it's funny you should mention that. Truth is, I'm doing my bit for queen and country, if you know what I mean."

Targutai pricked up his ears at that.

"You are an agent of Queen Victoria?" He frowned. "Then you have played a cruel trick on me. You are spies after all."

"You've seen right through me," Ulysses said, holding up his hands in surrender. "*Mea culpa*. But we never meant to trouble you, oh great khan. Between you and me we were on the tail of another airship that was skirting your lands."

"Another airship?" Targutai said, his brows knitting. He suddenly directed his gaze into the thick of the throng gathered around the edge of the light cast by the cook-fire. He shouted something in his native tongue and, at his summons, a lean warrior extricated himself from the arms of a pug-faced woman and, bowing low, approached his lord and master.

Warlord and bondsman shared a brief exchange, during which the tribesman shot Ulysses a disparaging look more than once. But the man was soon sent away, with a wave of the hand and a barked command, and Targutai turned back to Ulysses.

"Temüjin confirms your story. He says there was another blimp, heading north over the Sayan Mountains. Temüjin says it bore the crest of the Bratsk bat."

"That's it! That the one!" Ulysses exclaimed, relief flooding through him. "Do you know this crest then?"

"I do," Targutai confirmed, lowering his voice, Ulysses' conspirator once more. "It belongs to the region ruled by the Dark Prince."

"The Dark Prince?" Ulysses suspected that he was talking of Prince Vladimir, but with Targutai in such a voluble mood, he didn't want to say anything that might limit the information the khan might otherwise choose to share.

"His lands lie north of here, on the other side of the mountain wall. But it is a cursed land. Many evil things are said of the place."

"What kind of a place is it?"

"A place of brooding forests and deep shadowed valleys. Its peasant folk live in poverty, begging scraps from their master's table. I treat my slaves better than the Dark Prince treats his people. The prince is a recluse. It is said that he never leaves his castle, which stands on an outcrop over-looking the whole of his domain. It is known as the Winter Palace."

"That's the place!" Katarina suddenly interjected.

Targutai scowled at her in response. "And what business do you have there?"

And so, between them, Katarina and Ulysses told the khan everything.

"I see," the khan said at last.

"I don't suppose you could see to helping us on our way again, could you, brother? Time is, as they say, of the essence."

"Yes, I can help you," Targutai Khan said. "As you yourself said, brother, one good turn deserves another."

"Of course, and as soon as I'm back on English soil I shall make the necessary arrangements to have a Rolls delivered to you forthwith."

"But that might be months away, brother. And what if you are not successful in your mission?" the khan asked. "I would rather have my reward *now*."

"O-kaay... What precisely did you have in mind?"

"Your butler, Nimrod, stays with me."

"Wha-!" Ulysses began but Targutai silenced him by raising a hand.

"No, hear me out. Nimrod stays here with me, so that he might further educate me in the finer points of English etiquette and in return I will help you and your woman reach the Winter Palace."

CHAPTER THIRTY-FIVE

On The Wings of The Night

By dusk the next day, the wreck of the Potemkin had been recovered from the gully in which it had come down – pulled free by a team of harnessed triceratops. The horde's tent-makers had repaired the damage to the airship envelope, and the fuselage had been roughly beaten back into shape by the Khan's factory-sized workforce of skilled armourers. Nimrod and Ulysses had been able to help Agent K make what few repairs were necessary to the dirigible's engines and, with a fresh load of fuel to stoke the firebox under its boiler, by sunset they were ready for the off again.

It was a rush job – the best they could manage in the time available to them and it was amazing that the Potemkin was fit to fly at all.

With the envelope filled from the emergency gas tanks and the gondola securely tethered, Ulysses Quicksilver and Katarina Kharkova – along with the guide Targutai had provided them with – prepared to embark.

Yesugei, their guide, seemed very unsure about travelling on board the airship. It was as if he was of the opinion that if you were going to fly then whatever you flew should have wings. But he didn't have much of a choice, unless he wanted to endure a flogging at the hands of his master.

Katarina was already onboard, grumbling to herself, and none too quietly either, as she ran a final instrument check.

Ulysses turned back before mounting the disembarkation platform himself, so that he might bid Targutai Khan and his faithful manservant farewell.

"Thank you again, Khan," Ulysses said, waving with the bloodstone-tipped cane he had managed to retrieve from the Potemkin.

"Don't mention it, what?" the Khan smiled.

The dandy turned to his personal valet and oldest companion. "And, Nimrod, old man, don't go having too much fun now, will you? Remember, this arrangement is only temporary. Don't get too comfortable in that tent."

"Perish the thought," Nimrod replied, his face the picture of disgruntled indifference.

"You had best be on your way, sir," the Khan said. "Under cover of darkness and all that, what?"

"Indeed."

And with that, Ulysses turned on his heel and boarded the Potemkin.

Moments later, anchors were weighed and, engines labouring a little, Katarina Kharkova's zeppelin took to the skies once more, with a shout of "Tally-ho!" from the Khan.

The Winter Palace lay north of the Mongol warlord's lands on the other side of the Sayan Mountains, which made travel by air by far the quickest and most effective way to approach it.

The barren black wastes beneath them gave way to rugged foothills and then the white scree and snow-clad slopes of the mountains themselves.

"There," Agent K said, an hour after moonrise.

It was a full minute before Ulysses could make out the looming castle, perched on its outcropping of rock over the forested valley below. It looked like something out of a Murnau-inspired picture, the sort of over-exaggerated magic lantern documentary reels that played in the kinemas before the main feature started, such as the recent runaway hit *Nosferatu.*

The first any of them knew of the attack on the airship was when the Potemkin inexplicably began to lose height.

"What is it?" Ulysses demanded, joining Katarina at the controls.

"I don't know!" she snapped. "I think we're losing gas. Your friends didn't do such a slap-up job as you obviously thought."

"Now don't be like that," Ulysses said, coming to the Mongols' defence. "You saw their needle-work. You tested the seams for yourself."

"Well, at this rate we are going to hit the forest before we reach the castle."

"Look!" the Mongolian guide suddenly shouted.

"I am looking, thank you very much!" Katarina retorted, adding something in mumbled Russian.

"No, I think he means look at *that,*" Ulysses said, grasping Katarina's arm and guiding her round.

The clear, midnight blue vista that had been before them was now filled with a storm of black wings. The Potemkin hit the flock head on, the force of the impact shattering the glass of the cockpit and filling the gondola with a chill, biting wind and a maelstrom of bats.

Squeaking like demented mice, the creatures set about those trapped inside, clawing at them with their savage talons, biting their exposed skin, flapping wings getting entangled in hair as they descended upon them with malign intent.

Ulysses stumbled backwards, beating at the bats that surrounded him. He caught a glimpse of the cone of the Potemkin's envelope through the shattered cockpit. Clinging to it were more of the black-winged monstrosities, worrying at the fabric with claws and teeth.

The engines coughed and the dirigible juddered. Ulysses could only guess that yet more of their nocturnal assailants had got drawn into the workings of the airship's turbines.

The Potemkin was going down, and there was nothing any of them could do to prevent it.

Hearing a scream, Ulysses batted the bats from his face to see the wretched Yesugei stumbling for the door, blinded by the creatures tangled in the thick mane of his hair. The falling airship lurched again, throwing him into the door with a crash.

A window smashed as the spear-tip of a severed branch penetrated the cabin. A tree top snagged the deflating balloon, jerking the falling airship round, sending it into a spin.

With a scream of rending metal the door was wrenched open, torn from its hinges. The Mongol gave another scream as he tumbled backwards out of the opening.

The crump of an explosion shook the tumbling airship as an engine exploded.

Ulysses and Katarina were lifted off their feet by the ball of fire that chased them through the fuselage of the vessel as they hurtled into the night.

For a moment everything was light and dark and noise and silence and then Ulysses hit the ground, the deep snow capturing him in its smothering embrace.

Woozily he opened his eyes, and in the moment before blissful unconsciousness took hold, he saw Katarina Kharkova there above him, hanging from a tree like a marionette with its strings cut. The pine needles were wet and red where the splintered branch had punched clean through her chest, impaling her.

CHAPTER THIRTY-SIX

Prince of Darkness

"Mr Quicksilver," came a voice as clear and sharp as crystal, accompanied by a slap to the face, "wake up!"

Ulysses lifted his lolling head and slowly opened his eyes.

Shapes began to form in the darkness in front of him. From the echoing quality of the voice and the deepening space that grew with every blink of his eyes, he imagined he was in some great vaulted chamber underground; or inside a large, solidly-constructed building.

The castle, he thought as his memories began to return.

And standing there in front of him was a man, no more than a black silhouette against the nimbus of light that dimly illuminated the vaulted chamber.

A dull, throbbing ache permeated every part of his body. He was suspended by the wrists, from the rusted frame of some torture device. He could feel the rough, flaking metal as it scrapped against his back, the manacles biting into the flesh of his wrists and the muscles of his shoulders singing with pain.

"How do you know my name?" Ulysses managed.

The man laughed. It was a sharp, cruel sound. "It is my business to know. And besides, you do not get to be one of the most powerful noblemen in Russia without learning a thing or two."

"Vladimir," Ulysses spluttered.

The man slapped him across the face and Ulysses felt his arms tense with the desire to slap the man right back.

"I think you'll find that's *Prince* Vladimir."

"What do you want? Whatever it is, was it really worth waking me up for?"

The prince glared at him and took a step backwards, moving into the hazy nimbus of light cast by a guttering candle-flame.

Ulysses was surprised at the man's appearance – even after all that he had already witnessed in his time as an agent of the throne of Magna Britannia.

Everything about him was as pale as porcelain, from his slender fingers, his skin, his hair – which was set in a sweeping side parting – his bloodless lips. Everything, apart from the irises of his eyes, which were as red as rubies. His clothes were of a sombre cut and funereal black.

The albino observed him, his mouth set in a frown, and lifted two items from where they had been lying on a barrel. Ulysses' eyes widened a notch. One of the objects was a stoppered phial, its contents dark, the other a well-thumbed notebook.

"These were found about your person," the prince stated, "both of them formerly the property of Dr Victor Gallowglass. Now, as I understand it, this is a sample of blood and this," – he held up the notebook – "is of incalculable value. Or at least it would be if anyone could translate it. And *you* will translate it for me.

"And what makes you think I can do that?"

"Translate it for me," the prince repeated softly.

Ulysses became aware of the other person in the room with them for the first time. He was a tall man, taller than Ulysses by a head, heavily-bearded and dressed in the rough clothing favoured by Cossack warriors. Everything about the man's posture and build spoke of violence done or violence waiting to be done.

A raw chuckle escaped Ulysses' throat. "You can hurt me all you want. I won't help you."

"No, I rather thought you wouldn't," he said.

Vladimir clicked his fingers and the hulking, hairy Cossack standing behind him left the room only to return a few moments later.

Within the Cossack's bear-hug embrace was Miss Wishart.

The dandy felt sick to the pit of his stomach.

"Don't!" he hissed.

The Cossack – his right eye a blind white orb, the brow above and the cheek below it knotted with a pink welt of fresh scar tissue – let one hand slip from before the wretched woman's face, ungagging her.

"Ulysses!" she screamed, tears streaming from her eyes.

"Lillian!"

He turned his gaze on the albino prince, eyes burning with a passionate fury.

"If you touch a single hair on her head..." he spluttered bloodily.

"Oh, *I* shan't touch a hair on her head. Not a single one," The prince stated with cold honesty. "Instead I shall let Dmitri here have his way with her, and then, I shall have him start to remove... pieces of her. Her fingers, ears and nose to begin with, I think, and we'll see how long she lasts. But then again, of course, you probably wouldn't be interested in having back what's left of her after that. And by the time he gets to her hands and feet, or her arms and legs, killing her will be a mercy."

Ulysses sagged upon the torture frame. "Then it doesn't look like I have much of a choice, does it?" He said. "I'll help you. I'll translate your code."

CHAPTER THIRTY-SEVEN

Codename Caliban

And so, that night, Ulysses set to work retranslating the contents of Victor Gallowglass's precious coded notebook, exposing the details of the late haematologist's greatest work for the benefit of his incarcerator, Prince Vladimir of Bratsk.

Having been taken down from the torture frame by the growling Cossack – none too gently either – he had his head plunged into a bucket of freezing water, his forehead being used to break the skin of ice that crowned the water. The fight had gone out of him by then. Exhausted and beset by all manner of cramps, along with other aches and pains, he felt certain that his fate had already been decided.

He had not seen Miss Wishart since accepting the futility of his situation and he hadn't seen or heard of what had befallen Miranda.

He was led to a dank cell, its walls black with algae, its stone flags strewn with rotting straw, and set to work with pencil and paper, straining his eyes as he worked by the light of a lone guttering candle. Locked away as he was in this manner, the only indicator he had as to the continued passage of time were the irregular meals that were shoved through the door and the occasional emptying of the slops bucket.

More than once he cursed the fact that he had rebelled against De Wynter's authority – as was his wont – and pursued the Russian connection, wishing that he had never left Blighty at all. There were even moments when he regretted ever agreeing to help his old school chum.

But what kept him going was the thought that, sooner or later, when this work was finished there would be an end to it all.

As he set about transcribing Gallowglass's notes, racing through some of those sections he had already attempted on the Trans-Siberian Express, the enormity and daring of his old friend's endeavour was revealed to him. It threw into question not only Gallowglass's patriotism but also what state of mind he had been in to even attempt such a thing. What kind of a man had Victor Gallowglass become in the years since he and Ulysses had fallen out of touch?

For what was revealed was a scheme on a par with something the megalomaniacal Uriah Wormwood might have come up with.

Having pieced together the various footnotes, appendices and addenda – even though he could make little sense of the blood science and biological engineering – the sample contained within the stoppered phial, Gallowglass's 'thing of darkness', was nothing so simple, nor so innocent as blood.

It was a bio-weapon, a blood agent codenamed, appropriately enough, Caliban.

The genius of the Caliban bio-weapon was that it had been engineered to target those of a specific bloodline.

This realisation left Ulysses in a state of shock and sleep did not come easily to him that night.

How could he pass such knowledge into the hands of a man as utterly without morals as the sociopathic Prince Vladimir?

Having lain upon the damp straw, wringing the stinking

horsehair blanket in his hands, he rose and, lighting a fresh candle from the flickering stub of the last, he took up the notes he had made and burnt them.

He then set to work re-transcribing some of the sections of the journal, before moving on to translating the passage following the one containing the terrifying truth. He worked as quickly as he could, hoping that this flurry of activity might help hide the fact that something was missing. As Ulysses resumed his work, he came across something else that provided him with the faintest glimmer of hope.

And so, at last, after God alone knew how many days or nights of desperate, feverish work, Ulysses found himself standing before Prince Vladimir, forced to watch as the nobleman went through his work.

"Fascinating. Fascinating," the prince said as he scoured page after scruffy page of Ulysses' translation.

Eventually, the albino looked up and, fixing Ulysses with his blood-red stare said, "I take it the vital component that you have left out is the fact that this weapon was created to work only on your own dear Queen Victoria and her descendents."

Ulysses stared at him in horror. "You knew."

"Of course I knew." Vladimir laughed. "Why do you think I went to so much trouble, and at no little cost to myself either, to get hold of this?"

A page was missing from the journal, torn out for some reason. Following that one missing leaf was something that was just as startling a revelation as the discovery that Caliban had been designed to kill the monarch. As well as creating the weapon that could wipe out Queen Victoria and her descendants, Victor Gallowglass had created a cure.

Victor Gallowglass didn't have a daughter; his late wife Marie had died before she could provide him with an heir and her husband had, it seemed, remained faithful to her all the time that they were married. Certainly, from reading the doctor's journal, Ulysses was in no doubt as to the fact that Miranda was not his biological offspring.

The truth of the matter was that Miranda was the product of a test tube experiment, although one that must have required no small feat of medical and scientific skill for it to have been such a success. Ulysses and Victor Gallowglass, along with his so-called 'daughter', had a common acquaintance – a certain Dr Pandora Doppelganger.

Victor Gallowglass had been Queen Victoria's haematologist, Ulysses had known that, but what he could not have begun to even guess at was what his old school friend had got up to with the blood samples he had taken from Her Majesty.

Using the biological information encoded in the DNA present in just one drop of the mighty monarch's blood, Dr Doppelganger had been able to grow an exact replica of Her Majesty, the perfect test subject for the appalling experiment Gallowglass had been conducting.

How many Mirandas had there been? How many had unwittingly been used and tossed aside in Gallowglass's quest to develop the perfect form of the traitorous bio-weapon?

Ulysses found himself wondering how Gallowglass could even countenance producing such a thing of darkness, but then other pieces of the puzzle began to slot into place. The truth was that he couldn't countenance such a thing, forcing whoever it was that had been coercing him into producing the weapon to step in. Now Ulysses understood at last why Miranda had been a target for kidnappers. It had all been a set-up to force the wretched Gallowglass into completing his even more wretched work, just as Ulysses was now himself being forced to sell his own soul in the vain hope that he might save the life of another.

But should Ulysses reveal the existence of a cure to the tyrannical prince? Could he bring himself to do it? If he did, what dreadful fate would befall the child? If he didn't, Vladimir had made it perfectly clear what would happen to his erstwhile lover, Miss Wishart.

Should the knowledge that the child wasn't even Gallowglass's own flesh and blood change how Ulysses himself felt about her? Victor Gallowglass had effectively made Miranda Ulysses' ward and he had already saved her life on one occasion. No matter what her origins, she was still an eleven year-old child in need of love and protection. Could he really turn his back on her now, in favour of a woman he had seduced once on a monotonous train journey? But then what right did he have to forfeit either of their lives?

"You have what you wanted. It's all there," Ulysses lied as he stood before the prince. "I have kept my part of the bargain."

"Like a true English gentleman."

"Now it's time to show me that you've kept yours. I need to know that she's safe, that Miss Wishart is alive and well."

"What do you take me for, Mr Quicksilver? I am not a monster."

"That's not enough," Ulysses said. "I need to see her. Let me see her."

The prince looked at him coldly. "I had thought it might come to this."

Vladimir snapped his fingers. "Would you come here, my dear?"

As Ulysses watched, a figure rose from the chair facing the fire in the corner of the room. He did not realise who it was until she turned and crossed the room, hips rolling seductively. Everything about her was a million miles away from the staid governess he had first met on the steps of his house in Mayfair.

"What have you done to her?" Ulysses railed.

Vladimir laughed. It was a harsh, humourless sound.

"Done? Prince Vladimir has done nothing to me." Miss Wishart said.

Ulysses felt sick to the pit of his stomach as the truth of the matter became clear.

"That's right," Vladimir pronounced, as the temptress slipped an arm around his shoulders and pressed herself close against him. "You might say she was my woman on the inside, from the moment she started working for the late Dr Gallowglass."

"But Lillian, how could you?"

"Don't you understand, Ulysses, my poor dear?" the seductress said. "There never was a Lillian Wishart. There was only ever me."

"But I am forgetting my manners," the prince said, "let me introduce you. Mr Quicksilver, meet Lilith – Lilith de Báthory."

CHAPTER THIRTY-EIGHT

Bloodlines

"So you were onto that poor bastard Gallowglass from the start," Ulysses said.

"I have eyes everywhere. We knew that Gallowglass was working on a potent weapon."

"Caliban."

"But we didn't know what form it took and, due to the late doctor's eccentric method of note-making, we could not play our hand too soon, for fear that the work was not yet complete. But thanks in no small part to you, Mr Quicksilver, we now have the means to achieving our goal."

Ulysses' mind reeled. That could only mean one thing – the assassination of Her Majesty Queen Victoria. There had been no fewer than twelve attempts on the Queen's life during her 160 year reign, and Ulysses had saved her from one of those attempts himself. However, he doubted that he would be able to do anything to foil this latest challenge to her authority.

Ulysses turned to face Miss Wishart – the viper at the breast of the Gallowglass family. "You bitch!"

"Now, now, Ulysses," she chided. "That's no way to speak to a lady."

"You're no lady. You're nothing but a conniving serpent."

"So, I should thank you, Mr Quicksilver," Vladimir said, an icy smile on his bloodless lips, "for without your dogged pursuit of the truth and your unstinting work, I would not be where I am now, ready to put my master plan into effect."

"And now, I take it, I am a dead man," Ulysses stated, eyeing the Cossack disdainfully.

"Eventually," Vladimir agreed. "Frankly I couldn't care less what happens to you now."

The Cossack turned and strode up to the dandy. Ulysses turned his head away, but the brute grabbed his chin in one hand, forcing him to look up into his face, a face scarred by the tip of a rapier blade. Ulysses felt the Cossack's rank breath – redolent with the aroma of spoiled meat and sour blood – gust into his face, and had to fight the urge to retch. The brute bellowed something in the Balachka dialect.

"What did he say?" Ulysses managed.

"He said, he owes you," Prince Vladimir chuckled.

"Oh, but can I keep him?" Lilith de Báthory said. "Can I keep him, Vlad? I'll be so lonely here with you away, and you know how... hungry I get."

"You and your... appetites," the prince said.

"Please?" she wheedled.

"So you've had one taste and now you want to go back for seconds, hmm? Oh, very well. Keep him as your plaything. Do what you will with him, but when you've had your fun, make sure you have him properly disposed of, hmm?"

"Oh thank you, Vlad, thank you," she gushed, kissing the prince on the cheek.

She moved across the room, her hips rolling provocatively. To Ulysses' eyes she almost seemed to glide. As she stood before him, she leaned forward, her shapely breasts barely contained by the gown she was wearing. She put a baby-soft hand to his face and stroked his cheek. "We're going to have such fun."

Ulysses turned away, disgusted with himself as much as by her. Lilith laughed.

"Make him comfortable in my quarters," she told the Cossack. "And Ulysses, I'll be seeing you later."

"Yes," the dandy snarled. "In hell, if I have anything to do with it!"

When Ulysses regained consciousness he found himself in what appeared to be a cross between a whore's boudoir and a dungeon cell. Velvet drapes hung from the rough stone walls and a fashionable Japanese silk-screen stood close to an extravagant four-poster bed. A fire crackled in the grate at the other end of the room.

Ulysses was upright, arms stretched out to each side of him, legs splayed, to a sturdy wooden saltire cross.

A door opened somewhere behind him and a voice as soft and as sensual as silk said, "Good, you're awake. Now, where did we get up to?"

He felt Miss Wishart's – no, Lilith de Báthory's – caressing fingertips circle his nipples; his body thrilling to her touch no matter how much his rational mind might rail against it. He felt her hook a leg around his from behind, the rise and fall of her knee stroking his thigh.

And then she was there in front of him, bosom heaving, her gown practically falling from her shoulders, the split dress revealing her own creamy thighs.

Ulysses felt himself stiffen despite his exhausted, wrung out state.

A scream sounded from somewhere within the castle and Ulysses snapped out of his ecstasy in an instant, but the only sign his seducer showed of having even noticed was a brief hiatus as she tensed before resuming again.

The scream came again, a horrible, animal sound.

Lilith grunted in annoyance. "Ignore it."

"That's quite normal, is it?" Ulysses asked.

"It's nothing. Besides, soon we shall drown out their shrieking with our own screams of ecstatic pleasure."

The scream was met with a brief burst of machine gun-fire.

"What *is* going on? This is most off-putting." Lilith broke off.

Crushing her lips hard against his, her tongue forcing its way into his mouth, she grabbed hold of him and said, "Hold that thought," before making for the door.

He heard a door open behind him. Lilith screamed in fury. There was the ring of steel and then a sound like someone burying a spade in a cauliflower. A moment later Ulysses heard two distinct thuds as something – two somethings – hit the floor.

And then – as Ulysses' mind reeled at the impossibility of it all – there was a woman with bobbed blonde hair, releasing him from his bonds.

"Katarina?" he said, as he stared down at the black, bloodied hole in the front of her tunic. She was now wearing a bandolier of weapons across her chest – pistols and knives mainly.

"You were expecting someone else?"

"But you're dead. I saw you impaled on a tree branch."

"As yes, you did indeed see me impaled on a tree branch," she smiled, "that is correct. But as you can see for yourself, I am not dead. You see the branch failed to pierce my heart."

"B-But... You're a..." Ulysses stammered.

"Yes, I am."

"But what's a vampire doing on the trail of a crazy Russian noble?" Ulysses floundered.

Agent K looked thoughtful for a moment as she undid the last strap and helped him down from the cross-frame.

"You... How do you say? Ah, yes. You set a thief to catch a thief."

CHAPTER THIRTY-NINE

Dark Discoveries

"Well I think she got the point, don't you?" Ulysses said as he looked down at the decapitated body of Lilith de Báthory, a startled look of surprise locked on her features forevermore. What looked like a broken chair leg had been rammed into her heart. "Was she a... you know...?"

"Do all your relationships end so abruptly?" Katarina asked.

"I hope not," he said.

"You might be wanting this," she said, passing him his sword-stick.

"Oh," he said. "Yes. Thank you."

He slowly found his gaze being drawn back to the savage wound in her chest.

"Do you mind?" the vampire said, pulling her jacket tight about her.

"Sorry, it's just that... well..."

Katarina fixed the exhausted Ulysses with those piercing eyes of hers. "Our quarry is getting away."

"H-He is? How do you know?"

"I saw him leave, along with that one-eyed bodyguard of his."

"The Cossack?"

"They left by train, from the prince's own private station."

"He has Caliban with him."

"He has what?"

Ulysses hesitated for only a moment before telling Katarina everything. After all, he decided, he owed her. She had saved his life twice now.

"Do you know what he plans to do with the Caliban bio-weapon?" she asked when he had finished.

"He only wants to wipe out the monarchy of Magna Britannia."

"But why?"

"Who knows, but we can't risk finding out the hard way. We'd both be out of a job for a start."

"Then there's all the more reason to leave now."

"No, we can't." Ulysses stopped at the door to Lilith de Báthory's chamber.

"What? Why not?"

"The child," he said, "Miranda. She'll be here, somewhere."

"How do you know?"

"She's the key to all of this. She is as much an artificial creation as the weapon. She's the antithesis. She's the cure. If we're going to take on Vladimir and win, I have a feeling we're going to need Miranda with us."

"I see."

"Besides, how did you intend us to chase after the prince if he's travelling by train with the Potemkin gone?"

"One does not survive as a vampire throughout the darkest three centuries of the history of our kind without learning a trick or two. We'll find a way."

"Or we could just find the airship that led us here in the first place and put that to good use."

"Very well," the vampire replied.

"Then if we are going to look for this child, we had best get moving."

*   *   *

They found her deep within the dungeons of the Winter Palace, in a laboratory, hooked up to some arcane piece of machinery that was all wheezing compressors, gurgling pumps and rusted valves.

It was there that Ulysses also found the enigmatic Dr Pavlov. The moon-faced man was working at a bank of monitoring equipment when the dandy and the vampire entered the humid chamber.

"So, we meet again," Ulysses growled and then flung himself at the porcelain pale doctor, who simply snarled and hurled the clipboard he was holding at him. Ulysses batted it aside and was on the doctor in a second.

Pavlov fumbled for something in a pocket until Ulysses wrenched his arm free, slamming his wrist against the edge of a cogitator unit. The man gave a cry and the hypodermic in his hand fell from his hand, smashing on the stone-flagged floor.

Ulysses grabbed the doctor around the throat with his free hand, pushing the man's head back.

"Why?" he shouted into the doctor's face. "Why? Just answer me that!"

Ulysses felt Katarina's hand firm on his arm, holding him back.

"We won't learn anything like this. Let me talk to him."

Ulysses glared at her and then the tension in his face eased. "Use your womanly wiles on him, you mean. Good idea."

Relaxing his grip on the man, Ulysses took a step backwards. Agent K stepped forward, fixing the panting man with her aquamarine gaze.

The scalpel was in Pavlov's hand in a second, its blade shining silver in the strange light of the chamber. He sprang at the vampire, the tip of the scalpel pointing directly at her heart.

As the point appeared about to enter the gaping hole in the vampire's chest, Ulysses was suddenly between the two of them again, pushing Katarina out of the way and sending Dr Pavlov tripping over his legs to land awkwardly on the floor.

He lay there, doubled up, groaning.

"Right, I want some answers," Ulysses said, pulling the doctor over onto his back. The end of the scalpel protruded from the man's side, blood soaking his clothing all around it. There was only an inch of the surgical instrument still showing. The rest of it was sunk into the man's lung.

With one final rattling breath, Pavlov's eyes glazed over and the sadistic doctor took whatever secrets he was party to, to the grave.

Grabbing the limp body by the lapels, Ulysses pulled Pavlov's slack-jawed moon-face close to his and screamed, "Damn you to hell!" Then he let the corpse drop.

A faint whimper drew his attention back to the arcane contraption fixed to the wall and the helpless child suspended within it.

Miranda was still alive, but only barely.

Tubing attached to her wrists was draining her very lifeblood drop by precious drop. She was dressed in nothing more than the nightie she had been wearing when she had been whisked away from her berth aboard the Trans-Siberian Express.

She was deathly pale, her twitching eyes sunken within deep black rings. Beneath her, bottles caked in crumbling brown deposits were filled with sticky, red liquid.

Having released her from the giant wheel of the arcane device, they laid her on a gurney and Ulysses set about extracting the catheters and tubes. He cleaned and dressed the wounds as quickly as he could. Then, with the girl laid across his shoulders, the two of them set off for the stairs that would lead to the upper levels, where they hoped they would find the prince's private airship hangar.

"I can hear something." Katrina brought them to a halt.

Ulysses listened. All he could hear was the echo of dripping water and the distant wheezing and gurgling of unknowable mechanical processes.

"There's someone else down here."

Before Ulysses could comment, Katarina was away, moving swiftly through the labyrinthine tunnels of the Winter Palace dungeons.

Ulysses hesitated, but only for a moment, before following.

Katarina stopped again at an iron-banded dungeon door. "Can you hear it now?" she asked, turning to Ulysses. Not waiting for an answer, she tested the door. It was locked.

Laying the unconscious Miranda on a table, Ulysses helped Katarina search for a means of opening the door. As they searched, Ulysses noticed that a number of untarnished copper pipes fed through the ceiling of the deeply buried chamber, through the wall and into the room that lay beyond the door.

"I have it!" Katarina said and Ulysses, hearing a key rattling in the lock, turned his attention to the door, sword-cane in hand.

"Smells worse than an open sewer," Ulysses pronounced as the stink of the cell hit him.

As the light from the wall-lamps in the main chamber wormed its way into the cell, what looked like a pile of sacking and hair shifted and gave voice to a pitiful wail.

"What is that?" Ulysses said, peering in fascination at the decrepit creature. "Is it even human?"

But he could see what it was now that the light had reached it. It was, or once had been, a man, but now was little more than skin and bone buried beneath the unruly mass of a beard run wild.

Slowly Katarina approached the cell. She was repeating something over and over in her native tongue as the wretch incarcerated within muttered and gibbered away incoherently. The old man abruptly ceased his muttering and looked at Katarina through the red slits of his eyes.

"Not what, but who?" the agent said, eyes fixed on the wretched thing.

The old man was silent for a moment and then mumbled something into the messy growth of his beard. Katarina heard, put a hand to her mouth and staggered away from the door.

The man mumbled again, but this time Ulysses heard him clearly.

"Rasputin. Grigori Yefimovich Rasputin."

CHAPTER FORTY

The Curse of Rasputin

"Did he just say what I think he just said?" Ulysses asked.

"Yes," Katarina replied. "Rasputin."

"But he can't be. I mean, that's impossible. He would have to be 130 years old!"

"The evidence would suggest otherwise. And he would be 129, actually."

"But I've visited his tomb."

"And was he there?" Katarina asked.

"Well no, now you come to mention it." He paused. "It must be a set-up, he can't possibly be *the* Grigori Rasputin. Can he?"

"The world is full of impossible things, Ulysses. I would have thought a man like you knew that already."

"Alright, so assuming that this is the original mad monk himself, what's he doing here?"

As he continued to stare at the dishevelled specimen, Ulysses noticed how the curious pipework that he had already spotted came down inside the cell, ending at what looked like a water dispenser. Only it wasn't water that had dried in black flakes around the tap.

Turning back to the mad old man, Katarina spoke to him again in Russian, but he simply stared at her, uncomprehending.

She repeated herself once more, fixing him with her penetrating stare.

She sighed. "His mind is gone, broken by decades of captivity," she explained, her shoulders sagging. Her mask slipped, just for a moment, and Ulysses saw how tired and weak she was.

"Look, you don't need to do this," he said gently, putting a hand to her arm.

"It's alright, Ulysses," she said, managing a faint smile. "He might know something that could be of use to us."

Turning back to the stinking old man squatting amidst the filth of his squalid cell, she struggled to wheedle the truth out of him, matching her hypnotic gaze with his dead-eyed stare.

At last the old man began to talk. And now that Katarina had got him talking, there was no stopping the bearded bag of bones.

As Rasputin talked, Katarina listened and translated for Ulysses' benefit, teasing the truth from the old man's lunatic gibbering.

Ulysses Quicksilver, like any educated Englishman, knew the story of the mad monk Grigori Rasputin. He had been born in 1869, in Siberia, and a vision of the Virgin Mary set him on the path to become a wandering pilgrim-mystic.

But it was when he came into contact with the banned Christian sect known as the *khlysty* – an orgiastic sect who favoured the practices of self-flagellation and the mortification of the flesh as well as unnatural carnal couplings – that his life was changed forever. For the sect was merely a facade of something even darker - and this was where accepted history and the old man's recollections began to diverge dramatically.

The young Rasputin had actually joined a blood cult that venerated its own dark pantheon of diabolical saints, along with the first of their line, the fifteenth century Prince of Wallachia, Vlad Tepes himself. History also remembered this bloodthirsty tyrant as Vlad the Impaler, but to his own people, those who suffered the nightmarish consequences of his murderous psychoses, he was known by another name. Dracula.

In time Rasputin rose to a position of power within the cult, and under his charismatic influence the *khlysty* regained the sense of purpose that had been undermined by the baser instincts and appetites of its devotees. Their original ambition had been forgotten, but Rasputin made them remember and desire it again.

And so it was that, in 1903, Rasputin arrived in Saint Petersburg and his reputation as a holy healer and prophet developed and grew.

The story went that Rasputin was travelling through Siberia when he heard of Tsarevich Alexei's illness. The legacy of the Tsar's great-grandmother, Her Majesty Queen Victoria, was a blight upon the Russian royal family, for Tsar Nicholas's only son and heir to the throne of Imperial Russia suffered from haemophilia. Rasputin already had the Russian royal family in his sights and the Tsarevich's condition provided him with the perfect means of infiltrating the Tsar's inner circle.

And so the famed peasant healer came to court and laid his healing hands upon the Tsarevich Alexei and worked his charismatic magic on the boy's mother and father as well. Thanks to the monk's ministrations, Alexei did indeed begin to show signs of improved health. Steadily Father Grigori worked his way into the family's affections and that was how a peasant mystic managed to come to exert such control over the ruling house of Russia.

Nicholas's wife, the Tsritsa Alexandra, came to believe that God spoke to her through Rasputin and so his personal and political influence upon her continued to grow. Controversy followed.

And all the while, in the shadows, Rasputin and his fellow cultists prepared for the time when one of Dracula's bloodline would ascend to the throne of Russia. Slowly but surely Rasputin moved his pawns into position, in readiness for the moment when their scheme would at last bear bloody fruit.

Even the onset of the First Great War did not halt Rasputin's schemes. And then, one night, Rasputin imparted his healing gift to the young Tsarevich Alexei, curing him with a kiss. And so, the boy was inducted into the bloodline of the great Vlad Tepes. But where Tepes had merely been Prince of Wallachia, the destiny laid out for Alexei was for him to be nothing less than the ruler of all the Russias, with Rasputin the real power behind the Imperial throne.

But Rasputin's rise to power had not gone unobserved. In fact it had been closely followed from several different quarters. On the night of December 16, 1916, his enemies made their move against him and the *khlysty*. Quite possibly having uncovered the cult's plan for the empire, with help from the British secret service, the now infamous group of nobles led by Prince Felix Yusupov, the Grand Duke Dmitri Pavlovich and the right-wing politician Vladimir Purishkevich, lured Rasputin to the Moika Palace and set about trying to do away with the beast, not understanding his true nature.

But Rasputin's vampiric metabolism meant that he survived the conspirators' attempt to poison him with cyanide and their vain efforts to shoot him. When they discovered that he was still alive, he was beaten, castrated, bound and bundled up inside a carpet before being thrown into the icy Neva River.

When his body was recovered from the river three days later, an autopsy was carried out, with the coroner declaring that Rasputin's supposed death had been the result of drowning.

As soon as was seemly, the Tsaritsa Alexandra – a member of the cult herself by this point and aware of Rasputin's true nature – had his body taken to Tsarskoye Selo and had Rasputin interred inside his own vault, along with the bloody means by which his body might continue to reconstitute itself.

After the devastating events of the failed February Revolution, Rasputin's enemies, also now aware of Father Grigori's true nature, broke into it and dragged his body into the woods where they attempted to finish the job begun by the vampire's would-be murderers, by consigning his mortal remains to the cremating flames of a funeral pyre.

His body aflame, Rasputin was roused from his sleep of ages. In excruciating agony, he leapt from his pyre and fled the scene.

Those who had attempted to burn his body set off in pursuit, but the vampire evaded them and managed to escape at last. Not wanting the world to know of their failure, the conspirators perpetuated the story that Rasputin was dead, his body burnt, and then waited for the day when he would surely re-emerge once more.

Rasputin went into hiding, along with the rest of the cult. Two years later – during the turmoil of the attempted Bolshevik Revolution – the enemies of the *khlysty* made their move on the Russian royal family itself. Captured at Ipatiev House in Yekaterinburg, the cultists were eliminated, but other survivors of the vampiric purges, sent by their overlord Rasputin, came to the Romanov's aid. Alexei went into hiding, along with his father in darkness, the latter having made sure to fake the death of the young prince, while Anastasia, his sister, survived to continue the royal Romanov line, although the rest of her family did not.

The boy grew to manhood, but the vampirism affected him in ways that Rasputin could not have imagined, resulting in mutations that only occurred in one out of thousands, rather like the haemophilia he had suffered from in the first place. Alexei developed albinism and, rather than curing his haemophilia, the vampirism merely gave him an unusual means of compensating for it, the prince having to undergo regular and painful blood transfusions simply to maintain his cursed twilight existence.

Condemned to such a miserable and painful existence by the mad monk's actions, driven to the brink of madness by this endless torment, as Alexei grew so did his hatred of the man who had cursed him.

In time the 'son' had usurped the 'father' – as is the way of things – and his first act upon seizing control of what remained of the degenerate *khlysty* cult was to denounce Rasputin as their enemy, betrayer of them all, sentencing him to an eternity of incarceration. And so he had been interred within the deepest dungeon beneath the Winter Palace, the arcane machinery drip-feeding him the blood he needed to survive, but only enough to keep him alive to endure his eternal sentence, and never enough to give him the strength he needed to escape his bonds.

But after eight decades, Alexei had had enough of hiding in the shadows. And so, at last, he was re-born as Prince Vladimir of Bratsk – taking the name of the primogenitor of his vampiric bloodline and the cult's infamous forebear – ready to put into operation the plan that would deliver him the Imperial crown of Russia. But in his years in hiding, the scope of Alexei's ambition had grown. Russia was only to be the beginning.

It was with this knowledge that he had tormented his former mentor. The prince had taken pleasure in taunting the old man with his schemes, knowing that he would never be Rasputin's puppet now and that he had, in fact, become the puppet master.

"I can see where this is going," Ulysses said.

"He means to assassinate the Tsarina!"

"Indeed. And it's up to us to stop him."

CHAPTER FORTY-ONE

Cry Havoc

"We must away to Saint Petersburg," Ulysses said. "We don't have a moment to lose."

"But our quarry will not find the Tsarina Anastasia there," Katarina said, eyes flashing as she turned them on Ulysses.

"Then where is she?"

"She is due in Prague for a state visit."

"Of course!" Ulysses said, recalling the newsreel footage.

"And that is where he will have gone too."

Miranda stirred momentarily as Ulysses took her up in his arms but her eyes thankfully remained shut.

Without a moment's hesitation, the agent of the British throne and the agent of Imperial Russia – the dandy and the vampire – turned their backs on the damned monk and left Rasputin with only darkness for company.

* * *

The castle was eerily quiet. Ulysses, carrying Miranda, followed as Agent K led them through drawing rooms, solars, ballrooms, dining chambers and reception rooms; directing their way with such confidence that it was as if she was making use of some other sense beyond the accepted five.

In the stillness of the castle, the tapping of their hurrying heels on the polished marble floors, Ulysses' rasping breath and the beating of his own heart seemed traitorously loud.

"What was that?" he hissed, suddenly tensing.

Katarina skidded to a halt. "I cannot hear any –"

The blood-curdling howl cut through the still night air like a rapier blade.

"The wolves," she said, sniffing the air. "Come on. We have to keep moving. It is not far now."

They passed another ballroom and then they were through a glazed solar and into a battlemented courtyard. On the other side stood an ornate ironwork hangar, looking out over the forests beneath it.

Ulysses paused before the battlements and peered over them at the foot of the cliff a hundred feet below. Behind them, sheer walls of icy black rock rose up behind the palace, making it look as if the hawkish edifice had been sculpted from the face of the cliff itself.

Ulysses could see shapes moving in the shadows below. Sometimes they appeared as wolves and then, at other times, they looked more like men. From the way they kept following the same, regular, looping pattern through the trees and around the craggy protrusions, he would have said they were patrolling the castle grounds.

"Look at them all," he gasped. "There must be hundreds of the things."

"The pack are loyal to the prince and him alone," Katarina stated.

"Well, I for one am glad that we're travelling by air," Ulysses remarked. "I wouldn't fancy having to battle my way past that lot."

Katarina sniffed and spun round, her eyes fixed on something beyond Ulysses' head.

Ulysses turned, gasped and dropped to the ground, the child slipping from his arms onto the cold stones of the battlements..

Snarling, the man-beast sailed over their heads, having misjudged its leap from where it had been perched, gargoyle-like, atop a gothic window arch. It crashed onto the battlements in a flurry of grasping claws, raised hackles and murderous intent.

Ulysses' hand immediately went to his sword-stick and Katarina pulled a primed and loaded flintlock pistol from the bandolier of weapons strung across her chest.

The werewolf tensed to spring but then something slammed into it with the force of a cannonball.

Snarling and snapping at each other, the huge sabre-toothed cat and the werewolf tumbled over the battlements, the sharp crack of snapping branches reaching them a moment later as the creatures crashed through the canopy below.

A terrific trumpeting reverberated from the sheer walls of the rock face and Ulysses and Katarina both looked west as, with a groaning crash of falling timber, a bull mammoth smashed its way through the trees towards the Winter Palace. Clinging to a howdah lashed across its mighty shoulders was its Mongol handler and a team of warriors. Other war mammoths came after the bull, clad in armour and other creatures too; styracosaurs and hunting cats, slipping lithely between the lumbering pachyderms.

The wolves at the foot of the cliff rushed forward to meet the charge head-on and were the first to be savagely cut down, feline claws tearing them open from gizzard to gut, human-wolf intestines spilling into the snow, the hot ropes steaming. But the sabre-tooths did not stop to feast; at a command from their handlers they moved on to cull the next wave, those they had already wounded left lying in the snow to be crushed under the huge feet of the mammoths and the lumbering dinosaurs.

Snarls and roars echoed from the trees below.

Ulysses looked up. Black shapes crowded the sky too as great winged things approached the castle.

One of the huge pterosaurs swooped down over the battlements and, wings beating furiously, the rider alighted.

Ulysses could not help but smile as a hairy-faced mountain of a man dismounted and approached him with his great bear arms outstretched.

"Ulysses, my brother!" the warlord proclaimed.

"Targutai!" Ulysses said as the khan caught him up in a great bear-hug. Having half squeezed the life out of him, the warlord broke from their embrace.

"You smell worse than a yak's arse!"

"Do I? Sorry about that."

"But you are alive!" Targutai proclaimed delightedly, clasping Ulysses' shoulders again.

"It would appear so."

"And I have brought someone else with me who will be very pleased to see you."

The Khan stepped to one side.

Alighting from the back of a squawking pterosaur was a pale-faced and slightly shaking Nimrod. From his ashen expression, Ulysses guessed that his manservant hadn't particularly enjoyed the flight.

"Nimrod!" Ulysses exclaimed. "Boy, are you a sight for sore eyes!"

The two men took a step towards each other, Ulysses making as if to hug his ever-faithful manservant and Nimrod looking like he was about to do the same. Then they both paused and restrained themselves, settling instead for a firm handshake.

"It's good to see you, old boy," Ulysses said.

"And you, sir."

Then Targutai was at their sides, his huge arms encircling both of them around the shoulders. "It's thanks to this man here that we came at all."

"Really?" Ulysses said.

"Well, we hadn't heard from you for so long, sir," Nimrod mumbled.

"And he was bally-well worried, weren't you, old chap?" Targutai said.

"Well, I was a little," Nimrod said, his cheeks reddening.

"Kept badgering, day after day, trying to persuade me to come to your rescue."

Nimrod glowered at the warlord, who continued, oblivious or indifferent to the butler's discomfort. "So persistent was he, in the end I just had to give in, didn't I, what? Took us days to get here mind."

Below the battlements the cries of the Mongol warriors, the snarling voices of the wolves and the trumpeting of the mammoths all merged into the clamour of battle.

Within half an hour the howls of the routed pack were fading, as the first light of a new day painted the cliff-face behind them and Ulysses' mind returned to the chase.

Nimrod looked up as Ulysses boarded the prince's zeppelin and could hardly hide his concern. The dandy was still emaciated after days of malnutrition and his eyes were sunken within grey-ringed hollows. But nonetheless, he still looked one hundred percent better than he had done before.

Agent K had dressed her own wound and found herself a clean, undamaged, tunic from somewhere.

"Ready for the off then, are we?" Ulysses addressed those assembled within the airship. Katarina Kharkova was at the helm, making her final checks while Nimrod supervised a bucket-chain of Mongols loading the airship with all manner of supplies.

"Just about, sir," Nimrod said, happy to be back in the thick of things.

"Excellent! Excellent!" Ulysses replied.

"You're looking much better, sir, if I might say so."

"Thank you, Nimrod. You may say so. I must admit that I feel like a new man." He stopped and gazed out of the cockpit, through the yawning hangar doors, at the last vestiges of night that were slipping away over the horizon far to the west.

"We have a journey of thousands of miles ahead of us to stop Vladimir from murdering the crowned head of Russia. He has a five-hour head-start and is on board a train, whereas we are going to be travelling by airship. Do you think we can catch him in time?"

"Indubitably, sir."

"That's the spirit. Right then, Agent K, chocks away."

"Thanks again, my brother," Ulysses called from the open door of the cabin as the airship's engines ran up to speed and the dirigible was cleared of Mongols.

"Don't mention it, old boy! Wouldn't have missed it for the world, a battle like that," Targutai grinned back from his place on the battlements. "That was always the problem with this area – too many damned vampires and werewolves running about. Nimrod!" he shouted as Katarina slowly guided the zeppelin out of the hangar, "You're sure you won't stay? I would pay you a prince's ransom."

"Thank you, Khan, but I am afraid I shall have to politely decline your offer!" Nimrod shouted. "You've seen what happens when I let him out of my sight. Begging your pardon, sir."

"Not at all, old boy; not at all."

"Tally-ho!" Targutai shouted from the courtyard. "And good sailing!"

"Offered you a job, did he?" Ulysses said, a wry smile on his lips, as he waved at the Mongols ranged along the battlements before pulling the cabin door shut.

"Yes, sir," Nimrod said, his cheeks flushing.

"Tempted were you?"

"Well the pay was good."

"I can imagine."

"But I couldn't stomach the gaseous anal-exhalations of ruminants... I couldn't have stuck it, sir."

"Oh, I see. It was like that was it?"

"Yes, sir."

Ulysses returned to gazing out of the glass bubble of the cockpit. "Jolly good," he said, half under his breath as he gazed out at the endless expanse of the Central Siberian Plateau. "Jolly good."

CHAPTER FORTY-TWO

Blood Relative

The horse-drawn carriage rattled to a halt on the cobbles outside the imposing entrance to Prague Castle. A door opened and Ulysses Quicksilver got out. He looked very dapper in black tie and a red velvet-lined cape – a necessary indulgence considering he was about to be hobnobbing with the heads of state of at least half a dozen European countries. The only thing his outfit was lacking was a suitable mask for the ball he was about to infiltrate.

Second out of the carriage was Nimrod, wearing a fresh suit of anonymous black and grey that marked him out as a gentleman's valet.

His bloodstone-tipped cane in hand, his pistol loaded and holstered beneath his dinner jacket, Ulysses turned and addressed the two ladies remaining in the cab.

"Right, this is the plan. We'll have a gander inside, find the villain and stop him before he can harm the Tsarina. You stay here and watch the exit in case he tries to make a break for it. Okay?"

"Okay, Uncle Ulysses," Miranda replied. The colour had returned to her cheeks now and she didn't look as horribly emaciated as she had when they had discovered her hooked up to Vladimir's blood-letting machine. He gave her a warm smile and ruffled her hair.

"Are you sure you don't want me to come with you, and have your man stay here?" Katarina Kharkova suggested, fixing Ulysses with her baleful gaze.

Ulysses squeezed his eyes shut tight and shook his head. "Don't try that on me now. I'm not as susceptible as I was, you know."

The vampire looked away sulkily.

"I need you to keep an eye on our prize asset here," he said. "And if you have to look after yourself without back-up, you've got a much better chance in a fight against whatever Vladimir might have to throw at you."

"Good luck, Uncle Ulysses."

Ulysses turned and set off along the torch-lit path , joining the other well-dressed guests as they made their way inside for the evening's main event.

"Come on, Nimrod," he called back over his shoulder. "You're my plus one."

They had arrived in Prague only that morning. The journey from the Winter Palace had felt as though it had taken far too long. But at least the flight from Siberia had given them all a chance to recover their strength – Miranda and Ulysses most of all, considering what the former had been through and the sacrifice the latter had made to save her.

And yet there were more than simply physical scars to heal there and Ulysses was impressed by Miranda's mental fortitude in the face of all that she had had to bear.

But the length of journey had also meant that, upon arriving at the Czech capital, they had spent a frantic day doing their darnedest to discover the whereabouts of Prince Vladimir.

The dandy detective had decided against contacting the

authorities – he wasn't entirely convinced of the abilities of the police forces of Europe; London's Met was bad enough.

While Ulysses and Nimrod had raced about town – checking hotel reservations and train arrivals – Katarina had been left with the still recovering Miranda. By mid-afternoon, with time fast running out, Ulysses had realised that their only chance of stopping the murderous prince now was to be there in person, ready to leap into action when he made his move on the Tsarina Anastasia at the masked ball that was being held in her honour within Prague Castle. With that in mind he had paid a visit to the British consulate, playing on his reputation as the hero of the hour and using his royal-ratified ID to talk his way into an invitation to the royal function.

And so, back at the Ambassador Hotel they had held their own private council of war to formulate their plan of attack, or counter-attack as it was more likely to be.

"Any joy?" Ulysses asked as the two men re-convened in a balcony vestibule, looking down into the ballroom.

Having moved through the crowds of political animals, diplomats and other assorted VIPs, accepted a glass of champagne from a frighteningly realistic porcelain doll-faced serving droid, and made polite small talk, having failed to spot their quarry, the first opportunity they had, they decided to split up to track their prey instead. Between them they had explored every nook and cranny of the castle, moving among the hundreds of guests in the vain hope of locating one individual who was wearing a mask to conceal his identity and who no doubt knew that they were onto him.

"There's no sign of the devil, sir," Nimrod stated.

"Damn it all to buggery!" Ulysses swore. "I can't just stand here doing nothing, waiting for him to make his move!

"If only there was some way to force his hand, sir."

"Indeed, Nimrod."

Ulysses looked up from his musings, an expression of startled near-delight on his face.

"By Jove. I think I've got it!"

"What do you have in mind, sir?"

"Well you know what they say about desperate times, old boy."

"That they call for desperate measures, sir?"

"Well, they've never been more desperate."

"Ambassador!" Ulysses announced as he approached the cowering, weasel-faced man simpering and fawning before her majesty the Tsarina Anastasia III.

Ambassador Lionel Snelgrove looked round, his look of startled surprise quickly giving way to one of indignant annoyance. He had been waiting all night for the opportunity to ingratiate himself into the guest of honour's company and now that upper class twit from the mother country was here, making a fool of himself.

"Oh. Mr Quicksilver. What a pleasure it is," Snelgrove said. "I was just speaking with the Tsarina about our mutual concerns regarding the German issue. Your majesty, Ulysses Quicksilver, Esquire."

"Ah, good evening, Mr Quicksilver," the Tsarina said in heavily-accented English and offered him her hand.

Ulysses took it and, bending, laid a kiss upon her silk gloved fingers. "Enchanté."

"He's considered something of a hero back home in England," the ambassador went on.

"Ah, I see," the Tsarina said, smiling blankly, patently having no idea who Ulysses was.

"That's right, your majesty, and I would be grateful if you could bear that in mind," Ulysses said, giving her a rakish smile.

"I am sorry," the Tsarina replied, "my English is not so good. What do you mean?

"With everything that's about to happen."

"No, I am sorry, I still don't –"

In one fluid movement Ulysses pulled his pistol from its holster, grabbed the Tsarina and pulled her to him, putting the muzzle of his gun to her temple.

The Tsarina gave a stifled cry, while Ambassador Lionel Snelgrove and Nimrod gave gasps of disbelieving horror.

"I'm very sorry, your majesty," Ulysses said softly, "but you are now my hostage."

CHAPTER FORTY-THREE

Blood Simple

With gasps of horror, guests began to back away from Ulysses and his hostage.

There was a bustle of confusion and panic, and a barking of orders as the royal guard put lockdown procedures into action and that, Ulysses realised, meant that Prince Vladimir was locked in there with them.

Ulysses spun himself around with the Tsarina clasped in front of him, making sure that any have-a-go-heroes were in no doubt as to what would happen to the Tsarina if they tried anything.

"What do you think you are doing, man?" Ambassador Snelgrove protested

"What are you doing, sir?" Nimrod mouthed at him silently. Ulysses flashed his manservant a look loaded with meaning.

"Listen up, all of you!" Ulysses shouted. "Now I am sure that nobody here wants to see the Tsarina dead, so I would suggest that it would be most unwise of anybody to do anything rash.

So, first of all, I want everybody to drop any weapons they might be carrying."

There came a clatter as the anxious guardsmen shed themselves of their rifles and ceremonial swords.

"And the rest of you!" Ulysses said. "Very good. And now I would like your help with the small matter of an assassination attempt."

The masked guests looked at him and then at one another in bewilderment.

"I see you are confused. But you see there is a man here who wishes to see Her Majesty dead and I would ask this man to step forward now."

The atmosphere palpably thickened.

"No? Not going to do the honourable thing?" He sounded almost disappointed. "Prince Vladimir?"

Ulysses hesitated for a moment, giving the Machiavellian schemer a chance to step forward.

He didn't.

"Well, it was worth a try, I suppose. Then your various majesties, my lords, ladies and gentlemen, I would ask whether you might help me uncover this traitor. Please, take off your masks."

More murmurs passed through the ballroom but one by one the masks were removed.

"He shouldn't be too hard to spot. White hair, red eyes; stands out in a crowd rather. Nimrod, take some of these fine gentlemen," Ulysses indicated the twitchy guards, "and scour the crowds, would you?"

Nodding to a pair of guardsmen, Nimrod did as he was instructed and started moving through the assembled onlookers, searching out their prey.

Ulysses' attention was directed towards the area beneath a large stained-glass window as guards converged on the spot. Cries of alarm came from those nearby, and a new space formed within the ballroom as the tide of people shifted, desperately moving out of the way of the scuffle.

There were more shouts of protest and then four steely-faced guards, led by a determined Nimrod, frogmarched their white-haired, white-skinned, red-eyed captive towards the spot where Ulysses stood, the Tsarina still in his grasp.

"Ah, there you are, Prince Vladimir – or should I say Tsarevich Alexei Romanov?"

The albino stiffened.

"Alexei?" the Tsarina gasped and, knowing that his work with her was done, Ulysses lowered his gun and released his hold. "Great-uncle Alexei?" The Tsarina took a step towards the captive albino, her scrutinising eyes uncovering the family likeness lurking there.

"You're no niece of mine. I have no family, pretender!" he spat.

"Search him, quickly," Ulysses ordered. "He will be armed I can assure you."

Relief flooded through Ulysses. He and Nimrod had revealed the villain and saved the day – again.

With a crash, the great stained-glass window exploded inwards, a hail of tiny shards of rainbow glass whirling through the air.

Women screamed and men cried out in alarm. There, crouched within the fractured glass remains was something large and lupine. The beast had something slight and limp flung over one massive, muscular and fur-covered shoulder.

In a single bound the werewolf left the ruins of the window and landed lithely in the middle of the ballroom, not ten feet from the captured Alexei.

It was only then that Ulysses could see properly what it was that it had brought into the castle with it.

The feral thing fixed Ulysses with a savage glare, one eye burning an angry red, the socket of the other scarred, the eye it held cataract white. A growl escaped from the monster's jaws and it almost seemed to Ulysses as if the creature were laughing.

The beast released its hold on the child's body, letting Miranda fall to the floor.

Ulysses put his hand to the bloodstone hilt of his sword. But in the end it was Alexei, and not the wolf, that made the first move.

With a roar of anger and frustration, Alexei threw off his guards and sprang towards the astonished Tsarina, pulling something from a jacket pocket as he did so.

Ulysses' horrified gaze darted from the werewolf to the syringe now in the vampire's hand, saw the fluid contained within, saw Alexei's thumb ready on the end of the plunger and, in that split second, made his choice.

In a single fluid motion Ulysses turned his gun on the raging madman, and fired.

The was a sharp crack as the bullet hit the hypodermic needle, exploding the glass, and the blood agent it contained.

CHAPTER FORTY-FOUR

Kill or Cure

As droplets of blood filled the air around them, Alexei and the Tsarina couldn't help but breathe the red vapour.

The crack of the gunshot had shattered the tension of the moment and people fled from the ensuing chaos, those behind pushing those in front out of the way. Some threw themselves to the ground, but most charged for the doors.

People were crushed in the stampede to escape as they came up against locked doors. Bones were broken. One of the guards died under the press of people desperately trying to force the door. The panicking crowd were now significantly more of a danger to themselves, than either the megalomaniacal vampire prince or his hulking one-eyed Cossack lycanthrope guard.

There was the splintered crash of a door being forced as ornaments and statuary were employed in opening suitable escape routes.

As the screaming guests fled, they left behind them, in the middle of the ballroom, a cluster of eight desperate individuals.

There was Ulysses Quicksilver, rapier blade in hand as he faced the heaving mass of the transformed Cossack, hunkered down over the motionless body of the child. Then there was the quivering wreck that was all that remained of Ambassador Snelgrove, a pool of piss spreading across the polished marble floor at his feet.

Out of the corner of his eye Ulysses saw one of the guards rush to the Tsarina's side as she coughed and gagged. Nimrod looked on too, trying to work out whether to try to pull the child clear, go to the aid of the choking Tsarina, or take the fight to Alexei.

Which qualified as more valuable, the life of the Tsarina of Russia or the clone-child of the Empress of Magna Britannia?

As Ulysses and the wolf began to circle one another, the Tsarina's and her attacker's condition continued to deteriorate. The Tsarina's breathing had become a rasping gasp, while Alexei was wheezing horribly, the agent working its ill-effects on both of them.

Alexei appeared to be suffering the most. For a second he locked his gaze with Ulysses, a mad look in his wild red eyes, accusing and horrified at the same time.

"Nimrod, see to the Tsarina," Ulysses said, not once taking his eyes off the werewolf. "You know what to do."

Nimrod obeyed at once. Kneeling down beside the stricken Anastasia, he pulled his own hypodermic needle from a jacket pocket and – silencing any protests the guard might be thinking of making with a glare – wasted no time in finding a suitable vein.

Ulysses noticed the vampire staring at the unconscious Miranda. His throat tightened in dread.

Alexei threw himself upon the child and, before anyone could stop him, sank his teeth into her neck. Blood, rich and red, oozed from around Alexei's lips and, with a great slurping, sucking sound he began to feed.

Ulysses lunged for Alexei, but the werewolf's swing hit him squarely in the stomach, punching the air from his body and sending him hurtling backwards.

The beast followed him across the room and crouched over

him. The feral stink of its blood-matted fur was sharp in Ulysses' nose and made him want to gag. But the wolf did not finish him. Its snout mere inches from the dandy's face, its eyes – one seeing, one blind – locked with his, Ulysses could see its lips curling back from its fangs as if it were smiling.

Sword-stick still in hand Ulysses thrust the blade upwards, into the monster's heaving ribs, hoping to find its heart.

The werewolf gave a savage roar, and then, lashing out, snapped its jaws closed around Ulysses' head.

Or at least it would have done, had Nimrod not got there first with the cast-iron candelabra.

The wolf bit down hard on the unyielding iron and there was a crack as several teeth broke. The candles spluttered out and tumbled to the floor.

The werewolf yowled again and turned its attention to Nimrod, who was swinging the heavy iron candelabra to defend himself. Against the sheer mass and power of the werewolf Nimrod was losing.

Ulysses was able to pull himself clear and he was on his feet again in seconds.

And then the Tsarina's bodyguard was there at Nimrod's side, thrusting the legs of a chair at the werewolf's muzzle.

With both Nimrod and the bodyguard keeping the Cossack busy, Ulysses turned his attention back to the Tsarina, the child and the vampire.

He noticed then that the Tsarina's condition thankfully appeared to be improving. She sat at the edge of a dais, staring in horror at the bloodletting of the child taking place before her.

Knuckles whitening around the pommel of his rapier, Ulysses turned eyes blazing with barely-contained anger on the guzzling leech-thing.

Alexei suddenly sprang back from the child, letting her pallid form slip onto the floor. Standing tall, the prince wiped the back of his hand across his blood-stained mouth.

A wild look was in his eyes, and a cruel smile split his face.

"I win! I have done what I set out to do!" he shouted. "The Tsarina is dead, long live the Tsar! Today Russia, tomorrow... the world!"

"Are you sure about that?" Ulysses challenged, nodding towards the recovering Anastasia.

The vampire tensed and a look of panic entered his blood-red eyes

"It must just take a moment to take effect."

Alexei suddenly doubled up in pain. He fell to his knees and threw back his head, giving voice to an agonised howl, veins throbbing at his temples and in his neck.

"But the cure!" he spluttered.

"Ah yes, you mean the one Nimrod just administered to her royal highness. Appears to be rather effective as it happens. Thank God."

"But the child..." Gagging, Alexei began to shake violently.

"You're right, of course, she was the cure, but note my use of the past tense. I'll tell you what happened, shall I?"

It seemed to Ulysses, as the vampire fixed him with a look of black hatred, that Alexei's face was swelling like a balloon. His eyes were bulging painfully and his skin was flushed, as if engorged with blood.

"When we found her, after what you and that bastard Pavlov had done to her, she was dying; the blood loss had just been too great. So you know what we did? We had to give her a blood transfusion, or rather I did, to be precise. Took it out of me too, I can tell you, but the blood flowing through her veins now is Quicksilver blood. The last sample of her own blood, the cure, my man just used on the Tsarina."

"You..." the vampire gasped.

"Bad luck."

Alexei's nose began to bleed and blood began to leak from his tear ducts, running down his face in crimson tears. Finally, in a torrent of internal haemorrhaging, filthy black liquid poured from his trousers as blood gushed from his bowels.

"Curse you!" Alexei screamed. His final words were transformed into one protracted howl of pain and bitter hatred.

Ulysses found himself unable to tear his eyes from the vampire as every last drop of blood escaped him, his body withering, white flesh becoming grey as his eyes disappeared back into their sockets before melting and pouring from his face.

As the vampire's desiccating corpse crumbled into flakes of skin and grey dust Ulysses smiled, the look in his eyes as cold as marble.

"Have a nice death now, won't you?"

CHAPTER FORTY-FIVE

Children of the Night

Ulysses turned to the child lying at his feet and his expression softened into one of almost parental anxiety.

He knelt down beside her. Blood soaked her clothes and matted her hair.

He put two fingers to her neck and waited for what seemed like a long time before he felt the faint flicker of a pulse. He knelt closer, his cheek practically touching her partially open mouth, and felt the faintest breeze of a breath. She was going to live, he was sure of it.

"Over here, your majesty," Ulysses called to the stunned Tsarina. She stared at him in bewildered shock, but then got to her feet. "I need you to apply pressure to the wound," he said, taking off his jacket, tearing out its lining and placing the folded pad of silk over the bite.

Moving as if in a trance, the Tsarina made her way over to where Ulysses crouched and did as she was told.

Hearing a crash of splintering wood and a change in the pitch of the wolf's snarling behind him, Ulysses turned to see the Tsarina's bodyguard fall back before the cornered beast.

"Bad dog!" Ulysses snarled, as he strode across the room.

The beast turned, fixing him with its single blazing red eye.

"What are you going to do now?" Ulysses goaded. "Your master's dead and you've been a *very – bad – dog.*"

With one almighty bound, the huge creature launched itself at the wall, its powerful leap carrying it to within a claw's grasp of the broken window frame and, with another bound, it was gone into the night.

"Come on!" Ulysses ordered his manservant as he started to move towards a door. "We can't let that thing run riot through the streets of the city. We have to stop it."

He suddenly hesitated, looking back to where Miranda lay cold and motionless on the floor of the ballroom, with the Tsarina doing her best to staunch the blood.

"Look after her," he told the Tsarina. And then turned to address the still reeling bodyguard. "Stay with them," he said. "Keep them safe. And don't worry, we'll be back."

Ulysses sprinted into the square to be confronted with the brutality of the werewolf's handiwork.

The cab they had arrived in lay on its side, the carriage door torn off its hinges. The horse lay dead, still in its traces, its throat ripped out. The driver lay on the grass beyond.

Ulysses ran to the wreck and, pulling himself up on top of it, peered inside. Katarina was gone.

A scream cut through the night.

"This way!" Ulysses said, setting off down the steps that ran parallel to the castle.

He hesitated only briefly at the bottom, scanning the streets around him for any sign of the werewolf. Black blood glistened in the greasy orange gas-glow of a streetlamp.

The two hunters passed the ornamented facade of the High Baroque Church of St Nicholas, past the gently decaying squares and once picturesque palaces, churches and gardens that lay on either side the Mostecká bridge street, until the trail of blood spots and screams brought them within sight of the pitch-roofed towers that marked one end of the Charles Bridge.

A thick mist was rising from the river. Hearing a snarling ahead of him, Ulysses knew they had caught up with the wolf at last.

Through the mist he could now see two shadows circling one another; one tall and heavily-muscled, the other svelte and female.

Ulysses started to run, Nimrod hot on his heels.

As the dandy closed the distance between them he watched as the wolf made sweeping lunges for the woman as she spun and danced out of the brute's way. Ulysses heard yowls of pain as the blade in her hand moved in darting, sweeping strokes and stabbing lunges, finding its mark again and again.

With a savage roar the werewolf sprang, catching the swordswoman as she made her own flying leap, bowling her across the bridge.

Ulysses had his own sword in hand now, not daring to use his pistol when he might hit either friend or foe.

There came a sudden savage snarl from the beast which didn't quite cover the ghastly ripping noise that sounded unmistakably like flesh being torn open.

Slowly the monster rose up on its hind-legs and turned to face the approaching dandy. Agent Katarina Kharkova lay spread-eagled on the cold cobbles and didn't move.

The Cossack gave Ulysses a bloody smile. Its furious red-eyed gaze seemed to burn through the mist.

Suddenly, to Ulysses, his sword didn't seem like the right tool to finish the job. He had plunged several inches of its tempered steel into the brute's chest already and it barely seemed to have bothered it. It certainly didn't appear to have caused it any lasting harm. But what else was he going to do.

"Come on then, you Cossack bastard!" he shouted. "Let's finish this right here, right now!"

The beast sprang.

Ulysses was already spinning out of its way as it landed and laid the edge of his blade across its broad shoulders. The wolf snarled in pain and twisted, lashing out at the dandy with raking claws. The tip of one bony talon snagged Ulysses' dinner jacket, tearing through the fabric.

The beast lunged again and Ulysses took another dancing step backwards, bringing his blade down this time on the monster's wrist. It howled in pain, but followed with a clubbing swipe of its other meaty paw, that sent Ulysses stumbling into the side of the bridge.

A pistol crack sounded from somewhere close by, curiously deadened by the fog. The werewolf's head snapped sideways, blood spraying from the ragged remains of one ear. The brute reeled, recovered and then launched itself in the direction of this new threat as another pistol shot echoed from the walls of the bridge.

"Nimrod!" Ulysses bellowed as he pushed himself away from the wall, hurling himself after the monster, the sword-stick gripped tight in his hand becoming an extension of his arm as he lashed out again. This time he caught the werewolf across its flank.

The enraged beast turned once more, unsure which attacker to take on first, being goaded as it was by both the dandy and his manservant.

Ulysses stumbled to a halt behind the transformed Cossack, almost losing his balance and coming dangerously within reach of its muscular arms.

Something flashed silver in the suffused glow of one of the gas-lamps that lined the bridge. Out of the corner of his eye Ulysses caught a glimpse of spidery movement as something clambered up over the side of the bridge and onto the cobbles behind the beast.

With a snarl the werewolf went for Ulysses –

– as the Ripper pounced too.

The Ripper-thing landed on the brute's broad back, the weight of it sending the werewolf stumbling forward as Ulysses threw himself out of its way.

"Slice and dice," he heard the cackling voice say as it set to work with its silver-coated blades.

A terrible sound escaped the monster's jaws and the beast arched its back; its body contorting in agony as the razor-sharp knives of the automaton dug and gouged at its unnatural flesh.

Where the blades cut the werewolf's body the flesh burned. Blood bubbled from its wounds, only to hiss and evaporate at the Ripper's continued caresses.

The Ripper worked fast, hacking and snapping at the creature's body with its scissoring blades. An ear flew here, a piece of pelt there.

The werewolf pawed at the thing latched, limpet-like, to its back, eventually managing to get a grip on the automaton. With a bellow of fury and pain the creature hurled the cyber-organic assassin clear across the bridge, the Ripper's bladed hands tearing through its flesh.

The Ripper clattered across the cobbles and came to a sudden stop, crouched on all of its multi-jointed limbs. A split second later it sprang back onto the werewolf and set to work again.

The beast was weakening now. As Ulysses watched, it seemed to him that the werewolf was shrinking in stature as it slumped to its knees. The werewolf's fur was disappearing back into follicles in its skin, its long lupine feet and ankles re-shaping themselves into something more human.

In one deft move, the Ripper-thing put a pair of blades against the werewolf's flesh and slit its throat from ear to ear.

A final, gurgling cry bubbled up from somewhere within the beast's chest as thick, black blood bubbled from the fatal wound. The Cossack fell face-first onto the ground and did not move. As the dead man's blood steamed in the cold night air, the cyborg scuttled clear of the corpse, fixing Ulysses with a sinister needling stare.

"Goodbye, silver man," the Ripper giggled, a sly smile bisecting its face. Then, it darted back over the side of the bridge and was gone.

For a moment Ulysses almost considered following his saviour but then thought better of it. He turned and hurried to the side of Agent K.

"Ulysses? Ulysses, is that you?"

"I'm here."

"I think it is my turn to die now," she said.

"You're not going to die," Ulysses told her.

"I have lived a long time, Ulysses."

"And you're going to outlive all of us."

"No, not this time, I think."

"You're not going to die!"

"Hold me, Ulysses. I do not want to die alone."

"I'm here. I'm holding you," he told her. "But you're not going to die. You're not going to die!" he hissed urgently into her hair as he held her close, cradling her head as she pressed her face into the hollow of his neck.

CHAPTER FORTY-SIX

Brave New World

Under a clear blue sky, a Rolls Royce Mark IV Silver Phantom rolled along the private road that led to a large Gothic pile set within sixteen acres of flat green fields, oak and beech-studded woodland.

It was some weeks after the traumatic events surrounding the attempted assassination of the Tsarina and the late April sun shone like an irradiated pearl, giving the mansion a honeyed glow.

"Do you think she'll be alright here?" Ulysses asked his driver.

"Indubitably, sir," his manservant replied, although there was a certain anxious tension in his face, despite his suggestion to the contrary.

Ulysses turned to regard Miranda, the uniform she was wearing making her appear suddenly three years older.

"Now, you're sure you've got everything?"

"Yes, I told you, Uncle Ulysses; I'm sure," Miranda Gallowglass replied.

"You've got all your games kit?"

"Yes, Uncle Ulysses."

"And your hockey stick? Tennis racket?"

"They're in the boot."

"You'll remember to brush your teeth?" Nimrod threw in.

"Don't worry, Nimrod, I will."

"And wash behind your ears."

"I will."

"And don't forget to keep your fingernails clean."

"I won't."

"And do remember to write," Ulysses told her.

"Every Saturday."

"Have you got your toothbrush?"

"Yes."

"And you've got my personal communicator number, and Nimrod's, should you need anything?"

"Yes."

"Anything at all, you understand?"

"Look, don't worry, Uncle Ulysses. It's going to be fine. In fact, I'm looking forward to it."

"We probably sound like a pair of old women, don't we?" Ulysses said, smiling.

"Speak for yourself, sir," Nimrod said.

There in the shadow of the school chapel a black limousine, was already parked. Its blacked out windows and lack of number plates immediately told Ulysses that it was a Ministry car. Nimrod pulled up alongside it, turned off the engine and got out, opening the rear passenger door for Miranda to exit the vehicle as Ulysses let himself out.

A middle-aged woman awaited them at the foot of the steps which led to the grand entrance. She was grey-haired, dressed in a tweed twin-set and pearls and had the physique of a beanpole. Standing next to her, his face set in a disgruntled grimace was a large man – thickset, darkly handsome, rugged in the classic sense of the word, looking like the quintessential English country gent in his tweed jacket and breeches.

As Nimrod unloaded Miranda's trunk and a plethora of other luggage, Ulysses guided the suddenly hesitant child towards the steps and the prim and proper headmistress.

It was Lord Octavius De Wynter who spoke first.

"Quicksilver," he said curtly.

"De Wynter," Ulysses replied.

"I'd like you to meet Miss Haversham."

"Mr Quicksilver, a pleasure to meet you," the middle-aged woman said, bending stiffly and offering Ulysses her hand. He took it and was momentarily startled by the force of the headmistress's handshake.

"Likewise," he replied.

"And this must be Miss Gallowglass," Miss Haversham said, turning to Miranda and offering her hand. Miranda took it uncertainly and bobbed a curtsey, blushing nervously.

"Oh, how charming," she said.

"What do you say?" Ulysses prompted.

"Good morning, Miss Haversham."

"Good morning, my dear," the headmistress said.

"Thank you ever so much for finding Miranda a place here at your school," Ulysses said.

"Oh, it was the least I could do after all she's been through," the woman said. "I am sure that St Trinnian's will be lucky to have her."

"Thank you."

"Thank you, Miss Haversham," Miranda parroted.

"Now then, my dear, I must introduce you to your housemistress. After all, lessons are already well underway and we need to get you to your dormitory and unpacked before the lunch bell. Gentlemen, if you will excuse us."

"Of course," smiled De Wynter.

Putting a guiding hand on the girl's shoulder, the headmistress took Miranda under her wing and led her towards the open front door.

Ulysses watched them go.

When she was halfway up the steps Miranda suddenly stopped and, slipping out from beneath the headmistress's guiding hand, skipped back down the steps to where the two men stood watching. Flinging her arms around Ulysses she caught him in a great bear-hug, squeezing him tight.

"Goodbye, Uncle Ulysses," she said through the tears now streaming down her cheeks and, standing on tiptoes, planted a kiss on his cheek.

"Goodbye, Uncle Octavius," she called to De Wynter, and then turning her gaze on Ulysses, blew him a kiss.

Then she turned and was gone at last.

"Right. Job done," De Wynter said. "Walk with me, Quicksilver."

As Nimrod struggled up the steps after the departing Miss Haversham and Miranda, dragging the child's trunk and other belongings, Ulysses and De Wynter set off at a gentle stroll .

"Thank you for arranging the place for her here," Ulysses said.

"Look here, Quicksilver, I'm not here to make small talk and I don't want your thanks. You're lucky we're even having this conversation."

"What do you mean?" Ulysses said, taken aback.

"What did you think you were doing?"

"I'm sorry?"

"When I expressly told you to leave the matter alone?"

"Ah, I see. You mean following up the Russian connection."

"Of course I bloody well mean following up the Russian connection!"

"Now hang on a minute, I saved the day!"

"You think you're some kind of hero? You made a bloody shambles of things is what you did."

"But thanks to me another dangerous megalomaniac was thwarted before he could put his damnable scheme into operation, not to mention that Tsarina Anastasia of Russia is still alive, thanks to me."

De Wynter stopped walking and turned to look at Ulysses with a face like thunder. "You put a loaded gun to her head!"

"It was the only thing I could think to do to save her life. I would never have pulled the trigger."

"But she didn't know that! I've spent half my time since your return trying to smooth things over with the Russians and they're still not happy. They want your balls over this and if it wasn't for the apparent soft spot the Queen seems to have for you, you'd be languishing in some Russian gulag by now!"

"Oh. I see."

"I told you to leave the Gallowglass case well alone."

Silence descended between them.

There was obviously nothing Ulysses could say to make things any better.

But as quickly as it had arisen, the storm passed. De Wynter took out his pipe and began to fill it. He turned and gazed out across the courts where two teams of teenage girls were trooping out into the sunshine for a game of netball.

"Your actions may only have delayed the inevitable," De Wynter said as he gazed into the distance, as if to some secret horror that was lurking there just out of sight, beyond the horizon.

"I beg your pardon?"

"War is coming."

"Oh. I see."

"Dark times lie ahead, and of one thing you can be certain, things will never be the same again."

Managing to light the wad of tobacco at last, De Wynter gave it a few puffs and then, exhaling a great cloud of smoke said, "Does she know what she really is?"

Ulysses found himself glancing back to the grand facade of St Trinnian's and wondering when he would see Miranda again.

"What, that she was only created to be the cure to a lethal bio-weapon or that she's a clone of Queen Victoria?"

De Wynter gave a grunt that might even have been something like laughter.

"Don't you think she's been through enough already?"

"Good. Let's keep it that was then shall we?"

"With pleasure."

At a shrill blast from the games mistress's whistle, the netball match got under way.

"She'll be alright you know," De Wynter said.

"I know."

"It's a very good school."

"Yes, I know."

"And we'll be keeping a close eye on her."

"I'm sure you will."

"Anyway, I can't spend all day talking to you. I have a meeting back in London."

He turned and set off back across the green sward, leaving Ulysses watching the netball game, his mind swimming with a whole host of new concerns.

"You know that holiday we talked about," De Wynter suddenly added, turning back to face Ulysses for a moment. "Now might be a good time to get away, don't you think? But somewhere further away this time, where you can't get into any trouble, at least until all the fuss and furore has died down a bit."

"My brother's recently moved to the Moon," Ulysses offered.

"Perfect," De Wynter returned. "Can't stand the place myself. No atmosphere," he said, and obviously meant it. There wasn't any hint of mirth in either his expression or his tone.

As the head of Department Q made for his waiting limousine, Ulysses went over what his employer had said again, one nagging thought coming to mind more than any other.

Things will never be the same again.

"Well, you got that right," Ulysses said, putting a hand to the cravat that was hiding the two small yet distinct puncture marks that were still healing in the side of his neck.

"How right you are, indeed."

He could feel her inside him now. What it just childish fancy or did the two of them really share a unique bond? Just as there was a bond of blood between him and Miranda now, it was his blood that had saved the vampire.

Even though she had been prepared to die, Ulysses had offered his blood willingly, after all that she had done, and Katarina had drunk deeply. He had been on the verge of losing consciousness when Nimrod had stepped in and pulled him away from the voracious vampire.

After that she had slept the sleep of the dead, and had remained in that state for four days. Ulysses had split his time between her bedside, in their suite at the Ambassador, and that of the child. Miranda's recovery astounded them all, so much so that Ulysses wondered whether her erstwhile father and Dr Doppelganger hadn't added something else to their incredible science experiment.

On the fifth day, Ulysses woke to find himself still in the chair by the vampire's bed, a blanket draped over him, and Katarina gone. He hadn't seen her since, but he still fancied he could feel her inside him, and the scars of her feeding remained.

He had done a little probing, curious to know what consequences there might be to having a vampire feed on him, and of course Miranda had suffered the same indignity, but he had been assured by those with more knowledge on the subject than he that as long as they had not ingested vampiric blood themselves they would remain unchanged. He certainly didn't feel any aversion to sunlight and didn't have a craving for raw steak, but, as the netball game advanced before his dead-eyed stare, Ulysses Quicksilver couldn't shake the feeling that De Wynter had been right.

Things would never be the same again.

The footman, looking splendid in the livery of the Inferno Club, opened the door and admitted Ulysses to the small, opulently decorated room beyond. "If you would like to wait in here, sir?"

He tipped the youth who bowed graciously – "Thank you, sir." – and pulled the door closed behind him.

Alone again, Ulysses made himself comfortable in the padded leather armchair and fixed the large, gilt mirror with a needling stare.

"Hello?" he said, after a few minutes had passed. "Anybody there?"

"Good evening, Mr Quicksilver."

"Ah, Hermes, there you are."

"You wanted to speak with me."

"Yes, as it happens." Ulysses continued to stare at his own mirror image, imagining who it might be that lay behind the glass. "I played your little game and now I want some answers. I take it that the outcome of my trip to the continent was to your liking."

"As I said at our first meeting, it was in both our interests that you get to the bottom of the mystery."

"Right, and considering what my little jaunt cost me, by my reckoning you owe me some answers."

For several long seconds the speaker beneath the mirror remained silent before humming into life again.

"What do you want to know."

"Let's start with Pavlov. What was he doing offing royals on the Isle of Wight?"

"As I explained, he was trying to recreate Dr Gallowglass's work."

"But why take such risks? Why expose himself like that?"

"He was desperate. He had not managed to secure the necessary formula from the good doctor before Gallowglass set about destroying all evidence of what he had done."

"But I still don't understand."

"Really? Tell me, what did you find in the dungeons of the Winter Palace, other than the child."

"You know about Rasputin?"

"I know that Tsarevich Alexei Romanov had kept him alive for close to eighty years in perpetual torment as punishment for condemning his to his twilight existence. If you had been in Dr Pavlov's shoes, would you not have done all you could to stay on the right side of him?"

"But he still failed his master."

"He also showed great determination."

"Very well. Moving on to Gallowglass, there's something that's troubled me more than anything else about this case and that is what was Victor doing creating a weapon that could kill the Queen? And what was Dr Doppelganger doing helping him?"

"Ah, now you've hit the nail on the head. Why would two eminent and trusted physicians work to bring about the collapse of the empire?"

"That's what I'm asking you?"

"Answer me this," the disembodied voice went on, "why do you believe Miranda Gallowglass was kidnapped?"

"Blackmail, pure and simple. Somebody felt compelled to force him to complete his work?"

"Very good. Meaning...?"

"Meaning that Gallowglass was working on the Caliban weapon against his will."

"Precisely."

"So it is possible that Dr Doppelganger was in the same position."

"You might think that; I could not possibly comment."

"But what could anyone have over her? And who is this mysterious blackmailer anyway?"

"That, as they say, is the sixty four thousand guinea question."

Ulysses had the distinct feeling that there was only so much Hermes was prepared to divulge and that he was probably pushing his luck probing much further. But there was still one more aspect of the mystery that puzzled him.

"The Ripper," he said. "It murdered Gallowglass, it tried to kill me, then it didn't and then it ended up saving my life. What was all that about?"

"Gallowglass had blown his cover and had to be silenced."

"By the blackmailer, you mean?"

"You might think that; I could not possibly comment."

"And he was trying to confuse the killer – and whoever set it on him – by apparently destroying the bio-weapon when he had in fact sent it to me. But that still doesn't explain how it changed its tune so suddenly when it had me up against a wall, as it were."

"You have friends in high places, Mr Quicksilver –"

"I know that."

"– and you are useful to them."

"How high are we talking here?" Ulysses asked, fingers steepling before his face.

The speaker remained silent.

"Hello? Are you still there? I said, how high?"

Still nothing. Realising that the interview was over Ulysses rose and left the room without further ado. It was only as the door click shut behind him again that Hermes' voice whispered from behind the mirror, "Higher than you could ever know, my boy."

"I think we can say that the trial was a complete success, don't you?" Lord Octavius De Wynter said as he peered through the inches thick glass panel at the cyborg, secured within its harness and in a state of near suspended animation once more.

"Yes, sir," the chief technician replied.

"And it appears to have come through relatively unscathed."

"Yes, what damage it sustained was relatively superficial."

"And with our new measures in place, we won't be having any more potentially embarrassing repeat performances with regard to the offing of street-walkers now, will we?"

"No, none whatsoever," Xavier Sixsmith assured him.

"I wonder why it did that in the first place."

"Old habits die hard," the technician said. "It was following previously established patterns of behaviour. You can hardly blame it really. After all, that is why the subject was chosen for this venture."

"How right you are," De Wynter said. "Aberline did a good job with that one. Just a shame the world will never know that the inspector really did always get his man."

"What about Quicksilver?" Sixsmith interrupted.

"What about him?"

"He must have his suspicions. He's not going to let this one lie, is he?"

"Leave Quicksilver to me."

Sixsmith opened his mouth to speak again and then caught the look in De Wynter's eyes and thought better of it.

The towering presence of a man turned to the technician again. "And the other units?"

"Ten are already in production, sir, with another ten to follow as soon as Dr Doppelganger has been able to cultivate enough cloned cerebral tissue."

"Brains, you mean."

"Yes, sir, brains."

"Excellent." De Wynter turned and strode away from the vault, leaving the technician and Xavier Sixsmith to their own dark thoughts. "As you were, gentlemen. I must be off; matters of state await."

Secured behind eighteen inches of solid steel, the Ripper slept within its sepulchral vault, while visions of street-walkers danced in its head.

"Slice and dice, little red bag," it whispered in its sleep as its knife-fingers twitched. "Slice and dice."

> *How many goodly creatures are there here!*
> *How beauteous mankind is! O brave new world,*
> *That has such people in't.*
> (*The Tempest*, Act 5, Scene 1)

THE END

Ulysses Quicksilver will return in *Pax Britannia: Dark Side.*

Jonathan Green lives and works in West London. He is well known for his contributions to the *Fighting Fantasy* range of adventure gamebooks, as well as his novels set within Games Workshop's worlds of *Warhammer* and *Warhammer 40,000*.

He has written fiction for such diverse properties as *Sonic the Hedgehog, Doctor Who, Star Wars: The Clone Wars* and *Teenage Mutant Ninja Turtles*.

He is also the creator of Pax Britannia and *Blood Royal* is his fifth novel for Abaddon and the sixth in the series.

If you would like to find out more about the world of *Pax Britannia*, set your Babbage engine's ether-relay to **www.paxbritanniablog.blogspot.com**

PAX BRITANNIA

White Rabbit

Jonathan Green

Abaddon
Books

WWW.ABADDONBOOKS.COM

I

1901

The door opened and the single candle within the shuttered room guttered in the breeze. The door was closed again quietly and the new arrival joined the four men already seated around the table.

"What news, doctor?" one asked.

"The Queen is dying, Prime Minister," the new arrival replied.

"Then it is as we suspected," said another.

"I fear so."

For a moment nobody said anything, the silence disturbed only by the ticking of a clock on the mantelpiece above the cold hearth.

"Then the Angel of Death hovers over Osborne House, even now," said a third.

"Do you have to be so bloody elegiac?" snapped the first.

"Sorry, Prime Minister. But I am Poet Laureate, you know?"

"There are dark days ahead of us; the darkest. The Queen is adored – venerated even. With Her Majesty gone, with the figurehead of our great and honourable nation lost to us, the rot will soon set in."

"You speak as if she's already dead, Salisbury," the second said.

"She is as good as, is she not?"

"There is nothing more *I* can do, certainly," the doctor added. "And I doubt there is more *anyone* could do for her."

"'You are old, Father William'," the second added with a smile.

"Really!" the first fumed. "I hardly think that comments like that are appropriate at a time like this!"

"You do not know your Carroll then?"

"What? You would talk of childhood nonsense at a time like this? What's wrong with you man?"

"It's one of Her Majesty's favourites. Did you not know?"

"And what, sir, is the relevance of this bowdlerising?"

"I was merely making the point that age is nothing but a number, thinking that we might look for inspiration elsewhere."

"She is an old woman," the first stated emphatically. "She is eighty-one years old. She has reigned for an unparalleled sixty-three years. She is tired and she is ill. She is not long for this world."

"And what happens when she is gone?"

"Why, all the nations of the world will be circling the corpse of our once great empire ready to move in for the kill."

"Precisely. The glory days of the British Empire – our Magna Britannia – will be over. Our noble Queen is not known as the grandmother of Europe for nothing. Her descendants will all consider themselves owed a piece of pie when the greatest monarch the world has ever known goes into the ground at last."

"That is the future as I see it, yes," confirmed the first.

"But what if Her Majesty were not to die?" The second left the thought hanging.

"Man, you're talking nonsense again. This is poppycock! You talk in riddles like your beloved Carroll."

The second turned to the doctor. "You said that there is nothing more you can do for her, doctor."

"That is right, sir."

"I would beg to dispute that fact."

"I beg your pardon?" the doctor managed.

"Quicksilver," the second said, addressing the last member of the party seated at the table, a portly middle-aged gentleman with wire-rimmed spectacles, "would you care to explain?"

"Gladly," Erasmus Quicksilver replied.

He shuffled to his feet and straightened the front of his frock coat. His moment had come at last.

"Gentleman, during Her Majesty's glorious reign we have seen advances in science and medicine that we could not have predicted when she first came to the throne. Now we have Babbage's Analytical Engine, the Lovelace Paradigm and we have even taken the first steps in cybernetics. There are even those who say that, in another sixty years, we'll all be living on the Moon. Who knows what another hundred years of such scientific advances will bring? Perhaps we will even be able to create perfect replicas of living human beings from the smallest samples of biological tissue."

"And your point is?" the first fumed.

"My point is that the Queen need not die."

For a moment nobody spoke.

"But you said it yourself, man," the Prime Minister managed at last, "that such accomplishments are all in the future. They remain the preserve of writers of fanciful tales and penny dreadfuls. And yet we are on the verge of a national crisis right *now*. We teeter at the brink of disaster!"

"Be in no doubt; the Queen is dying," the doctor persisted. "Her lungs are riddled with pneumonia. Her major organs are simply worn out."

"Gentlemen, things have already progressed far further than the man on the street knows, than even you may have realised. So her lungs are useless – we replace them with something better. Her heart gives out – we fix a steam-powered pump in its place. Gentlemen, the Queen need not die. We can rebuild her – we have the technology. We have the technology available *now*."

"Go on," the first said, slowly.

"Gentlemen, I present to you, a little something of my own invention. I give you, the Empress Engine!"

II

Through The Looking Glass

He was falling again.

The gondola dropped like a stone through the freezing fog, stinging ice crystals – like a million tiny knives – whirling all about them as they fell through the white hell of the blizzard.

And then the sensation of falling halted abruptly and he was thrown clear of the shattered wreckage of the hot air balloon's basket.

He lay in the snow, his whole body numb, dimly aware of the fact that Davenport's body was lying next to his, the man's blood freezing black in the sub-zero temperatures of the mountaintop. As the cold took hold, he closed his eyes, welcoming the embrace of oblivion...

He opened his eyes.

He was falling again, his view of the dirigible and the noted London landmark expanding as he dropped towards the oily black river. A gaseous flame blossomed like an orange rose above him.

And then he hit the surface of the cloying Thames and the waters closed over his head...

He opened his eyes.

He was inside the airlock now, the huge pressurised suit he had been bolted into barely fitting inside the conning tower of the submersible. The smaller sub was closing on the other at last; against all the odds, or so it seemed.

He waited with bated breath, his heart thumping against the cage of his ribs, every sense heightened by the rush of adrenalin surging through every fibre of his being.

It was now or never. His mouth suddenly dry, he punched the emergency eject and the airlock opened in a torrent of swirling seawater and bubbles. The abominable pressures working on the craft sucked out the air, the pressure suit and him within it...

He opened his eyes to see the beast rearing above him, its impossible anatomy exposed for all to see. Sticking out of its reptilian flesh was the glinting pommel of his sword. Reaching up, he grabbed the bloodstone hilt and pulled. The blade came free with an obscene, sucking gasp.

Pulling himself upright within the embrace of the abomination, he brought the blade to bear and neatly parried the creature's own chitinous blade. As the talon slid free of the sword again, he twisted his wrist sharply to deliver a downward cutting stroke and a pallid, pilfered arm flopped onto the windswept grass at the cliff's edge.

The dreadful screams of the beast suddenly ceased, replaced by a single, breathless cry as it reeled backwards, gouts of thick black blood pumping from the severed limb.

He stepped in again, bringing his blade up in a sweeping arc, the tip making contact once more. The severed stem of the creature's snaking neck writhed in silent agony, and then the creature's body began to fall towards him...

He opened his eyes, half closing them again almost immediately against the full force of the gale howling through the falling Weather Station. Eyes streaming, he started to run along the sloping corridor, searching for the emergency exit.

At the end of the corridor a framed sign, half hanging from the wall read: "Emergency Lifeboats – THIS WAY." Beneath the words an illustration of a hand pointed to the right.

He followed the hand's helpful directions.

The wind grew stronger as the passageway continued to bear right, and then, as he rounded the bend he saw that it came to an abrupt end ten yards further on. Beyond the sheared metal superstructure there was nothing but the cold rushing air and the rapidly approaching Thames.

As the churning brown river-water rushed up to meet the plummeting Weather Station he skidded to a halt. Grabbing the handrail to stop himself tumbling out into the yawning void, he braced for impact...

He opened his eyes to see the woman being crushed by the great weight of the beast now on top of her.

There came a sudden, savage snarl and he heard the ghastly, wet ripping sound as the monster tore out her throat.

Slowly, purposefully, the monster rose up on its hind-legs and turned to face him. The beast gave him a bloody smile, its baleful stare burning through the mist and into his own appalled eyes.

Suddenly his sword didn't seem like it would be enough. And then, with a snarl, the werewolf pounced...

He opened his eyes, blinking the crusted sleep away as he tried to focus on the ceiling. He blinked twice and continued to stare hard at the peeling paint and cobwebs as the memories fled from him.

He blinked again. His eyes felt sore – the light in the room was too bright. He could feel the nauseous tide of a rising headache at his temples.

The aroma of antiseptic and urine cloyed the air. It was the smell of bleach and incontinence.

He tried to sit up, fighting to hold back the wave of nausea that threatened to overtake him as he did so, but found he couldn't move his arms. He had to settle for swinging his legs off the tubular steel cot on which he'd been lying, the momentum helping him sit upright. Then he looked down at himself. His fringe flopped into his eyes and he instinctively went to brush it aside, but once again his arms wouldn't respond. And then he saw why.

Groggily he got to his feet, wincing as a veritable tsunami of sickness threatened to overwhelm him.

Every step an effort, he walked barefoot across the cushioned floor until he was standing in front of the locked and bolted steel door of the cell.

"Hello?" he shouted at the pane of wire-reinforced glass. "Excuse me! Can anyone hear me? There seems to have been some mistake. For some unfathomable reason I've been checked into the rubber room and been given the special jacket with the extra long sleeves to wear. Is this Bedlam? I bet it is," he added to himself. "Look can you just run along and find Professor Brundle? Tell him that Ulysses Quicksilver would like a word, then we can get this all sorted out in a jiffy."

Rant over, he listened for a reply, but all he could hear was an asthmatic rattle coming through the grating of a ventilation duct in the ceiling and the distant, tuneless whistling of an attendant as he clattered with his trolley through the corridors.

"Hello!" He called again. "Room service! You appear to have confused my reservation with somebody else's. I distinctly remember booking the Emperor Suite! *Hello!*"

But still there was no reply.

He shuffled away from the door and back to the wire-sprung discomfort of the bed. He stared forlornly at the seatless lavatory bolted to the wall and couldn't help feeling that something had gone horribly wrong.

"And how are you feeling today, Mr Quicksilver?" the white-coated psychiatrist said without looking up from his clipboard.

"Well, Doctor. I'm as fit as a fiddle, whatever that means. I would even go so far as to say I'm chipper. So I'm glad you're here, because there appears to have been some mistake."

"Hm?" the doctor mumbled, his pen scratching across the chart clipped to the board.

"Yes. I mean I've been incarcerated in this madhouse when there is patently nothing wrong with me!"

"Really?" For the first time since entering the padded cell, the psychiatrist peered at Ulysses with piggy eyes, sunken into the flabby flesh of his face.

"I'm no medical man, Doctor, but I know whether I'm feeling under the weather or not, and I feel fine. Bright as a button, I am."

"Really."

"That's what I keep trying to tell you. There's nothing wrong with me."

"Hm." The doctor returned to note-taking.

"Look, where am I? Is this Bedlam? It's Bedlam, isn't it? Just run along and find Professor Brundle, there's a good chap, and tell him that Ulysses Quicksilver would like a word with him at his earliest convenience."

"Fascinating," the man observed. "Good day to you, Mr Quicksilver," he said, turning for the door.

"You'll speak to Brundle for me?" Ulysses called after him.

But the psychiatrist left the cell without saying another word, the bruiser of an orderly following after.

The door slammed shut with a resounding bang and Ulysses heard the metallic grating of the key being turned, followed by the *shunk* of deadbolts. He had the unnerving feeling that he wouldn't be going anywhere anytime soon.

III

Down the Rabbit Hole

It seemed like another forty-eight hours had passed before the psychiatrist returned. Another two days with nothing for company but his own increasingly wild thoughts.

"Did you speak to Brundle?" Ulysses asked him before the tubby little man had even managed to bustle his way into the ammonia-reeking cell.

The psychiatrist fixed Ulysses with his beady black eyes. His jowls wobbled as he spoke. "Ah, yes, Mr... Quicksilver," he mused, as he scanned his notes. "And how are you feeling today?"

"Same as I was when you last saw me. Right as rain."

"Right as rain? Interesting."

"Yes, so did you speak to Professor Brundle?"

"Tell me, Mr Quicksilver, do you know what year it is?"

"Er... Nineteen ninety-eight. I think."

"Good." The doctor wrote something down. "Very good. And your name? Your full name, I mean. Can you remember?"

"Y-Yes," he said cautiously, for fear that the recollection

might vanish again if he acted too hastily. "Ulysses Lucien Quicksilver."

"Good."

"Now I've answered your questions, doctor, perhaps you'd like to answer mine? Professor Brundle – did you speak with him?"

The psychiatrist looked up from his notes.

"I'm sorry. Who is this Professor Brundle?"

"You know, the Director of this place. I asked you to have a word with him. I asked if you'd pass on a message – get him to come and see me at his earliest convenience."

"You did not."

"I did!" Ulysses shrieked. "I remember that quite clearly!"

"And what else do you remember?"

"What?"

"It is a straightforward enough question, Mr Quicksilver," the psychiatrist tutted.

"Do you mean, what else do I remember about our last meeting? Or –"

"But we have not met before, Mr Quicksilver," the doctor stated calmly.

"I can assure that we have!"

"Ah, I understand now. You are confusing the semblance of a thing for the thing itself."

"You *understand*? Well I don't!"

The psychiatrist stared at Ulysses a moment before speaking.

"You have not met me before, but you may have met my brother. Until today you were his patient."

"Oh," said Ulysses, the wind taken out of his sails.

"He looks like me. Contrariwise, I look like him."

"Well now that we've got that cleared up, please can you tell Brundle I need to see him and we can get all this unpleasantness cleared up without any further ado. I'm known to him, you see. He's an acquaintance of mine."

"Ah, another of your fictional acquaintances, is he? Yes, I understand now. He is another symptom of your psychosis."

"I beg your pardon?

"You have suffered a terrible trauma, Mr Quicksilver, and,

as a result, you have retreated into a world that exists wholly within your own mind, populated by a complex and varied cast of characters, and in which you have cast yourself in the role of a heroic agent of the crown, undertaking daring missions on behalf of Queen and country. Is that not so?

"What?" Ulysses was flabbergasted.

"But, Mr Quicksilver, if we are to see you make any progress then you must accept the fact that you are making it all up, that you have imagined it all. You are, in reality, a clerk working for a firm of accountants, and have been for the last fifteen years."

"But I'm not making it up. It's true, I tell you! Every last word of it! I demand to see my lawyer!"

The psychiatrist regarded him with the severe expression of a disappointed headmaster.

"It was Mr Screwtape who had you sectioned in the first place. Now take one of these," he said, passing Ulysses a blue pill, "and get some rest. Good day, Mr Quicksilver."

Ulysses lay on the lumpy, wire-sprung mattress, hugging himself tightly, but then the straightjacket gave him little choice in that matter.

Am I mad? he wondered, flexing his aching shoulders as much as the jacket allowed. *I didn't think I was, but then if I'm not mad then everybody else must be. But does thinking you're the last sane man in the world mean that you* are *mad?*

No, he couldn't think like that. Give such thoughts credence and it would drive him insane. He had to have faith in himself. Why, only that morning he had... he had... He couldn't remember. What had he been doing that morning? Or had it been the day before? Or was it last week?

"I have to get out of here," he said to himself. "But isn't that the first sign of madness, talking to yourself?"

Ulysses felt that he was never going to be able to think straight again, locked away in this place, wherever this place was. It was as if there was something inside his head, playing with his thoughts.

Without even realising he was doing it at first, Ulysses subconsciously tried to put a hand to the back of his head – he was sure there was something there. But the attempt was immediately hampered by the straight-jacket.

Had it been another cruel trick of his mind, or had there been a little more give in the jacket this time?

"So," he resolved, "before I am going to be able to do anything else, I have to somehow get out of here. And if I'm going to do that then I'm going to have to convince them I'm cured, in their eyes at least. I'm going to have to play along with the doctors' little game. But which of the two is most likely to be convinced by my little charade?" he pondered, as he stared at the blank white ceiling.

Two eyes blinked into existence between him and the flaking paint.

Ulysses started in disbelief and horror at the disembodied greeny-yellow orbs. The pupils of the eyes were black slits.

The eyes were soon joined by a grinning mouth.

"Dee-dum, dee-dum, dee-dum," it said in a sing-song fashion. "See either you like. They're both mad."

"But I don't want to go among mad people," Ulysses said.

As he continued to stare at the grinning mouth and the blinking, mesmeric eyes a face materialised around them. It was a broad face, furry and bristling with whiskers.

"Oh, you can't help that," said the cat, "we're all mad here. I'm mad. You're mad."

"How can you know I'm mad?"

"You must be, or you wouldn't have come here."

But that doesn't prove anything, Ulysses considered. "How do you know that you're mad?"

"Because otherwise I wouldn't be here. Q.E.D." the cat smiled, and vanished.

"So, you no longer believe yourself to be an agent of the crown?" the white-coated psychiatrist asked him again, a week later.

"No, no – of course not. That, if you don't mind me saying so, is a preposterous idea, doctor."

"And do you still wish to speak with this Professor Brundle?"

"Why should I?" Ulysses asked. "He was nothing but a figment of my fevered imagination."

"And your manservant – Nimrod, was it? – and this Lord De Wynter?"

"A manservant, doctor? Since when do accounts clerks have personal valets? And what would a man like me be doing talking with a nob like his lordship?" Ulysses fixed his gaze on the scribbling psychiatrist. "Doctor, they were nothing but a fiction, the lot of them, the product of an over-active imagination and an exhausted, broken mind. But I'm better now. You've cured me. I no longer suffer from that... delusion."

The man finished scrawling something on the paper in front of him – and was it his over active imagination, or his exhausted state of mind, or was his scribbling hand really moving from right to left across the page as if the man were writing backwards?

He swallowed hard, struggling to keep the carefully cultivated look of serene composure on his face.

"Very good. Very good. Well I am pleased to say you are making excellent progress, Mr Quicksilver. Continue like this and we may even have you rehabilitated into conventional society within the next five years, or so. We may even be able to take you out of that jacket in a week or two."

"Five years?"

"Yes. A most positive prognosis, don't you think?"

Ulysses felt his shoulders sag and he sank back onto the bed, feeling more fatigued and defeated than ever.

Five further years of incarceration within this stinking institution, with no contact whatsoever with the outside world.

His eyes took on a distant quality, as if he were staring at something nobody else could see, and then they widened as his face took on an expression of anxious disbelief.

"Doctor," he said weakly. "Can I have another of those nice blue pills you gave me?"

"Why?"

"Because a white rabbit with pink eyes just took a watch out of its waistcoat-pocket and remarked that it's going to be late."

IV

The Knave of Hearts

When he woke again – from a dream in which he was falling, over and over, down a well-shaft deep underground, his fall never ending – it was to discover that he was alone and lying on the uncomfortable, squeaky bed.

He sat up, levering at the waist, his arms still strapped fast across his chest, and quickly scanned the cell. He looked up at the ceiling and down at the floor, peering into all the corners of the room. Mercifully, there did not appear to be any grinning cats or waist-coated rabbits waiting for him there.

He relaxed and let out a weary sigh, as the reality of his situation hit home all over again. Five years, the doctor had said. And that was taking a glass half-full attitude.

He stared forlornly at the door – he had never felt so utterly without hope – and it was then he noticed that the door was very slightly open.

Ulysses' pulse began to quicken. It was now or never.

Springing off the bed, Ulysses darted over to the door and, easing it open with one shoulder, peered through.

There was nobody in the clinical white corridor outside. From somewhere in the distance he could hear the indistinct voices of doctors, nurses and orderlies going about their business. But there was nobody on guard outside the special guest accommodation with the rubber wallpaper.

To his left, ten yards away, the corridor came to a T-junction and he could see one end of the nurse's station within the adjoining corridor, the paper-hatted woman sitting there absorbed in the register she had open on the desk in front of her.

To the right there was another intersection and, beyond that– glory of glories – he saw natural daylight streaming through the glass panes in a pair of swing doors.

A way out!

"Alright, Bill!" he heard someone call, and then the voice retreated into the distance again. The coast was clear.

Here was his chance.

Glancing back at the nurse's station and seeing that the woman on duty was still deeply absorbed, barefoot, he crept out of the room.

Although there was no one to see him – as long as the nurse didn't look up – Ulysses still hunched his body, as if by making himself smaller he would have a better chance of getting away.

Then there were footsteps from ahead as someone approached the intersection.

Ulysses jerked at his arms but, although he was sure he felt the tension in the sleeves slacken slightly, the buckles behind his back remained securely fastened. A flurry of strategies suggested themselves to him. Was there time to make it back to his cell before he was spotted, so that he might make his escape attempt later? Could he jump the person approaching and still get away? Or was his escape plan doomed to failure?

He froze.

As the footsteps came closer still, Ulysses' attention was suddenly drawn to a door on the other side of the corridor, not three yards away, and there stood the white rabbit. It was the same rabbit he had seen before, dressed in a waistcoat and tapping at the pocket-watch it held in one paw whilst it looked at Ulysses meaningfully with its bulging pink eyes.

Ulysses felt himself wilt. It seemed that the psychiatrist twins had been right. He must be mad, and if he truly was mad, there was no point trying to escape from this place after all. But then, Ulysses reasoned, if he was doomed to spend the next five or more years of his life here, surrounded by the same four rubber walls, what did he have to lose?

As the toe of a shoe appeared around the corner, Ulysses threw himself through the gap in the door, closing it behind him with a nudge of a shoulder. His heart racing, he let out his pent-up breath in a long, heartfelt sigh.

"Are you the Knave of Hearts?"

Startled, Ulysses turned, followed the sound of a child's voice to the centre of the room.

The chamber was larger than the one in which he had been incarcerated. It looked to be an operating theatre or a treatment room of some kind. Gleaming stainless steel gurneys and wheeled stands with saline drips had been pushed to the sides of the room, along with what looked like a large battery connected to two metal paddles.

Ulysses' eyes took in all of this in an instant, but his gaze lingered longer upon the child bound to the wheelchair in the middle of the room.

She couldn't have been more than eleven or twelve years old. She was wearing a blue pinafore dress with a white apron over the top of it. Her hair was dark and straight and hung down to her shoulders. She was bound by a series of leather straps that had been buckled tight around her ankles, her wrists, head and chest. She was only able to move her eyes and mouth.

Of the rabbit there was no sign.

The girl fixed Ulysses with an intense stare.

"Who did this to you?" he gasped as he stumbled towards her.

"Are you the Knave of Hearts?"

"No, I'm not."

"Then what's your name?"

"Ulysses. Ulysses Quicksilver." She reminded him of someone, although he couldn't quite remember who. "What are you doing here?"

"Why, with a name like yours, you might be any shape almost."

There was blood on her dress, splashes of red like rose petals. "What have they done to you?"

"Why is a raven like a writing desk?" the child said

"I don't know," he said as he pushed against the restraints of his straight-jacket. "Because it can produce a few notes, though they are very flat, and it is never put with the wrong end in front?"

With a rattle and a click, and the smell of hot leather, the straps of the straitjacket sprang free.

Ulysses shrugged off the straight-jacket and then fumbled at the catches securing the girl, the straps leaving distinct red marks on her when they came free.

"They're all mad here, you know," she said, smiling at him as he helped her up out of the chair.

"That fact hadn't escaped me," he said in hushed tones. "I'm getting out of here and I'm taking you with me. Now, stay close."

Holding her by the hand, he led over to the door.

Easing it open a fraction, Ulysses prayed that the hinges were well-oiled and that they wouldn't creak and give the game away. They didn't.

Peering through the gap, Ulysses glanced up and down the corridor. Whoever had interrupted his escape attempt before was gone. The way was clear.

"It's now or never," he whispered to the girl, "and, personally, I'm in favour of now."

She gave her smiling consent and the two of them were through the door in an instant.

Scampering along the corridor, trying to make as little sound as possible, they made it to the double doors without being spotted. And then they were through them and away.

V

Curiouser and Curiouser

They found themselves in a paved courtyard and, from there, followed the failing sunlight into the grounds that spread out behind the hospital. Broad stone steps led down to luscious lawns criss-crossed with gravel paths and dotted with curiously shaped pieces of topiary – all of them looking like over-sized chess pieces. Beyond, Ulysses fancied he could see the sea.

He glanced behind him as they ran. There was something strangely familiar about the hospital building, with its belvedere towers and mock Italian Renaissance look. Ulysses was sure he had been here before, but when he tried to recall precisely when, the memory fled from him.

"Why can't I remember?" he muttered to himself, and absent-mindedly, his free hand strayed towards the base of his skull.

"What are you trying to remember," the girl said, not sounding at all out of breath, "something that *has* happened or that *hasn't* happened yet?"

"I can't remember things before they happen," he said. What had the doctors done to her mind to leave her like this?

"It's a poor sort of memory that only works backwards."

"Look, we have to keep moving."

He was sure it would be only a matter of time before the hospital staff discovered that either he or the child had absconded and put out the call for them to be recaptured.

If they continued across the open lawns they would be in full view of anyone coming after them. Heading left would expose them to the entire rear aspect of the house. To the right, the interestingly shaped hedges and gravel paths ran up to the boundary of a brooding forest offering far more cover.

"This way," he said, pulling the girl after him as he set off for the shadowed perimeter of the ancient woodland.

"What's your name?" he puffed as they crossed into the premature twilight of the forest.

"Alice," replied the girl. "I think. Yes, Alice. I always liked the name Alice. I think I had a daughter called Alice, once upon a time."

Ulysses' concern for the child deepened. Her mind was unravelling like a ball of wool being toyed with by a kitten. Here was a damaged soul, if ever Ulysses had seen one. Whatever diabolical experiments the doctors had carried out upon her, there would be hell to pay when Ulysses was back to his old self.

He suddenly froze.

It was as dark as dusk between the trees. Above them, glimpsed through the branches, the sky was the colour of a putrid bruise.

"What was that?" Ulysses said.

"What was what?" the girl said happily.

"It sounds like people talking."

Slowly, Ulysses advanced further into the wood.

Gradually the close packed knotty boles of the wood gave way to the crumbling wall, lichen-scabbed gateposts and rusted iron railings of a fenced-off flower garden. Descending a few mossy steps, Ulysses found himself standing between flowerbeds riddled with weeds and rife with countless curious blooms that swayed above him like the fronds of palm trees.

He gazed up and suddenly felt very small.

Alice gazed up at the swaying flower heads with wonderment in her eyes.

Ulysses wandered on, listening. And then the voices came again.

"There it is," he said. "It sounds like the rustle of petals, or the rattle of seed heads."

"But of course it does," the child piped up. "After all, it is the flowers that are talking."

Ulysses turned and stared at the girl. She was off again. "But flowers can't talk!"

"Yes they can."

"I can't believe *that*!"

"Can't you?" the child said, in a pitying tone. "Try again: draw a long breath, and shut your eyes."

"There's no use trying," Ulysses laughed mirthlessly. "One can't believe impossible things."

"I dare say you haven't had much practice. When I was your age I always did it for half-an-hour a day."

"*My* age?"

"Why, sometimes I've believed as many as six impossible things before breakfast."

"We can talk," said a Tiger-lily, "when there's anybody worth talking to."

Ulysses suddenly felt sick to the pit of his stomach. Was the child's madness contagious, he wondered, or were talking flowers merely another piece of evidence of his insanity?

In fact, come to think of it, was he even there at all, or was he merely a fantasy vision brought on in someone's mind by a piece of undigested cheese?

"Stop it!" he reprimanded himself. "Thinking like that could make a man mad, if he wasn't as mad as a hatter already."

Ulysses broke off, unnerved by his new habit of arguing with himself. He had thought he had heard something else altogether more threatening than the sound of gossiping gladioli. In fact, it had sounded unpleasantly like the growling of a steam-engine, or the snorting of some wild beast loose in the woods.

"Are there any lions or tigers about here?" he asked the child, who continued to smile at him knowingly.

"It's only the Red King snoring."

Ulysses looked about him, but couldn't see anyone, awake or otherwise.

"He's dreaming now, and what do you think he's dreaming about?"

"Let's not go there. We have to keep moving." He took hold of the girl's hand again, but then hesitated. "But I don't know the way."

"Don't worry. I know the way," the child said, leading him up the garden path.

They left the garden and set off deeper into the wood. In no time at all, it seemed, they were surrounded by a profusion of gigantic fungi. They walked on through the twilit gloom of this forest of toadstools.

They stopped in the shade of a particularly large mushroom, its fleshy gills mottled the colour of a week-old corpse. The long mouthpiece of a hookah pipe trailed over the edge of the mushroom's cap. Something wet and sticky, like sugar syrup, oozed and dripped from the top of the fungus.

His curiosity getting the better of him – having looked under it, and on both sides of it, and behind it – it occurred to Ulysses that he might as well see what was on top of it.

Stretching himself up on his tiptoes, he peered over the edge of the mushroom and found himself looking into the lifeless eyes of a large blue caterpillar. It looked like the creature had been opened up with a butcher's knife, from top to tail, the yellow paste of its ravaged internal organs oozing out onto the toadstool.

"Curiouser and curiouser!" cried Alice as she joined him on tiptoes.

Were the bloodstains on her dress larger than they had been or was it all just part of the delusion Ulysses was suffering?

He turned from the brutally gutted butterfly larva and stared into the girl's face.

"Curiouser and curiouser!" she said, and smiled.

VI

Malice in Wonderland

From the carnage of caterpillar's carcass, they made their way through the crowding fungi and back into the forest. Coming to a clearing, they came in sight of a curious cottage. The roof was thatched with fur and, just as bizarrely, the chimney-stacks were shaped like ears. The layout and proportion of the windows and the front door helped to give the cottage a distinctly rabbity appearance.

Under a tree, in front of the house, a large table had been laid for tea. Slumped in an arm-chair at the head of the table was a man wearing a check waistcoat, a large spotty bow-tie, a white wing-collar shirt and a top hat with a ticket tucked into the band that read, '*In this Style 10/⁶*'.

Slouched in a chair one place removed from the Hatter, its chin resting on the matted fur of its chest, was the March Hare. Neither even so much as moved as Ulysses and Alice made their approach.

The ropes of their intestines adorned the branches of the tree like party decorations. The rank stink of offal was hot in the air.

Ulysses gagged, and tried to shield the child from the horror that she had already witnessed, pulling her close to his chest.

But Alice simply pulled back and stared at the grim tableau of the tea party.

Ulysses heard the rattle of china as the child reached across the table and removed the lid of the teapot, its cracked glaze sticky with drying gore.

"Ah, and here's the Dormouse," she said. "At least I assume it's the Dormouse. Well, bits of him anyway. It's really just so much guts and fur now. How simply frightful! You don't want fur in your tea, do you? That would be disgusting."

"What is going on here?" Ulysses hissed.

The child studied him, a quizzical look in her eye, her head on one side.

"Why, I would have thought that was quite plain. It's tea, of course."

What had they done to the poor child to make her like this? She was utterly, utterly mad.

"Is this all real?" he asked himself as he gazed around the clearing, at the house and the forest beyond, "or is it all in my head?"

"Why does it make it any less real if it's just inside your head?" the child asked, her expression one of guileless innocence.

"Come on," Ulysses said, tugging at Alice's hand again, shooting fearful glances at the shifting shadows of the encroaching trees. "We have to get you to safety, and quickly."

The child fixed him with those wide, almost black eyes of hers and he felt the layers of his consciousness being peeled away. He could feel his agitation rising, his carefully created facade of cool, calm collectedness crumbling.

"But where to? Where can we go that's safe?" she asked, her eyes suddenly the imploring eyes of a fearful child, waking to find that the nightmare was real.

It was up to him now. He was the adult, she the helpless innocent. She needed him.

"Into the house!" he said, in a moment of decisive action, his eyes still on the tree line, the sky the colour of dried blood.

The two of them – the madman and the girl – sprinted across the clearing, kicking up dead leaves with every pounding footfall as they made for the front door of the cottage. Ulysses could see things moving within the tree-line now, he was sure of it.

And then they were at the door and he was barging it open with his shoulder, bundling the girl through, and then himself. Throwing all his weight against the door he slammed it shut.

He closed his eyes and slid down the door to the floor. The come down from his adrenaline rush was making his hands shake; and then the blackness of oblivion took him as he passed out.

Ulysses snapped his eyes open to be greeted by the gloom of the hallway. Night had fallen. How long had he been out for? He sniffed. The mouth-watering aroma of eggs and bacon reached him as the popping and sizzling of the frying pan hissed along the passageway from the kitchen. The delicious smell helped rouse him and, blinking the weariness from his eyes, he tried to stand. His back ached. His arms and legs were stiff. He had no feeling in his feet at all. But, nonetheless, he still managed to follow the tantalising scents to their source.

The large kitchen was full of smoke and steam, and there was a cacophony of sounds to match the miasma of scents. Bacon sizzled and popped, a cauldron of broth bubbled, while pots and pans clattered as the girl worked.

He could see her through the fug, standing before the range, a large ladle in her hand, stirring the contents of the cauldron. As Ulysses watched, Alice wiped a hand across her forehead, strands of dark hair, plastered to her skin, forming random fractal patterns across her face. As she stirred she sang to herself.

"Humpty Dumpty sat on a wall, Humpty Dumpty had a great fall. All the King's horses and all the King's men, couldn't put Humpty Dumpty in his place again."

"That smells good," Ulysses said.

Alice turned and offered him a smile.

"You prepared all this yourself?"

"Well somebody I know, not a million miles from here, was too busy snoring as loud as the Red King to help. Did you dream of him, by the way, dreaming of you? Let's consider who it was that dreamed it all."

"So," said Ulysses, peering over the girl's shoulder at the cauldron bubbling upon the range, "what are we having?"

As Ulysses stared into the pot, and Alice stirred the bubbling broth, a calf's head floated to the surface, its boiled eyes white and sightless, its cooked tongue lolling from its slack mouth.

Ulysses' grumbling stomach knotted and that same unpleasantly familiar sick feeling returned. He slowly took in the rest of the kitchen.

The largest eggshell he had ever seen – at least ten times as big as an ostrich's – lay cracked on the kitchen table. Beside it, on a plate, sat a suckling pig's head. When he caught sight of the skinned cat, he turned away in disgust.

"Soup of the evening, beautiful soup! Mock Turtle soup in fact," the child began. "Beautiful soup, so rich and green, waiting in a hot tureen!"

"Followed by oysters and frog's legs, and a ham and pepper omelette. There's also dormouse and roast flamingo and gryphon wings. Then there's jugged hare – or lamb chops, if you prefer – and sausages, with jam tarts to finish, only there's no jam in them."

"Why not?" Ulysses asked weakly, barely managing to hold it together as the world began to unravel around him once again.

"The rule is, jam tomorrow and jam yesterday – but never jam today."

"You killed them, didn't you?"

The child looked at him. "Oh yes," she said, smiling.

"And the Hatter, and the Hare."

"That's right."

"And the Knave of Hearts?"

"As dead as a dodo."

"You killed them all," Ulysses whispered, stunned. "It was you," he said as memories re-surfaced and facts he hadn't previously been aware of even knowing presented themselves to his conscious mind. "It was you that killed the visitors to the Phantasmagoria."

"Oh yes. I don't deny it."

"Then why didn't you say something before?"

"You didn't ask me before."

Ulysses suddenly felt horribly cold, despite the heat of the kitchen. He needed to sit down. Backing away, he collapsed into a chair.

"They all came to see *us*, you know," the child said, abandoning her cooking, slowly crossing the kitchen towards him, swinging her hips in a way that a twelve year old girl never should.

"Stop it, please," Ulysses wept. "You shouldn't have done it."

"But we were not amused," she said, her crocodile leer remaining firmly fixed upon her innocent face. "'Til we set about butchering them, of course. Then we found them most amusing."

Ulysses couldn't move.

"But none of them will have amused us as much as you will, I suspect. Mr Quicksilver."

The child's smile never stopped, the corners of her mouth stretching wider and wider. And her smile was full of teeth.

And a verse entered Ulysses' mind:

Beware the Jabberwock, my son!

VII

Jabberwocky

Beware the Jabberwock, my son!
The jaws that bite, the claws that catch!

A children's nonsense rhyme nothing more. Except that it *was* something more. Otherwise, why should such a thing come into his mind at this very moment?

Ulysses stared into the black, soulless eyes of the child as she continued to saunter towards him.

"How doth the little crocodile improve his shining tail," the child intoned, as she walked the length of the ever-lengthening kitchen.

"Please stop," he begged her, fear colouring his voice.

"And pour the waters of the Nile on every golden scale?"

"You don't need to do this."

The girl paused, putting her head on one side again, regarding him with the same quizzical expression. "Is this really the great Ulysses Quicksilver," she said, amused, "begging for his life like some abused workhouse urchin?"

"Look, I don't want to have to hurt you," Ulysses explained, backing away from her.

"You?" she smiled coldly. "Hurt me?"

A long purple tongue darted from between her teeth, running up and down her lips in hungry anticipation. "Come now, Mr Quicksilver, what do you take me for? You shouldn't judge a book by its cover, you know."

She was right, Ulysses thought. His eyes darted about the kitchen; he looked for a something to defend himself with. If only he had had his sword-stick to hand, or his trusty pistol.

The trouble was, the further he moved away from the child, anything even remotely approximating a weapon was further from his reach. The carving knives and cleavers were in a block on a work surface at the other end of the room, as were the frying pans and saucepans hung above the range.

What he really needed was a way out. Where was a rabbit in a waistcoat to direct you when you needed one?

As if reading his mind, Alice stepped to one side, providing Ulysses with an unobstructed view of the range and the saucepans crowding the coals. There was the cauldron, full to the brim with bubbling broth, the calf's head still peering blindly from it, and there, next to it, was another pan, the lid that had been forced down upon it rattling wildly as its contents boiled over. Flopped over the edge of the pan was one drooping white ear.

Alice followed his gazed and then smiled at him from beneath hooded eyes. "Oh, no, you're not getting away that easily. And didn't I mention it before? We're having boiled bunny too. It's my own invention, but it needs more pepper."

He returned his gaze to the girl as if she might leap at him any second. She was half his size, but something about her features gave him the undeniable impression that, as she herself had said, appearances could be deceiving.

At that moment Ulysses spotted the bread knife that had been left on the table – it was only an arm's length away – and he made a grab for it.

The transformation took place so quickly that Ulysses barely registered it. One moment, the child had been standing there rabbiting away, the next it seemed to Ulysses that she simply shot out her hand, as if to seize the knife before he could, even though she was still half a table's length away from it.

As his fingertips brushed the handle of the bread knife, a bony talon slammed into the tabletop, pinning his sleeve to the wood.

"Speak roughly to your little boy, and beat him when he sneezes," the Alice-thing chanted. "He only does it to annoy, because he knows it teases."

Grabbing the trapped sleeve with his other hand, Ulysses pulled and, with a tearing of cloth, he tumbled free.

Before he had even engaged his brain Ulysses was running out through the door, back along the passageway and out through the front door of the cottage.

Drawing in great ragged lungfuls of cold night air, Ulysses spun to his left and hared away from the house.

He found himself sprinting through a garden of cool tinkling fountains and carefully-trimmed rose trees. It might have been considered beautiful, were it not for the fact that it was also strewn with the bodies of playing card people, their blood having painted the white roses red, although, in the moonlight, the dripping blooms glistened blackly.

Ulysses dared not stop, despite the bloody destruction that had been wrought all about him, and he dared not look back. For he knew that Alice was in pursuit. Her sing-song voice carried to him over the beating of his own panicked heart and his rasping breaths.

"Twinkle, twinkle, little bat! How I wonder what you're at! Up above the world you fly, like a tea tray in the sky."

And then he found himself repeating the nonsense verse as he ran. "'Twas brillig, and the slithy toves did gyre and gimble in the wabe."

He was now running across what he took to be a croquet-ground, of sorts; pink-feathered bodies and balls of prickles discarded among the ridges and furrows like broken dolls and squashed windfall apples.

He could hear nothing from behind him now, but he kept running. He crashed through a privet hedge and back into the forest, branches reaching for him as they clattered together in the breeze.

There was something waiting for him there, in the cold and the dark.

"You!" he gasped.

"As large as life, and twice as natural!"

The creature fixed him with two piercing black diamond eyes, Alice's shark-mawed face smiling down at him from atop a sinuous, snaking neck that seemed strangely familiar, even though Ulysses couldn't for the life of him remember why.

Its whole body swayed, writhing hypnotically, from its saurian legs to its great skeletal claws. A huge pair of bat wings, the same colour as the darkness beneath the trees, flapped behind it and a long, snaking tail thrashed with an unspeakable life of its own.

"The time has come," the monster said, "to talk of many things..."

"Of shoes – and ships – and sealing-wax – of cabbages – and kings," Ulysses smiled. Harming a child was an anathema to him, but a monster...? You knew where you were with a monster.

"You can have no idea what a delightful thing a Lobster-Quadrille is."

"No indeed," Ulysses replied, "But I know you, and I name you Beast. I name you destroyer. I name you murderer. I name you Jabberwock!"

And, along with its name, his memories began to return.

The creature hissed, its forked tongue darting from between its glistening fangs, and lashed out with a malformed claw. Ulysses side-stepped it smartly, never once taking his eyes from the swaying child's head atop the snake-like neck.

"'Twas brillig," he began, his voice like steel, "and the slithy toves did gyre and gimble in the wabe: all mimsy were the borogoves, and the mome raths outgrabe."

The beast lashed out again, this time with a whip-crack of its tail. It was fast, but Ulysses was faster.

"Beware the Jabberwock, my son! The jaws that bite, the claws that catch!" he pronounced as he came out of the roll that saved him from being trampled by a heavy, clawed foot. "Beware the Jubjub bird, and shun the frumious Bandersnatch!"

Somewhere else, deep within his mind – disjointed, as if out of sync with the rest of the world – Ulysses heard a dispassionate female voice announce, "Jabberwocky protocol activated."

The Alice-thing gave a banshee wail of rage and frustration as Ulysses ducked another swipe of its claws and then rose up before it, assuming a fencer's stance. Reaching out his right arm, he uttered the words, "He took his vorpal sword in hand!" and his fingers closed around its hilt.

VIII

Alice's Phantasmagoria

MAY 1998

"So, Mr," Ulysses Quicksilver consulted the name written on the notepad in his hand. "Dodgson... Is that right?" The anxious looking whip-cord of a man in front of him nodded. "What appears to be the problem?"

The attraction owner had met them at the door himself and hastily ushered them inside, glancing up and down the street, the lurid neon sign lending his already unhealthy complexion a pinkish sheen. Having secured and bolted the door behind them, he led them upstairs to a cluttered office redolent with the smell of stale tobacco. The stub of a Cuban cigar still smouldered in the ash tray, precariously balanced on top of a teetering pile of cogitator print-outs.

"There's..." he began, rubbing his hands together, over and over, in agitation. "There's been a death."

"A death?" Ulysses repeated. Nimrod raised an interested eyebrow but made no comment. "But I wouldn't have considered the type of recreation you offer here as being hazardous to health.

"No. Neither did my associates and I."

"So where's the body?"

"This way. Follow me."

"So this is where the magic happens, is it?" Ulysses said in hushed tones, taking in the brass, coffin-like cabinets positioned equidistantly around the circular, teak-panelled chamber. In the dull red light it looked more like a mortuary, or a morgue, than a place of entertainment.

"Well, I suppose technically the magic, as you put it, happens up there," Dodgson said, pointing at the ceiling. "The analytical engine that creates and maintains the virtual environment experienced by our guests is housed on the floor above this one."

"Must be quite some machine," Ulysses remarked.

"And the floor above that, and the one above that."

A number of cable-bundles emerged from the middle of the domed ceiling above them and then spread out like the tentacles of an octopus, following the curve of the ceiling until each one ultimately connected to the top of one casket.

Through an archway Ulysses could see another chamber, like the one they were in. He wondered how many more there were like it located throughout the whole complex.

"Do you know much about analytical engines, Mr Quicksilver?" Dodgson asked.

"I've had dealings with one or two."

"Mnemosyne is one of the new generation of Turing machines."

"Ah, yes. I met one of those once. Its name was Neptune and it condemned some three thousand souls to a miserable death at the bottom of the Pacific Ocean."

Dodgson smiled weakly before continuing. "It utilises a series of chromodynamic processors and Bloch spheres to create and maintain a fully realised simulation of what is, to all intents and purposes – within the mind of the participant – an utterly real world."

"Can I stop you there?" Ulysses said. "Can you just remind me again, precisely, what it is you do here, Mr Dodgson?"

The nervously sweating Dodgson took a moment to compose himself, before commencing with what Ulysses took to be a pre-prepared speech, memorised for the benefit of the curious paying public.

"Here at Alice's Phantasmagoria we offer a unique recreational experience. Thanks to the latest bleeding edge technology we can immerse you in a fantastical world that, for all intents and purposes, appears to be real, and which is only bound by the limitations of your own imagination. With Dodgson and Digby's Patented Phantasmagorical Projector you really can live the dream!"

"And this... this virtual reality of yours, do you have a catchy name for it?"

"We like to refer to it as the In-Body Out of Body Experience."

"It's all based on *Alice's Adventures in Wonderland*?"

"At the moment. It is a classic, after all. But our environment engineers are already working on other worlds based on the writings of H.G. Wells, Jules Verne and Sir Arthur Conan Doyle's *The Lost World*."

"One step at a time, eh, Mr Dodgson? One step at a time. I wouldn't start counting your chickens just yet. After all, you can see dinosaurs in the wild for the price of a cruise ticket. And I don't expect this operation's cheap to run, is it? So basically, this is where overweight, middle-aged businessmen, with a thing for little girls, come to live out their fantasies. Am I right?"

"No!" Dodgson railed. "It is not that kind of establishment at all. We are a highly reputable company."

"But, I mean, come on. Alice's Phantasmagoria? That's rather a lurid title, don't you think? Admit it."

"It brings in the punters," Dodgson said, an awkward grimace on his face.

"Yes, I bet that sticks in your throat, eh, Dodgson? Your marvellous machine, your magnificent achievement, testament to the superior advances in technology, being corrupted by sleazy window salesmen for their own sordid pleasure."

"You said you wanted to see the body," Dodgson reminded him.

"Yes, I did, didn't I?"

"Well, it's this way."

The anxious attraction owner led Ulysses and Nimrod into the next circular chamber.

"Here," he said, pointing at the cadaver bound within one of the cabinets. The front of the casket was open, the reek of death coming from it unmistakable.

"Ooh, nasty," Ulysses commented, peering at the body. The dead man appeared to be middle-aged, and was wearing two pieces of a poor quality three piece suit, along with a white cotton shirt and distastefully-patterned tie. His jacket hung on a peg beside the casket. His face was locked in a rictus of terror. "Hmm, overweight, middle-aged businessmen. Cause of death?"

"The life-support systems that monitor our guests' vital signs recorded his cause of death as cardiac arrest."

"Heart attack, eh? Could have just been bad luck I suppose. I take it all of your 'guests' sign a disclaimer."

Dodgson nodded.

"How long's he been dead?"

"Only a matter of hours."

"And it was after this happened that you evacuated everyone else who was here at the time."

"Er, no. Not quite. It all happened so quickly!"

"What do you mean?"

Ulysses and his manservant followed as Dodgson led them into yet another chamber.

"How many people can you accommodate at any one time?" Ulysses said.

"Our current maximum is forty-eight but the demand for tube-time is increasing and we plan to have another four simulation suites ready by the end of next month."

They stopped in front of another of the cabinets. This one also contained a limp corpse.

"Another heart attack?" Ulysses said.

"No stroke."

Dodgson set off again, stopping beside another cabinet. The dead man's body there was contorted in agony, the whites of the cadaver's eyes crimson with burst blood vessels.

"And what happened to this one?"

"Brain haemorrhage," Dodgson mumbled, as if he were guilty of some heinous crime himself.

"Oh dear, Mr Dodgson. Oh dear, oh dear, oh dear." Ulysses looked the quaking man up and down. His skin had acquired an even more unhealthy pallor. "One death could be considered... unfortunate. But two? That's just careless. So what does that make three?"

"It wasn't my – our, I mean *our* – fault," Dodgson protested.

"That's what you're worried about, isn't it, Mr Dodgson? You're worried that the Met will get word of this and charge you with complicity to murder. That wouldn't be good for business now, would it, Mr Dodgson?"

"No, not murder. More like... an industrial accident."

"Oh, come on, Mr Dodgson. Now you're just pulling my leg. An industrial accident?"

"That's not what I mean."

"You should say what you mean."

"I did, I mean..." the man stammered. "At least I mean what I say – that's the same thing, isn't it?"

"Try telling that to the judge."

"But can you help me?"

Ulysses kept the man hanging on for a moment longer, before answering. "I can try."

"Good," Dodgson said, with a sigh of relief. "And, um, how much will that, um –"

"How much will it cost you to have me sort out this little mess of yours?"

"Yes."

"A not inconsiderable amount." Ulysses scribbled a figure on the page of a notepad, tore it off and handed it to the sweating gentleman.

"Oh."

"And that's my final offer. Take it or leave it."

"I'll take it."

*   *   *

"So, bottom line is," Ulysses said, after the three of them had gathered within Mnemosyne's control hub, "something's killing your customers and you need to find out what."

"You are a consulting detective, are you not?"

"Good. Then we understand each other." Ulysses stared at the meaningless columns of numbers scrolling across the monitor in front of him. "And you're sure it's not a glitch in the Lovelace algorithm?"

"We've gone through the code a hundred times and there's nothing there," Dodgson said, glancing anxiously at the lab-coated technician seated at the console.

"So, who do you think the killer is?"

Dodgson stared at him, flabbergasted. "I'm sorry. Haven't I just hired you to find that out for me?"

"Go on, humour me."

"Well, for starters, I would have thought that it was something from outside the system. There are all sorts of fail-safes in place. We've checked the Lovelace algorithms again and again and again, and there's nothing. Nobody should die in Wonderland!"

"And yet three people have."

Dodgson gave the technician another surreptitious glance. "We suspect that an alien algorithm has piggy-backed its way onto the system."

"Then why not simply shut the whole thing down and re-boot it?" Ulysses asked, incredulous that nobody more technically minded hadn't thought of that approach already. "I think the technical term is, turning it off and on again."

"We have," Dodgson hissed. "Three times. But every time we re-boot, and carry out another scan, the anomalous code is still present."

"So what can I do that you haven't tried already?" Ulysses asked, genuinely bemused.

"We've created a diagnostic tool. A virus-killer, if you like."

"So why haven't you deployed it?

"Because we cannot lock onto the anomalous string of code. It's as if it knows we're looking for it and keeps shifting position, using our original algorithm to disguise itself."

"Why don't you just pull the plug?"

"Because this technology has the potential to improve the lives of all."

"More brochure-speak?"

"This is a business, Mr Quicksilver," Dodgson said, "and I would prefer to stay *in* business."

"Ah, now we get to the truth of it."

"I already have the bank breathing down my neck as it is."

"Everything comes down to money, doesn't it? Anyway, I thought business was booming."

"It will be."

"Understood. Then you can add a nought to end of my fee."

Dodgson scowled, but said nothing. He was hardly in a position to argue.

"So, what you're saying is that actually you know what's responsible for this... this mess, and you just need some dupe to go in and excise the cancer, as it were."

Dodgson smiled but still said nothing.

Ulysses grinned. "Then you've got yourself a deal," he said, a manic timbre to the tone of his voice. "My interest is well and truly piqued and I quite fancy taking a trip to Wonderland myself. So let's see how far down the rabbit hole really goes, shall we?"

Dodgson stared at him, the utter amazement expressed on his face as readable as an open book.

"Are you sure, sir?" Nimrod asked.

"Yes, I'm sure. I'm not going in ill-prepared mind. I don't want to end up like our friends down there in the bunko booth."

"Don't worry, everything's ready," Dodgson said, animated again. "The system already has a back door built in. If things start to get out of hand, once you're actually inside Wonderland, you only need to follow the White Rabbit to escape. It's a fail-safe we put in right from the off-set."

"And you're sure that'll work, are you?"

"Absolutely sure. It's written into the base code. It can't fail."

"And what about this virus-killer? What if I manage to find the source of all your problems? What if I come across whatever it is that's been killing your clients?"

"To access the algorithm from within Wonderland you merely need to recite the first line of the third stanza of the poem *Jabberwocky*."

"Really? Why so convoluted?"

"It's a precaution, to make sure that the virus-killer is activated only at the right time. Do you know it?"

"'Twas brillig', and all that? Oh yes, have no fear, I know it. Chalky Chambers made us learn it off by heart. Third year English Literature class, last period before lunch on a Thursday. Good old Chalky."

"And you're absolutely sure about this, sir?"

"Stop fussing, Nimrod," Ulysses chided, as Dodgson fitted the electrode skullcap over his head. "You're like an old woman sometimes, really you are. Ready, Dodgson?"

"Ready."

"Right then, gentlemen, I'm going in," Ulysses announced, giving a thumbs up as he made himself comfortable on the cushioned backboard inside the cabinet. "Are you alright, Dodgson, only you're not looking at all well?"

"I-I'm fine," Dodgson stammered, even though he patently wasn't, and closed the door.

"If anything happens to him..." Ulysses heard Nimrod say as the tube sealed with a hiss of equalising pressures, and watched as Dodgson threw the switch.

And then he was falling again...

IX

The Bitterness of Life

Coal black eyes wide with fury, the chimerical creature went for Ulysses.

"Will you, won't you, will you, won't you, will you join the dance?" Ulysses chanted as he brought the blade up in one powerful movement, the bloodstone-tipped pommel tight in his hand, the metal singing as he did so.

The monster only just parried the blow in time, retracted its writhing head and thrusting a claw in the way of the slicing blade.

The Alice-thing gave voice to a blood-curdling wail as the razor-edge of the blade took off three of its distended fingers at the knuckle.

Its scream of pain became a roar of rage and the malformed child's head darted forwards like a striking cobra.

Ulysses deftly spun the blade back and thrust it upwards in a reverse swing. He felt resistance as it bit into the meat of the thing's neck, before pulling back sharply with all the strength he could muster.

"Off with her head," he snarled in bitter triumph.

Alice's head – jaws still stretched impossibly wide – landed with a soft thud among the litter of leaves at his feet, the massive, warped body toppling backwards onto the ground moments later.

Panting hard, Ulysses stared dispassionately down at the malformed head of the twelve year-old girl. Alice looked back at him.

"You know," she said very gravely, "it's one of the most serious things that can possibly happen to one in a battle – to get one's head cut off."

"So it would seem," Ulysses agreed.

He gazed at the midnight forest and the darkness of the world around him, as if expecting something to happen at any moment.

"So what happens now?" the child-monster asked.

"Now?" the dandy said, staring at the sky above, as the heavens turned the colour of snow. "Now we wait."

"What, isn't there a moral?"

Ulysses fixed the head with a stare as hard as stone. "Perhaps it hasn't one."

The Alice face frowned disapprovingly. "Tut, tut, child! Everything's got a moral, if you can only find it."

"Alright then, how about this? Don't *get* a life – *live* a life?"

"Oh no, that won't do. I don't like that at all."

"Very well then. How about, make hay while the sun shines? Or, there's nothing virtual about reality? Or *ego cogito, ergo sum*?"

"Hmm, perhaps," the child-head pondered. "But perhaps if you told me the story again I might be able to determine the moral that way."

"Tell it again? This was no story." Ulysses gave an exasperated sigh. "Besides, I wouldn't know where to begin!"

"Begin at the beginning and go on till you come to the end: then stop."

"Look, are going to keep this up all the time?"

"The time has come," the anomaly said by way of a reply, "to talk of many things: of shoes – and ships – and sealing wax – of cabbages – and kings – and why the sea is boiling hot – and whether pigs have wings."

Ulysses turned his back on the chattering child and slowly walked away.

"I'll be seeing you again," the child's voice called out after him, crackling like an old gramophone recording, "of that you can be certain, Mr Quicksilver. My champion."

There was a hazy quality to the air of the chamber and an all-pervading smell of pomanders and lubricating oil. In the crimson gloom, Her Majesty Queen Victoria – Empress of India, Monarch of Mars and Ruler de facto of the Lunar colonies – slept the sleep of the dead, bound within the confines of her steam-powered, life-supporting throne.

There was more machine than monarch now. The physical husk the old woman had become could never leave the Empress Engine that Erasmus Quicksilver had created for her all those years ago; ninety-seven, to be precise. The Widow of Windsor herself was just a withered, fleshless creature that had been kept alive long beyond her natural span, and for far longer than was good for her deteriorating mind.

But in her death-like slumber her eyelids flickered.

The peace of the chamber was interrupted by a delicate chiming coming from the throne itself.

In moments, a lady-in-waiting was at the sleeping monarch's side, deciphering the ticker-tape readout produced by the agitated engine.

Her eyes wide with incredulity, she hurried to the telephony device on hand, close by, and picked up the receiver.

There was a static click as someone picked up at the other end of the line.

"Doctor Malbuse?"

"What is it?" the Queen's personal surgeon-cum-engineer responded sharply.

"It's the Empress Engine, doctor, I... I've never seen readings like this."

"What do you mean?"

"It's... It's as if..." She trailed off, unable to find the words.

"What is it, woman? Tell me!"

"Doctor, I think you need to see this for yourself."

And in her sleep, the Queen smiled.

The long grass rustled at her feet as the White Rabbit hurried by and she could hear the rattle of the teacups as the March Hare and his friends shared their never-ending meal, and the shrill voice of the Queen ordering her unfortunate guests off to execution, mixed up with the distant sob of the miserable Mock Turtle.

So she sat, with eyes closed, and half believed herself in Wonderland, though she knew she had but to open them again, and all would change to dull reality.

And she considered how she would gather about her little children, and how she would make their eyes bright and eager with many a strange tale, perhaps even with the dream of Wonderland of long ago; and how she would feel with all their simple sorrows, and find pleasure in all their simple joys, remembering her own child-life, and the happy summer days.

Still she haunts me, phantomwise,
Alice moving under skies
Never seen by waking eyes.

Children yet, the tale to hear,
Eager eye and willing ear,
Lovingly shall nestle near.

In a Wonderland they lie,
Dreaming as the days go by,
Dreaming as the summers die:

Ever drifting down the stream –
Lingering in the golden gleam –
Life, what is it but a dream?

(from *Through the Looking-Glass, and What Alice Found There*, by Lewis Carroll)

THE END

PAX BRITANNIA

UNNATURAL
HISTORY

Jonathan Green

Visit www.abaddonbooks.com for information on our titles,
interviews, news and exclusive content.

ISBN: 978-1-905437-10-8
UK £.6.99   US $7.99

Abaddon
Books

Follow us on twitter: www.twitter.com/abaddonbooks

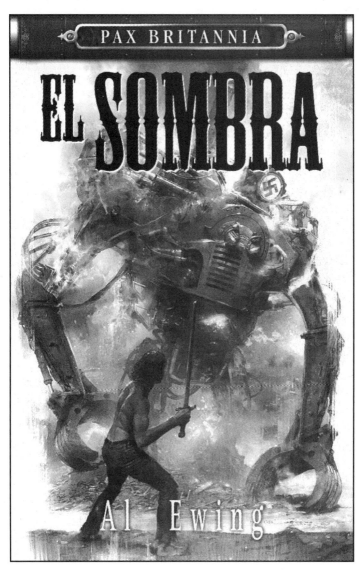

PAX BRITANNIA

EL SOMBRA

Al Ewing

Visit www.abaddonbooks.com for information on our titles,
interviews, news and exclusive content.

ISBN: 978-1-905437-34-4
UK £.6.99   US $7.99

Abaddon
Books

Follow us on twitter: www.twitter.com/abaddonbooks

PAX BRITANNIA

LEVIATHAN RISING

JONATHAN GREEN

Visit www.abaddonbooks.com for information on our titles,
interviews, news and exclusive content.

ISBN: 978-1-905347-60-3
UK £.6.99   US $7.99

Abaddon
Books

Follow us on twitter: www.twitter.com/abaddonbooks

PAX BRITANNIA

HUMAN NATURE

JONATHAN GREEN

Visit www.abaddonbooks.com for information on our titles,
interviews, news and exclusive content.

ISBN: 978-1-905437-86-3
UK £.6.99   US $7.99

Abaddon
Books

Follow us on twitter: www.twitter.com/abaddonbooks

Coming soon!

PAX BRITANNIA

GODS OF MANHATTAN
AL EWING